Quest for Kerouac

QUEST FOR KEROUAC

Chris Challis

faber and faber

LONDON · BOSTON

First published in 1984
by Faber and Faber Limited
3 Queen Square London WC1N 3AU

Filmset by Goodfellow & Egan
Typesetters Cambridge
Printed in Great Britain by
Whitstable Litho Limited
Whitstable Kent

British Library in Publication Data

Challis, Chris
Quest for Kerouac.
1. American literature—20th century—History and criticism
2. Bohemianism—United States
I. Title
810.9'0054   PS228.B6
ISBN 0-571-13356-8

Library of Congress Cataloguing in Publication Data

Challis, Chris
Quest for Kerouac.
1. American literature—20th century—History and criticism.
2. Bohemianism—United States.
3. Kerouac, Jack, 1922–1969—Criticism and interpretation.
4. Literary landmarks—United States.
5. United States—Description and travel—1960–
I. Title.
PS228.B6C46   1984   810'.9'0054   84-13493
ISBN 0-571-13356-8 (pbk.)

This book is dedicated to Heather Anderson, to Carolyn Cassady and, most of all, to Dreada Challis. In their different ways, they each know just what a long strange trip it's been.

Contents

Acknowledgements

My sincere thanks go to all those writers who gave me permission to quote from their works and correspondence. In particular, thanks to William Burroughs, Carolyn Cassady, Gregory Corso, Allen Ginsberg, James Grauerholz, John Clellon Holmes, Arthur and Kit Knight, and Michael McClure.

For permission to reprint extracts from copyright material I am grateful to the following: New Directions Publishing Corp., New York, for excerpts from *A Coney Island of the Mind*, Copyright © 1958 by Lawrence Ferlinghetti, *Her*, Copyright © 1960 by Lawrence Ferlinghetti, *Starting from San Francisco*, Copyright © 1961 by Lawrence Ferlinghetti, and *Who Are We Now?*, Copyright © 1976 by Lawrence Ferlinghetti; Harper & Row, Inc., New York, and the Andrew Wylie Agency, New York, for excerpts from the works of Allen Ginsberg; Harcourt, Brace, Jovanovich, Inc., New York, and André Deutsch Ltd, London, for excerpts from *The Town and the City*, Copyright © 1950 by Jack Kerouac; the Putnam Publishing Group, New York, and André Deutsch Ltd, London, for excerpts from *Desolation Angels*, Copyright © 1960, 1963, 1964 by Jack Kerouac, and *Vanity of Duluoz*, Copyright © 1968 by Jack Kerouac; the Sterling Lord Agency, Inc., New York, and André Deutsch Ltd, London, for excerpts from *On the Road*, Copyright © 1955, 1957 by Jack Kerouac, *The Dharma Bums*, Copyright © 1958 by Jack Kerouac, *The Subterraneans*, Copyright © 1958 by Jack Kerouac, *Lonesome Traveler*, Copyright © 1960 by Jack Kerouac, *Tristessa*, Copyright © 1960 by Jack Kerouac, *Big Sur*, Copyright © 1962 by Jack Kerouac; the Sterling Lord Agency, Inc., New York, for excerpts from *Book of Dreams*, Copyright © 1961, 1981 by Jack Kerouac.

Note of Thanks

What we'd really like to do is thank: Roger Shirley-Elgood and Christopher Terry for moral support; Bim and Mavis Brown and Tone and Susie Howarth for oiling the wheels; the East Midlands Arts Association for the research bursary; Frank Pike for staying a friend while being an editor; Carol Clarke for reading my writing, for typing above and beyond; all those whose time, correspondence and hospitality shaped this book (their monument lies around); and the late G. S. Fraser for the only postgraduate guidance I ever received.

C.C.
February 1984

I New York

Goodbye Hank Williams my friend I didn't know you but I've been places you've been

America is gray, flat, and bumpy with hangars on its far edges. Twenty years of reading and writing about the place and when I finally risk the psychic damage of seeing it first hand it looks just like any other damn country.

In the departure lounge bar at Heathrow a young man had come up and accused me of photographing him in a show. "You'll have forgotten," he said. "I was Benjamin Franklin."

Later, this author of the Constitution got the last two seats on the plane and Heather and I had to wait for the next one.

At the Immigration desk no cynically predicted discourtesies materialize. With a few shutterboxes around his neck and a very tall blond at his side it seems that even a long hair can get into the land of the free. The officer studies Her Britannic Majesty's request and requirement.

"Dr. Challis?"

"Yes."

"Purpose of your visit?"

"Writing a book about the Beat Generation. Mutual influence on and support for each other. Taking photographs for it, talking to a few people who'll feature in it."

"You're a Ph.D.?"

"Right. American literature: Jack Kerouac."

The Immigration officer does not say, "Jack who?"

He seems a little bemused that an Englishman should be writing a book on such an American phenomenon. He stamps my passport with permission to stay about six times longer than the money will last and tells us to enjoy our stay. America is one wheeze of a bus door away.

15

It's so darned cold in this here New Yawk

This is the biggest city in the richest nation in the world. The acknowledged leader of the West and consumer of a rumored 80 per cent of the world's energy. And it is full of mad people. It is full of shopping-bag ladies and contentious winos and blacks screwed up in the corners of plush shop fronts with old cracked shoes and awful greasy old pants rolled up and hair tied up in woolly tufts straight out of Mark Twain. Richard Brautigan would appear to have been right: crazy old women ride the buses of America today. Is the country so car-oriented that only the poor, the mad, or the desperate gravitate towards the public transport?

America, I am not sure I understand this.

America, is this real?

Have I, America, the right impression here?

America, on the bus this evening a youngish (perhaps in her thirties) woman in pancake makeup and a hopelessly sad blue patterned dress in some man-made fibre, her hair drawn straight back in a rubber band, sat berating an old man whose most recent shave had left patches of stubble and scraped rawness over the lower half of his face. He had taken her, or wanted to take her, to some kind of "theater show".

"Was it s'posed to be worthwhile?" she demanded. "Was that why?"

"Most of it's worthwhile." He just sat and looked straight ahead.

"I would have, you know, preferred to have gone straight home from there – I guess it was I should have made it – I mean, more positive, you know? Was it that I left it too open? I mean I have some things to take care of, you know? And the people who live in my apartment, they go to bed early. Why should I wake them up? When they're asleep? I mean, we could have taken a ride out to the airport. You know, La Guardia or Kennedy, you know, Kennedy Airport. We could have gone out there. And you see all the stores, and the people, y'know? I guess I should have *said*."

"The traffic is so terrible."
"I just suppose I didn't make it *clear*."

"Man, I'm beat to my socks"

HA HA HA HA HA HA HA HA HA HO (W. Cannastra, a
telegram sent by Western Union, 10 September 1942)

"Señor Gahr-va se murio" – He'd died up himself –
He who cried to me and Irwin and Simon on the last
day when we were running away to America and the
World and for what?

(Desolation Angels)

The members of the fledgling Beat Generation met William
Cannastra, Bill Garver and Herbert Huncke in the New York of
the forties. Possessing different attitudes and temperaments, they
were catalysts for the group, inspiring vivid characterizations
though not writers themselves. The published reminiscences of
Huncke, a renowned raconteur, tend to plod in print, as if they
rely for impact on being heard, not read.

Bill Cannastra's charisma was both intense and enduring.
Contemporary Alan Harrington characterized him as Bill
Genovese in *The Secret Swinger*.

He was puerile, foolish and gaily cruel: on a rough flight to
Provincetown, the most courteous passenger, suddenly an
imitation steward, coming down the aisle with a huge paper
bag, bowing to a gray-faced man: "Sir, would you prefer to be
sick now or later?"; to a team of neatly uniformed oil company
trainees running to their pumps: "Up your ass with Mobilgas!"

Twenty years later, interviewed for the *Paris Review*, Kerouac
chortles that very line and immediately launches into remi-
niscence of Cannastra's party piece – dancing barefoot on shards
of glass – the catch phrase triggering the memory.

Harrington's description of the Genovese milieu is everyone's idea of the bohemian lifestyle.

> Genovese's loft was sometimes strewn with broken glass. People made love in the bathroom (often, without realizing it, for a circle of spectators looking down from the skylight). They made love on the fire escape and on the roof . . . and Bill Genovese ate glass, and music roared out of the dark. . .
>
> Bill Genovese walked carelessly along the edge of the roof, saying: "It would be easy to fall off, wouldn't it?" . . . "I've asked you up here for a reason. Only you. Why don't you push me off?" Genovese, on the waterfront, entering a bar-room full of longshoremen, stepped up to the nearest one, saying: "Give me a big, wet kiss!" kissed him, and walked slowly out unharmed . . . (*The Secret Swinger*)

Both Kerouac and John Clellon Holmes had the same incidents stick in their minds.

> Bill was the guy who used to teeter off his roof – six flights up you know? He'd go – "you want me to fall?" – we'd say no, Bill, no . . . He says, "Jack, come with me and look down through this peephole." We looked down through the peephole we saw a lot of things . . . into his toilet. (*Paris Review, 43*)

> "I've just seen Agatson in the White Rose Bar, and you know what he did? It was fantastic! He was already very drunk, and right while I was talking to him, he turned away, positively wriggling, and went up to a tough-looking marine and said: 'Give me a big wet kiss!' . . . But imagine Agatson . . . You know he's not queer at all. It was just an imitation of course. But I tell you the whole bar was electrified!"
>
> "How did you get him out alive?" Hobbes exclaimed.
>
> "Nothing happened! Isn't it incredible? The marine was absolutely speechless, as though he was seeing a monster. . . "
>
> Pasternak refused to show his amusement at the story.

"That guy's going to get killed someday, crazy son of a bitch!" (*Go*)

The outrageousness fueled by a death wish impressed the poets as vividly as the novelists, even though they couldn't seem to spell his name. Allen Ginsberg wrote "IN MEMORIAM William Cannestra 1922–1950". To Robert Creeley he was "the most painfully vivid instance of one of 'the best minds of [our] generation' that one saw 'destroyed by madness.' Bill had the compulsive need to kill himself." (*Contexts of Poetry: 1961–1971*)

He finally fulfilled that need. As he tried to scramble out of a subway train leaving a station his head was smashed on the tunnel entrance. The shock was like a bucket of cold water to his friends in the lofts and bars. His last girlfriend "inherited" his loft: she was called Joan Haverty and she was soon to become the second Mrs. Jack Kerouac.

Over the top as he was, Cannastra nevertheless graduated from law school. Huncke and Garver, on the other hand, belonged to the criminal fraternity. William Burroughs met them in 1944 and put them both in *Junkie*. Thieving and intermittent prison sentences were almost inevitable for men like them, simply because of their dope habits. They exemplified a real "Beatness" which younger men from less desperate backgrounds often found fascinating. Portrayed by the Beats they symbolize the condition defined by John Clellon Holmes:

> the feeling of having been used, of being raw. It involves a sort of nakedness of mind, and, ultimately, of soul; a feeling of being reduced to the bedrock of consciousness. In short, it means being undramatically pushed up against the wall of oneself. A man is beat whenever he goes for broke and wages the sum of his resources on a single number. . . (*Nothing More to Declare*)

Huncke was Junkey in Kerouac's *The Town and the City*, Elmo Hassel in *On the Road*, Albert Ancke in Holmes' *Go*, and Herman in Burroughs's *Junkie*. Legend has it that it was he who first picked up the term "beat to my socks" from the jazz musicians.

Ginsberg dedicated *Empty Mirror* to him. He was the second, and last, of Neal Cassady's "Hip Generation." The best incarnation of Huncke as the essence of the unromanticized hustler is as Ancke in *Go*.

Ancke was only thirty-three, but everything about him seemed worn and faded. His head was large for the emaciated, almost girlish body, and his lank brown hair gave the appearance of being dry, even dusty. His skin was puffy, yellowish, and in his whole heavy face, with the wide, soft mouth, the small nose, and the pallid cheeks, only his eyes, that were large, dark and luminous, gave any sign of life. They burned fitfully under thick eyebrows. His thin arms and legs were scarred with the countless wounds of the hypodermic needle which had poured morphine into him for years, and the flesh seemed to have shrunk in upon his brittle bones. He quivered involuntarily every few minutes, as though he had chills. He was extremely dirty and smelled of sweat and decaying teeth.

Kerouac shared a house with Bill Garver in 1955, after the latter had quit New York permanently for Mexico. The man and the setting virtually dictated the form and content of Kerouac's most ambitious poetic work, *Mexico City Blues*.

Old Bill Gaines lived downstairs. I'd come every day with my marijuana and my notepad. He'd be high on opium. I had to get the opium in the slums from Tristessa. She was our connection. Bill's sitting in his easy chair in his purple pajamas, mumbling about Minoan civilization and excavation, I'm sitting on the bed writing poems. And through the whole thing some of his words come in. Like the 52nd chorus. Just idling all the afternoon. He talked real slow and I could put it all down. . . Allen Ginsberg said he talked too much. So I hit on the mad idea of listening to him. (*Kerouac Biblio.*)

Most of *Tristessa* and much of *Desolation Angels* is set at this

20

time. Both chronicle the narrator's relationship with Bull Gaines (not to be confused with Bull Hubbard), who transcends his sordid existence to become the archetype of the old addict.

– he lives there, thin, emaciated, long nosed, strangely handsome and gray haired and lean and mangy 22 in his derelict worldling ("student of souls and cities" he calls himself) decapitated and bombed out by morphine frame – . . . Old Bull . . . with his needles and his powders beside the bed and cottons and eye-droppers and paraphernalias – "When you got morphine, you don't need anything else, me boy," he says to me in the daytime all combed and high sitting in his easy chair with papers the picture of glad health – "Madame Poppy, I call her. When you've got all you need. – All that good O goes down in your veins and you feel like singin Hallelujah!" And he laughs. "Bring me Grace Kelly on this chair, Morphine on that chair, I'll take morphine." (*Tristessa*)

Kerouac's compassion and his romantic conviction that "all *la vida es dolorosa*" did not blind him to the waste and pathos of the junkie's existence. The Beats experienced that aspect of the human condition through rubbing shoulders with men like Huncke and Garver. The loss and the pity of it found its way into their work.

"Hey Bull, we're going now. I'll see ya – when I come back – I'll be back soon – "

"No! No!" he cried in the trembling sick voice he had when he tried to convert his addiction withdrawal pain to barbiturate torpor, which left him a mess of tangled bathrobes and sheets and spilled piss. "No! I want you to go downtown do somethin for me – It won't take long – "

Irwin tried to assuage him thru the window but Gaines started crying. "An old man like me, you shouldn't leave me alone. Not like this especially not when I'm sick and cant raise my hand to find my cigarettes – " (*Desolation Angels*)

"... *staying up for days in the Chelsea Hotel
writing 'Sad-eyed Lady of the Lowlands' for you. . .*"

On West 23rd Street the Chelsea Hotel stands tall and narrow, its frontage hinting at the special place it has in literary history, rather like an ornate bookcase. Since the great days passed into history Bob Dylan, Andy Warhol (*Chelsea Girls* was filmed there and Nico still lurks within), and Burroughs have given it notoriety to add to its fame. The plaque on the building's front recalls its association with literary lions of earlier decades. Brendan Behan raised some hell here, Dylan Thomas sallied forth to count the New York bars and die in the process, never knowing that the little bard from Minnesota would adopt the haunt as well as the name. Thomas Wolfe wrote novels here (with those long titles which Kerouac was to emulate when he first took up the craft – *Of Time and the River* begat *The Town and the City*). The Chelsea Hotel was one of the places Kerouac saw when, carried away by Thomas Wolfe, he "roamed his New York on crutches" after the broken leg on the football field. Some stories have him and Sammy Sampas on a pilgrimage out to a Wolfe holiday home, much like the kids with "Dharma Bums" emblazoned, teenage-hood style, across their shoulder blades, who would come knocking at his door in later years. In *Vanity of Duluoz*, the last novel, so desperately flawed by unreliable hindsight, Kerouac saw his young self as wide-eyed in search of a literary heritage. The small-town Canuck from the little mill town on the banks of the racing Merrimack seeking the great traditions of American letters. The New York he found in those wartime years was as different from that Wolfe knew as today's city is from the cradle of the Beat Generation in those heady days when Burroughs observed that it was a finkish world. Some of the New York Kerouac had read about was there still, though. Ghosts of the Jazz Age scuttling through the rain in a silk hat or a silver lamé wrap and into the Stork Club, uniformed doorman carrying a striped umbrella from the taxi to the canopy. Dorothy Parker storing up a week's witticisms for a meeting of the Algonquin's Round Table.

The old New York haunts of the Beat Generation are disappearing fast. The Pony Stable, the "dyke bar" where Gregory Corso was first "graced with a dark-eyed apparition" which turned out to be Allen Ginsberg (who he had watched performing with a girl across the street, unwittingly), is now a sedate sandwich bar with just one member of the staff who remembers the old name. Dylan Thomas's favorite bar, the White Horse on Hudson, retains its tin ceiling and retails bottled English beer and generally has an air of knowing that a great number of its clientele will be rubberneckers. The old Angle Bar on 8th Avenue and 42nd Street (the dips could enter from one side of the street corner and lose a tail by leaving on the other) bears no trace of its historic past. The Cedar Tavern is apparently newly sited and now has a roofgarden restaurant and a beautiful twenties bar which formerly graced the old Susquehannah Hotel. It is here, though, that one first gets an idea of the bar life of the forties and fifties and just how it colored and shaped the social groupings and relationships that the Beats were to celebrate. Closed for a bare two hours around dawn, the Cedar, like the other bars in the Village that keep similar hours, is a place to drift in and out of to see what's happening. Not like making a specific appointment to share one of Britain's sparse daytime opening hours. The long bar has stools for observing the street (occupied these days, still, by men in berets, shades, and checkered shirts, but they are ageing hipsters now) and the wall phone is a step away. The booths – for long and frenzied explorations of the theories of Marx or Descartes or the *Cantos* or the writings of Sartre – are dimly lit and have an aura of privacy conducive to confidences. The waitress in the leotard and tights will pad over when a refill is needed so that the talkflow need not be disturbed. Way up out of the Village and opposite the Columbia campus is perhaps the most famous Beat bar, the West End. In one of its booths one completely understands why Lucien Carr chose this confessional of dark wood and hushed groupings to tell Kerouac that Dave Kammerer was at that moment floating face down in the Hudson, his broken glasses in the weeds beside the river, the bloodstained Boy Scout knife down a drain. Kammerer, who behaved like a Sunday tabloid scoutmaster, and was killed by a Boy Scout knife.

The Village, the heart of Beat New York, has altered under the pressures of modern living. Even in broad daylight the mean and garbage-piled streets just out of Chinatown are as thick with menace as a Charles Bronson movie. Black girls come barefoot from a women's refuge, in nothing but thin wraps, to harangue insistent men in the street. A scavenger, his face set in a rictus of distant and incomprehensible greed, clambers teeteringly down a plank into the basement area of a deserted factory, knee-deep in moldering refuse. Face inflamed, swaying, a wino attempts to smear a filthy rag across the windscreen of a car nervously paused at a red light and reels into the gutter screaming imprecations as the relieved motorist eases off. A mile or two away, gazing out at the soaring arches of the Brooklyn Bridge, the cops cluster thick as flies, the mini-arsenals they carry on their belts dragging their weight down into short legs and spread asses. In the tough end of the East Village the despairing little crimes go unhindered in the streets of desolation.

In Washington Square, where poet William Morris, in his beatnik uniform of striped sailor shirt and sandals, was arrested one Sunday by the statue of Holley for reading his poetry out loud; students take video films of each other or crowd around a guitar under New York's own triumphal arch or jog in legwarmers around the square's four sides. Over the entire scene hangs the obvious and slightly sinister presence of the pushers, hands jammed into their coat pockets, exchanging the platitudes of the trade as they hover and cross on the pigeon-strutting paths.

In the Hotel Wentley the double glass doors at the lobby entrance are opened by the clerk from inside his bulletproof booth and the weed aroma is pungent in the elevator. From the window one can see the trees on the roofs of the buildings over on the Avenue of the Americas. It is a short step from the hotel through the bustling side streets of bookshops and sex paraphernalia emporia (expensive paperback Kerouac reprints and colored satin on the dominatrix outfits) up into the sex area of the

Village. Christopher Street, which the chains and boots trade seem to have made their own, the bikeboy black leather, switchblade, and singlet shops of MacDougall, past a deal for amphetamine on the steps outside what was once the Gas Light Café. Past Bleecker Street where the old newspapers blew like Kerouac's hopeless and damning fame. Up over Houston Street into New York's SoHo (the difference is the capital "H"). Holmes and Cannastra and Kerouac cut from bar to bar in these streets in the days before Kerouac drew himself up to his full height, took a deep breath, went and shut himself up in a loft in West 21st Street and poured out a beautiful book onto a continuous single roll of paper (shelf or teletype, or newsprint, according to which story you believe).

Since the Beats in wartime the Village has passed through its postwar bohemian phase (in the tradition of eccentric poet-salesmen murdered by axemen) through the New Left Activism to Flower Power to the disillusionment of the seventies and on to the determined sexual militancy of the eighties. From the *Village Voice* through the *East Village Other* to *SoHo News* and *Christopher Street*. In a way, the Beat Scene was over long before they all started to write about it – dying a little with Kammerer and a lot with Cannastra. In some of the quiet smoke of the chess-playing bars, in some of the long afternoon browsings in Brentano's or the West 4th Street Bookstore, in the inheritors in clown pants and spiky hairstyles and the cross-dressing parties at the Château, something of the tradition of Greenwich Village survives.

So the beginning was Times Square and the depths of a wartime winter. Army khaki and sailor suits among the jostling crowds and country boys burning at the word "hick." It was to this New York, with the glamor and graft and excitement of any big-city port but without the bombs that rained on London or Liverpool, that the boys came from Denver, from Paterson, New Jersey, and from Lowell, Massachusetts. Some came originally to smoke their pipes under ivied walls or make a touchdown on a red and smoky October afternoon. Some of them did just that. Some of them drifted into jobs as bartenders or pearldivers in Bickford's cafeteria, or into the Merchant Marine. There they met another kind of American, a character who might have felt at home in the moody, all-night atmosphere of an Edward Hopper painting (or, in the green light of the Pokerino that turned everyone into a geek, a Steadman drawing.) Not exactly Mom and apple pie and Norman Rockwell paintings.

The neons of the Pokerino, the last-ditch joint for the whores, hustlers, dips, panhandlers, and petty thieves thrown out of everywhere else, promised sleazy adventure. Here, where the dreamers and poets overlapped with the damned and desperate, the Beat Generation smoldered into existence. The jazz/poetry/painting coteries of Greenwich Village, North Beach, and Venice West were sired by an unholy alliance of street hoods and personal poet madmen: manic Bill Cannastra; car crasher and yacht sinker Lucien Carr; crazy Allen Ginsberg, suspended from Columbia for writing obscenities in the dust on his windowsill, hearing the sonorous tones of William Blake in his room.

Among the hoodlums were men like Phil White, who borrowed a Baretta, went on a spree, and shot an old man in a fur store who didn't have enough money. Broken up, the gun went down half the drains in Brooklyn. Little Jack Melody and his henchmen used Ginsberg's apartment as a Thieves' Kitchen. Convinced he was living the Dostoevskian low life, Ginsberg wrote it all down. Driving a car full of stolen property, plus Ginsberg and his journals, Melody started a quarrel with his woman, Vicki Russell, and missed a stop sign. A passing patrol car hit the siren. Melody hit the gas. The car hit a stanchion. Glasses smashed, the poet ran for it while the details of the capers and letters with his address on them fluttered in the breeze around the ankles of curious cops. With the assistance of family, friends, and Columbia professors, Ginsberg got out of that one with only eight months in shrink wards. Melody went to jail. So did Huncke.

Herbert Huncke (it even rhymes with junkie) was the archetypal hustler, the spirit of Times Square: walking the streets seen through the smeared window of the all-night joint, eking out a cup of coffee, sleeping in a fleapit movie theater. When the opportunity presented itself, he stole. When he was well enough, he hustled, turning tricks in the dim flop houses and ashcan alleys. Whenever he could get it, he shot up. Knocking on Ginsberg's door, snow on the ground and shoes full of blood, the blue cheese smoke of dying junk cells rising from him. When the frantic phone call after the car chase – "The cops are on the way! Clean up the place!" – reached him he got a broom and started to sweep the floor. Too wasted to comprehend or too wise for anything but resignation? Another time, when Burroughs took him in, he stole the rug. Inspector Lee looking at the bare spot on the floor was always "put in mind of his vile act." Later, of course, it would be Burroughs who would formulate that very junkie logic that makes burning *anyone* an acceptable equation in the algebra of need.

Bill Garver, famous and prodigious junkie and thief, was popularly supposed to steal an overcoat a day from the stores of Manhattan to keep up his habit. He moved to Mexico City for the ease of access to bent doctors, goofballs, and Horse. Later, Kerouac would visit him, writing in his adobe by candlelight.

So the Beat Generation's apprenticeship into minor-league crime and dope continued. A young hood who looked like George Raft, only taller, stole a sub-machine gun and asked if Burroughs could find a buyer. Burroughs and guns. Always a shooter or two about. Sure, he'd see what he could do. How about these? Morphine syrettes? It was shifting those on to Huncke and his sidekicks that gave Burroughs his first taste of junk. Meticulously folding his coat and rolling his sleeve. Rubbing alcohol. Blood blossoming in the syringe. Hmm. Fthunk. Verry innaresting.

Those, like Kerouac, who were leery of the needle, could still enjoy the kick of using something exotic and illegal. Marijuana was synonymous with blacks and black music – jazz. ("Don't let your children buy Negro records unless you wish them to turn into Dope Fiends!") The Freedom Riders and voter registration drives were a decade or two away when the original Beats were stomping their feet in the forties black clubs, eyelids and heartbeats synchronized with the music. There were two representative black beats.

Leroi Jones founded one of the best of the Beat mags -*Yugen*- and later signaled his rejection of "American" values by turning into Imamu Amiri Baraka. In the West Village of the eighties there are new handbills plastered on the hoardings telling of his latest clash with authority, the most recent nightstick on his skull.

Ted Joans was a poet and a painter and a taker of a white bride. "Goin' down South with a smile on his mouth and the sun shines bright on him all the day long." Bearded, bongoing, beret-wielding Rentabeatnik in the fifties when the whole thing really got going, he went back to Africa in another way. Literally. Letters to be forwarded to Poste Restante, Timbuktu, Republic of Mali.

Some, with precious hindsight, oversimplify the Beats–blacks camaraderie as white patronage, approving, for a change, the black stereotype of rhythm, randiness, and weed. In reality it was the beginning of a new consciousness.

As Jack Nicholson said in a film about a man who went looking for America (and couldn't find it anywhere), "they" will talk to you about freedom of the individual but show them a free individual and they'll get busy burning and lynching. This fact began to be realized. "Disaffiliated" was the technical term coined to cover the feeling of being used, raw, cheated. It was Huncke ducking a bar looking for a score, a john. A little change to slip off the counter, maybe. Some ill-considered trifles to snap up. In one door and out into another street. A pretty girl approaching him with an offer. Talk to a professor about sex, for cash. Huncke drawn but wary. After the first talk about his habits, Huncke recruited as an interview pimp. A few bucks for every interesting character who'd spill the beans on what he did in bed or under the fire escape. And that is how Dr. Kinsey came to compile the data for the book that scandalized

Americans by telling them they were all sex fiends. The straights in cold-war America howled in protest. The street Beats gave a sardonic chuckle.

Beat reality could scarcely have been less like the *Life of Riley*, *I Married Joan*, *I Love Lucy* sitcom fantasy that America was selling itself as the desirable norm. A cute and cosy world of Moral Values, material prosperity, and an icebox full of Eskimo Pies and Coke. The Beats and the hipsters turned away from William Bendix and Lucille Ball with a weary shrug. Small wonder the image makers could put a hypodermic in the hand of an ex-virgin co-ed and scream in shrill outrage until a million exposés were sold.

The hipster evolved. He was the street Beat with that spice of dangerous sex in him. The very early Elvis before the homogenization process ever began. Sometimes he got back at the straight world by being the invisible non-conformist, even leaving aside distinctive clothing to move unremarked through the streets, his power never tested because he never entered the arena. More often he adopted a touch of flash. Like the nihilistic type of Beat, the hipster eschewed regular employment and used grass. Unlike his counterpart, he was sexually aggressive (usually hetero), still drank, and was not averse to the odd bit of violence. When he stubbed out his joint he headed, not for endless philosophical discussion in a coffee shop, but for a bar with a whiff of action, the charge of danger in its air. The sociologists like to see his cousins in the Scandinavian hooligan, the Ted, or the *blouson noir*. The hipster was unconcerned about such distinctions.

Meanwhile, the A-trainers were picking up on the Bagel Babes and a Beat style was emerging. Snapping their fingers to Charlie Parker, Dizzy Gillespie, or Brew Moore, a copy of *Evergreen* or *Neurotica* slyly peeping from a pocket, sporting a goatee, shades and with a ponytailed chick in a black leotard, came a new breed of outcasts. From Parisian existentialism berets and a penchant for black were grafted on to the sandals, the windcheater, the Sloppy Joe sweater. A style of dress at once practical, distinctive, and a uniform of disenchantment.

It was disenchantment, partly, with a war just won and things little better for it. A former ally turning, overnight, into the All-Powerful Threat. Soldiers once more arching off, not to a war, but to a "police action" in some place called Korea.

Like all subcultures the subterraneans developed their own language – a blend of black argot, jazz terms, and dope lingo – in order to recognize their own. As soon as any term was picked up by the enemy (anyone who read the *Kenyon/Partisan Review* – or the cops) it was dropped. Some publishers, in a desperate attempt to merchandize the esoteric, brought out glossaries.

Their music was the music of revolt. The Bebop era arrived in answer to the bland ballads and lush orchestras of the swing years. A revolt against commercialized music asserting the individuality of the musician. Now was the moment of the sweating sax soloist, the frantic drummer, the subtle interchange of ideas between musicians *almost* over extending themselves in long sessions in hot, smoke-filled clubs with the audience breathless for that "Jazz Moment" which unites everyone in the room within the "It" of the music, black and white jammed together yelling "Go!"

Later still the Beats would be seen as having spawned a whole gallery of rebel styles. The Brando-Dean style hipster would segué into that bogeyman for the American matron, the leather-jacketed hood, eventually to recycle into outlaw biker, LSD-soaked prankster, or Weatherman. Down in the broken dreams of the Pokerino, in the spectral light of early morning, the progenitors of the Beat Generation, sleepless and waiting for a connection, a break, a sucker, a loan, cackled in mirthless pleasure as the last cowboy outlaw in America was run over by a truck full of toilet bowls. There's progress for you. The fêted outlaws of American legend – Billy the Kid and the Daltons, Butch and Sundance and Jesse James, ousted by the new breed of hero: Herbert Huncke, battered and bleeding on a blue day in the grimy snows of 42nd Street, stumbling down the block to score.

30

A *substance interesting as Bronx*

Heather is mildly surprised that Carl Solomon looks ordinary. He emerges from Dalton's bookshop after his shift, an unremarked man in his mid-fifties, wearing a Cossack hat in the Manhattan streets. He sits down over a plate of beans and franks in his usual restaurant and reads the inscription in the thick tome – the *Collected Neurotica* – I've just delivered.

"How is Jay?" he asks. He had two pseudonyms in the years when Landesman and Legman's idiosyncratic magazine was blazing its own particular trail: Carl Goy and Carl Gentile. It was his mother who gave the thumbs down to those. He lives with her, and an octogenarian uncle, in the Bronx. His two City Lights/Beach books, stocked, to his disenchantment, in a decreasing number of New York bookshops, display the surreal madness of Poor Tom, truth in the licensed mouth of the Fool.

The classic bright Jewish kid at school – 'A's for good conduct and a niche on the honor roll – he was a nineteen-year-old seaman's union Marxist when he jumped ship in France. There he lived by selling on the black market the U.S. currency bills his tailor grandfather had sewn in the lining of his jacket.

A couple of years later he met both Allen Ginsberg and Jack Kerouac on the same day, when the latter was visiting the former in New York State Psychiatric Institute. Their initial greeting became legendary: "I'm Myshkin," said Ginsberg. Solomon, probably very pleased that one of his fellow patients had read the Russians, replied: "I'm Kirilov." Ginsberg was just about to begin the "eight months in the bug-house" which followed his arrest. The following year, 1950, Solomon met Neal Cassady for the one and only time – at a New Year's party that went on for days. It was also, he says, the year of his first marriage, which was happy, while his second was not.

"Next, I had a spectacular breakdown." He shrugs. "Throwing my briefcase at cars in the street. Stress through work, I guess." It was about this time, circa 1955, that Ginsberg wrote "Howl for Carl Solomon."

Ginsberg, it turns out, was slightly off-course. American poetry garnered those ringing images by accident or poetic licence.

> Carl Solomon! I'm with you in Rockland
>   where you're madder than I am
> I'm with you in Rockland
>   where you must feel very strange
> I'm with you in Rockland
>   where you imitate the shade of my mother.
>
> *Howl*

Instead, by some peculiar irony, Solomon was sent to Pilgrim State, the same hospital in which Naomi Ginsberg, to whom *Kaddish* was dedicated, died.

In the precarious early fifties Solomon was employed as an editor at his uncle's paperback house. A. A. Wyn is long dead, but his name is still in the copyright notation on the colophon of a book it published by one "William Lee."

Ace Books were into the lurid end of the market. Pocket books for a hot read on Greyhound. Prodded by his old bug-house colleague, Solomon was trying to slip a few bits of quality writing onto Wyn's list, even though he recalls almost having a nervous breakdown just *handling* material like *Junkie* in the climate of the early fifties.

In 1953 Kerouac was given a $500 advance after Solomon read a description of a youthful Cody Pomeroy playing street football in Denver. This passage appeared decades later as part of *Visions of Cody*, but Ace Books never published any Kerouac.

In 1953, back to back with a "dope fiend" exposé by a narc (69/d, in Ginsberg's phrase), the first published book by William Seward Burroughs appeared. Expurgated (albeit slightly), layered with disclaimers (the original, prefaced by Ginsberg, has now appeared, spelled as *Junky*), it was not Burroughs' first novel (*Queer* remains unpublished) but it was a book in print. Burroughs had scarcely considered himself a writer; now he had 100,000 pocket books on the news-stands of New York. Dr. Benway owed his start to the shot nerves of Carl Solomon.

32

Kerouac, he recalls, he last saw in 1965. "I felt some animosity towards *On the Road*," he says, "because of its references to 'nanny beaters'." He has, apparently, had unpleasant experience of the species, although he is probably thinking not of *On the Road* but of *The Subterraneans*. Lucien Carr and Burroughs he saw at the Buddhist ceremony after the death of William Burroughs Jr. (author of *Speed* and *Kentucky Ham*) who only survived his liver transplant by five years. Ginsberg continues to take a kindly, somewhat avuncular interest in him.

Solomon's life is now chiefly divided between the bookshop (he just had his teeth fixed on a union plan) and his relatives at home in the Bronx ("increasing senility"). "I dislike the side effects but I keep taking the tranquilizers. They released me from hospital, finally, on the condition that I keep taking them, in 1964. It's a boost, you know, to receive some attention from England. Things are generally too eerie, I alternate between the impulse for health and safety and being drawn to danger."

Now, owlishly bespectacled and looking not in the least like a publishing pioneer nor the dedicatee of America's most notorious poem, Carl Solomon rises, shakes our hands and moves off, slowly, towards the Bronx.

I remember a market place

The West 4th Street Bookstore is on two levels, with light-colored wooden shelves and a public notice board. It's a browser's bookshop without the hidden closed-circuit camera feel imparted by some branches of B. Dalton's or Brentano's. Ginsberg and Lawrence Ferlinghetti each have five titles on display. Gregory Corso is conspicuous by his absence and of Holmes there is only the new edition of *Go*, the first novel wholly to depict the Beat Generation. Cassady's solitary volume is there. Burroughs leads the field with ten and a book of table talk. There's one book about Kerouac and five by him. A new edition of one of the Lowell novels. Tang of smoke on the wind of an autumn afternoon. Steaming coffee urns misting up the plate-glass windows of the diner. The shadow of Dr. Sax flitting down the redbrick alleyways of sunset.

Anthologies on the American small town manage to get by without mention of Kerouac's *Visions of Gerard* or *Maggie Cassady*. The King of the Beats persona has always overshadowed his picture of mainstream American life. Kerouac's father was an immigrant. No one tries harder to fit than the most recent arrival. "The country gave my family an even break," Jack used to say. The Lowell books illumine that stretch of American reality between the differing solitudes of wilderness and city. The intimacy of local communities: pride in a letter sweater; an older brother to buy your six-pack. American graffiti and Disney girls. The mill towns of Kerouac's Massachusetts.

Settled early by the British, Massachusetts is scattered with familiar English placenames: Worcester; Gloucester; Leominster; Boston itself. Jack's books, by the first of many coincidences, are dotted with names familiar to anyone from Essex: Chelmsford, Brentwood, Billerica (the Americans dropped the "y"). Even a Danbury. Now, far away on the other side of the Atlantic, just the thought of those names provokes a sudden wave of nostalgia.

The beach was gray rocks of irregular size. The overhanging cliffs were of reddish clay and walking along them at night the headlights from the road a hundred yards away flung giant striding shadows out on the dark and rustling surface of the sea.

By night the beach huts were the place for the heady taste of adolescent escape. Equipped with Calor gas stoves and paraffin lamps, constructed entirely of wood; it was forbidden to sleep in them. The fifties were scarcely out. Teenage Bohemianism was a duffel coat and blue jeans with six-inch turn-ups, a flagon of scrumpy and a packet of Player's Weights, Chelsea boots and the three-finger left-handed method of unhooking a bra.

The book was a thick paperback with a montage on the cover: a black jazz musician; a couple fighting (the girl, eyes and lips wide, falling backwards onto the seat of her jeans); a dreamer with a bottle of booze in his hand and, over all, a statuesque beauty with a steady come hither stare, the direct look of the woman who made her own sexual decisions (no demure downcast glances), wearing a V-necked sweater and a pair of hipsters that left a few inches of bare midriff to accompany the level eyes and the hand on the hip. On the back was a photograph of the author, a checked shirt and an untidy quiff of hair across the brow, a look one saw everywhere. Nobody dreamed he was forty years old.

A peeling stucco building on the edge of a teeming cobbled market place circled by pubs. All long gone under the interminable progress of the one-way system.

The folk clubs were a living for expatriate Americans. Champion Jack Duprees and Paul Simon, Spider John Koerner and Richard Farina. Average ticket price (for non-members) one shilling and sixpence.

The body of the hall and the balcony filled up with girls in beehives and court shoes, or straight hair with bangs and a tapered skirt. The men wore floppy sweaters with desert boots or boxy Italian jackets with cloth-covered buttons and very pointed shoes. Very few of the men wore beards and very few of the girls trousers. From the pubs where they had been drinking pints of cider and ginger wine or light and bitter and port and lemon, the audience came, smoking cigarettes without filter tips. Tobacco smoke only floated in the air. On the stage a man in a cowboy hat with his leg, in a plaster cast, resting on a stool, sat with his guitar across his thigh. He was Rambling Jack Elliot the Singing Cowboy from Greenwich Village and he was looked at with a certain awe. It was rumored that he hitchhiked with Jack Kerouac.

In most towns in Britain there was a pub that was the local equivalent of the Saracen's Head. Not all of them had the sort of aptness of name that brought Hassan i Sabbah to mind, but they were there. In a time when looking like John the Baptist was likely to get your head on a plate, it was essential that they wouldn't refuse to serve you because your rucksack took up space. In the quiet wastes of the Fens or the rolling Cotswold night you just stopped the first passing long hair and asked him where he went for a drink.

In the original Saracen's it was a hot July night and the long narrow bar was Cuban-heel deep in spilt ale and Crown Filter packets. A ten shilling note was floated for the next round. Threepenny bits rattled on the bar. Two new faces. One set in a permanent grin and one whose dark sideburns furrowed cheeks gaunt as a glacier. Extolling a writer who somehow expressed the idea and the force behind the life we were all leading. Some feller with a French-Canadian name. . .

He painted Lowell in colors of dark love and it ignored him in life. No statue under the elms when the critics were at their most vituperative. Barry Gifford and Marshall Clements, when researching *Kerouac's Town*, found, largely, ignorance of him on the second anniversary of his death. The pilgrims to his grave were outsiders. Then Dylan and Ginsberg sang over the gravestone that said "He Honored Life" in *Renaldo and Clara*, and now, safely dead and with a burgeoning legend, one that might bring in a few dollars, Lowell acknowledges its famous native son. In Père Lachaise I stood over a grave littered with trash, scrawled with graffiti. Since visiting the last resting place of Jim Morrison I have become increasingly uneasy about going to Kerouac's.

Across the West 4th Street Bookstore is the photo of Kerouac in Tangier taken by Burroughs. Still lean from the mountaintop and the traveling, checked shirt, very Gallic in a cap (the same one he photographed Burroughs wearing): Belmondo out of Brando. Eyes that follow you about. Printed on a folded beige leaflet. Inside, pious cant and a map of Lowell with numbers, key and a photo of the grave, scattered with bottles and Schlitz cans and precise directions of how to get there. Bring some tourists in now you're dead and can't be awkward, will you?

Heather looks over my shoulder. "That'll come in handy when we get to Lowell," she says.

"We're not going."

Sit down and weep

On impulse, in search of Primo del Rey and a look at Amtrak, we go to Grand Central Station.

Bang in the heart of the smart and mythic Manhattan is the decline and decay of the city's public sector. Once the middle classes have opted out of it, it runs rapidly downhill, whether it is public schools, public health, or public transport. The American middle class lives in a condo with a private security guard to protect it from the threat upon which this great vaulted roof, constellations twinkling, looks down; the vista of itinerants, winos, and junkies – the underclass. The men's room, underground, has two notices. The first, in dead and dusty neon tubing, unlit for years: "Hats Cleaned and Blocked While You Wait." Facing it: "Loitering or Standing Prohibited. Violators Liable to Arrest." Standing still is a crime. On the floor of the station I bump into a tall, fat man, and recoil from the squidgy impact of the floppy body under his expensive blazer and slacks. "Excuse me," I say. He staggers back, shock and panic on a face drained of color, his hand frantically groping at his hip before he scuttles off. I realize, slowly, that his instant reaction to a minor pedestrian shunt in Grand Central Station is a conviction that he was being robbed.

To the right at the top of the stairs out of the Gents' is a row of deserted stone thrones with worn boards in front. Where once Manhattan's commuter businessmen sat as their toecaps were made to twinkle, a lone black man, his bottle in a paper sack, sits looking down over the space where the subservient heads of his brothers gone before used to bob and think themselves lucky.

The place peels with former glories gone ratty, with civic

indifference, with the lurk and suspicion of petty crimes and miserable little violences. On a bench, someone sleeps, warmed by copies of *Women's Wear Daily*. Brooke Shields strutting and glossy across the sad greasy overcoat. "Well my boys, we'll be like that someday," Mr. Burroughs said. "Isn't life peculiar?"

By the station exit the music department of a store pumps the nasal accents of the industrial West Midlands into the winds scuttling down 42nd Street.

This town
Is coming like a ghost town. . .

Dreaming spires

They traveled a lot, so much of the writing has a strong sense of place: Git le Coeur, Orizaba, Raton Canyon, Corso's Greece, Ginsberg's India, Burroughs' South America. The observations of the outsider, different in style and feeling from roots writing: Kerouac's Lowell; Holmes' New England; Cassady's Denver. Then there is Sacred Time. That foreign country where they do things differently, a shared glorious past now irredeemably lost. The first and last year of the Beat Generation was 1956. Until then they had little support except that which they gave one another. Afterwards, they were famous writers, more or less. When it became common knowledge, moved into the domain of the media, it vanished. "Fame?" said Kerouac. "It's like old newspapers blowing down Bleecker Street." This is why they felt the need to analyze and examine that formative period so exhaustively in their work – a keening nostalgia for a lost golden age. A full decade after the parties in Cannastra's loft and Garver's daily coat thefts Ginsberg wrote a poem that catches the way that a place can embody an ideal as well as a physical reality. Hopeful confidence, wistful remembered support in the long years before recognition.

BACK ON TIMES SQUARE, DREAMING OF TIMES SQUARE

Let some sad trumpeter stand
    on the empty streets at dawn
and blow a silver chorus to the
    buildings of Times Square,
memorial of ten years, at 5 AM, with
    the thin white moon just visible
above the green and grooking McGraw-Hill Offices

a cop walks by, but he's invisible with his music

The Globe Hotel, Garver lay in
    grey beds there and hunched his
    back and cleaned his needles –
where I lay many nights on the nod
    from his leftover bloody cottons
    and dreamed of Blake's voice talking –
        I was lonely,

        Garver's dead in Mexico two years,
    hotel's vanished into a parking lot
And I'M back here – sitting on the streets again –
The movies took our language, the
    great red signs
A DOUBLE BILL OF GASSERS
    Teen Age Nightmare
    Hooligans of the Moon
But we were never nightmare
    hooligans but seekers of
        the blond nose for Truth

Some old men are still alive, but
    the old Junkies are gone –

We are legend, invisible but
    legendary, as prophecied (sic)

                    Reality Sandwiches

39

Don't do it if you don't want to
I wouldn't do a thing like that

When Walt Whitman died in 1892 Manhattan was no higher than ten stories. Since then the world has come to know that America is composed of skyscrapers – the Empire State with Kong swatting airplanes, the Pan Am with the helicopter pad on top and the heroine waving at Clint Eastwood, the lovely dotty spike of the Chrysler. The best place to see Manhattan is from the water, the island rising sheer out of the gray edge of the Atlantic and nothing in the way.

Over to the right France's vast verdigris congratulation waves her torch in the air. To the left the bright red fire boats bob on the waves slung low in the water with the cannon at half cock on their decks, saluting no one in smooth virile arcs today. In the setting where the first Beat novel ended, a lady with a Flatbush accent is dispensing hotdogs, and paper cups of coffee or beer to the commuters, who read newspapers, or the tourists, who take photographs. The shoeshine boy is a white man about sixty wearing a boiler suit as he walks around with his box. He takes my dollar and rubs cream and polish into my creased old Cuban-heeled boots and then he stands up with a grunt and wishes me a nice day and walks around a corner of the deck where he stops, takes out his false teeth, and carefully wipes them in a large buff handkerchief before putting them back in his face.

Goodbye, Big Apple

We have borrowed a cold-water walk-up to do some telephoning. The tenant, who emigrated to New York for the gay scene, has gone out to the men's baths where Bette Midler's career started. When his boyfriend phoned he was incredulous at hearing a woman's voice.

"Maybe I should have answered," I say.

"That," says Heather, "would have been even worse."

On the phone, she is in her element. Glasses on her nose and the receiver up under the spill of blond hair, juggling ballpoint, pad, package of Carleton's and the *Village Voice*.

"A Volkswagen, Thursday?" she asks, hand over the receiver.

"Lord no! I'm not driving three thousand miles with my knees under my chin. Get a gas guzzler before they're extinct. We'll do it the way they did it." I am standing at the window with a can of generic beer, watching New Yorkers on the sidewalk below and wondering why there is a pelican in the flat across the street.

She fingers the page and dials.

"What's an LTD?"

"Huge. Engine'd move a jet. Put a bowling alley in the back."

"We can have one from Richmond tomorrow."

"Great! Right. Take it."

She puts down the phone. "OK. Ready for us any time after two tomorrow."

The bus leaves the Port Authority Terminal fifteen minutes late. The three Puerto Ricans in front like the window open. New Jersey is mostly flat and grayish and throws new light on the world view of Bruce Springsteen. The Auto Driveaway office is in the charge of a pushy Italian with a black moustache. Something about the ostentatious way the framed photos of his wife and kids are displayed on his desk (turned *toward* the visitor) speaks volumes about his relationship with the snooty blond in the cubicle next door.

"I suppose," I say to her, "that you're always being told you're a look-alike for Stevie Nicks?"

She stops looking down her *retroussé* nose at my leather jacket for a moment. "Why no," she answers, trying to conceal her pleasure. "I've had Farrah Fawcett and Goldie Hawn. . . "

"Were they good?"

The LTD is maroon, half a block long and has only two pedals. The big Rand McNally road atlas says that you pick up Interstate 70 out of Philadelphia.

41

II   On the Road

Over easy

The six-wheeler stands gleaming in chrome and scrolled paint-work, incongruous in front of a field of kale and looking even more out of place since it has no trailer. Fuel tanks like crude-oil barrels, twin exhausts thrusting up into the sky, cab for the driver feet above anything else that uses the road. All that power and mystique and nothing to pull. Two bikers, full beards and fringed leathers, *Iron Horse* subscribers, come out and mount their Harleys, parked by the LTD in the rutted yard, give the Limey a friendly wave and roar off. The countryside settles quiet as their progress fades into the distance. The telephone poles teeter away down the side of the highway and the birdsong and the rustle of the kale is all there is. I make my call and go back into the diner. Heather is on her fill up of coffee and second cigarette.

"Did you get through?"

"Yes, they're expecting us. Did you order for me?"

"Yes. I waited to eat with you."

"No fried bootlaces, I hope."

"No, I ordered you fried potatoes, not hash browns."

"Thank God for that. Now I understand why Jack Nicholson meets too many bad-tempered waitresses. Having to serve up perfectly good potatoes turned into agglutinated bootlaces is enough to turn anybody stroppy."

The little girl in pigtails perched on the stool beside me giggles. She doesn't care that I think hash browns are indigestible and unappetizing, she just thinks I talk funny. It's the weekend and her father's brought her down to the diner for breakfast. Maybe he's giving his wife a lie-in or maybe he just likes to

45

spend some time with his daughter when he's not working, alone. He's talking Superbowl to the man beside him.

They are both wearing baseball caps and bobbing their heads at each other as they make their points. They remind me a little of those pairs of water-drinking ducks you sometimes see on window sills. I'm drinking coffee because Americans have no idea about tea. They don't seem to think it should have caffeine in it. My breakfast arrives. Strips of grilled bacon that look like what the British call streaky but taste very different; sausage, which is really a sort of oval patty of sausage meat, no skin, fried potatoes, two basted eggs, and a little container of huckleberry jelly. I've never had jam with fried food before. It is familiar and exotic all at the same time and it fills me with a warm and silly and spreading contentment.

The redbrick alleys of smalltown America

The frost belt of Pennsylvania is coal-mining country and most aspects of life are touched by that. When the center of Uniontown is sealed off on a Sunday the streets are lined with pizza stands and all the cheerleaders have names which end in "a" and the beer-bellied young fathers have dark sideburns and speak deferentially to the gray-haired men with moustaches who could consciously wish to look a shade more like Marlon Brando. The blacks were originally brought in as strikebreakers and the Italians haven't forgotten. The biggest Klan rally north of the Mason–Dixon line since the war was here a few years back, though local lore says the Imperial Wizard was rained off the last time he came here.

California, Pennsylvania, crouched near a famous bend in the Monongahela River, was founded and named in the year of the Gold Rush. Its epicenter and main employer is the State College, the life of which dominates the town. "ROTC" is the first logo on the road outside it, painted on the brick arch of an old bridge, and, in the mellow light of Kerouac's best month, the posters for the election of Homecoming Queen have spilled all along main street, in the bars and the windows of the stores. The girls glimmer out of their regulation-sized fliers, all teeth and smiles and coiffure whatever their ethnic origin. Their hair, luxuriantly abundant as only an American adolescence can make it, is as thick and perfect as it will ever be. Their grooming is as immaculate as the professional photos which are the basis of their campaign. Backlit, smiling, as wholesome and come hither as a fifties *Playboy* centerfold, crisply ironed and meticulously made-up they beam in proper promise and lash-lowering appreciation of the partisan banners flapping from windows of the men's dorms. They will have Erica Jong and Susan Isaacs and, certainly, Judith Krantz on their study-bedroom bookshelves (though they will mercifully, not have heard of Andrea Dworkin) and they all want to be Homecoming Queen. They want to preside over the celebrations when their gladiators return.

While Europeans are given the impression that the feminists have taken over America these dozens of pretty girls court rejection – of their looks and personalities, of their very definition of their femininity – in order to be *The* Most Popular. America has a safe supply of cheerleaders for the foreseeable future.

In California, Pennsylvania, the brass bell gleams on the fire station above the jetties of railroad ties that have been let into the river bank for the fishermen. What these gentlemen, in their mackinaws and baseball caps, would say if they knew that Allen Ginsberg knelt on their beached raft and asked the blessing of the river, is not known.

On the dappled surface of the Monongahela the combings of the fall lap red, russet, and gold at the shoreline. Above the river a single line of railroad track curves away across forever America, escorted by ridges of whitewashed granite chips. It goes through a gap in the bright trees and out under the wooded hills. Around the bend, the Hole in the Wall Gang wait to rob the mail car; Nick Adams, nursing his bruises, trudges along to his meeting with Bugs and poor, punchy Ad Francis. Right up at the head of

47

the track, way, way out of sight, the Chinese and Irish immigrant laborers race to meet in the middle of the plains.

The old cop walks by the placards for this week's special in the market, his gun, in the sleepy street and along with his homely cracker-barrel ambience, looking an inappropriate prop. Guns though, are very popular here. There are deer in the woods and the countryside is dotted with little forts, preserved or re-erected, dating from the British and Indian Wars. The little town boasts more than one gun club. In the prowl cars, parked in their reserved places along by the gas station, police in pairs carry heavier armament than handguns. Mostly though, their crews function as a combination of local bobby and campus cop.

Within twenty-four hours of coming in to California, Pennsylvania half the town will know of the presence of strangers and where they're staying. Depending on the standing of the host locally they'll probably be cashing a check or crossing the street to gossip, too. The smalltown friendliness epitomized by Andy Hardy and celebrated by Thornton Wilder. The stifling narrowness of a community looking over its own shoulder (often with a sniff) from Mark Twain to Sinclair Lewis or Grace Metalious.

Europeans usually think America is cowboy country and the cities (to many it is simply New York) but there are a lot of Americans who live in neither. Smalltown America came first. Little communities with a siege mentality (for good reason) banded together against the wilderness, the savages, and the wild beasts. No room for slackers or rebels. Scarlet letters for transgressors. That mentality can survive the shift of small town into suburb and it was a part of the American mentality that the Beats grew out of and kicked out at. It was certainly the part they most deeply offended. Ginsberg, wandering Paterson with its most distinguished chronicler, William Carlos Williams felt compelled to point out where he masturbated under the bridge. Kerouac made Lowell a microcosm of the virtues and values of this kind of life: roots, familiarity, settling deeply down into that supportive pattern of work and family and recreation. Big Papa Leo bustling to the print shop with his cigar and racing form yelling "Hi!" on the street. It was also Shittown-on-the Merrimack, with its petty jealousies, corruptions, and feuds, with Papa Leo building up enough grudges by publishing his little exposure sheet to eventually cost him his business. Dr. Sax cackling with laughter in the shadowed lots and grimy hills. It was the manifestation of the America that gave Kerouac's family that even break he used to talk about. He had to leave it to grow, even to see it clearly enough to write it, to give it just that hint of romanticized detachment that saves it from being merely its dreary reality.

He had to run away, as Peter Martin did, and when he tried to go back it started to kill him, hedging against him, according him the status of eccentric drunk and reinforcing his silly prejudices (Jews and Commies, later Hippies and Dope and Niggers). He even took a local girl for his third wife. Though most of the Beats were city boys (even if the cities were in the West or Midwest, Denver or St. Louis), they understood the smalltown mentality well enough. The literary Beats saw the literary establishment as the chief embodiment of the stale and sterile. The enclaves of North Beach and Greenwich Village and Venice railed against the attitude of mind that made Korea and the McCarthy witch hunt possible, and then followed them up with Vietnam. Made it possible out of a naiveté, out of the residue of a necessary Colonial response, a closing ranks against the invader without or the outlaw within. At its sinister extreme this is the America of the mob and the rope (historically, as likely to be found in a city as a small town). In *Easy Rider* and *Deliverance* the threat, representing both invader and otherness, is answered with direct and lethal violence. In reality the system of pressure and reward is usually subtler and more effective. Listen to the lyrics of "Harper Valley P.T.A." Naturally enough the response is ambivalent, even among the critics. It was that aspect of the U.S.A. that Ginsberg addressed in "America," the system that made one want to amount to something had made him want to be a saint. "America stop pushing I know what I'm doing." (*Howl*) It is that aspect of America that makes Lucy McAndrew, Libby Gonzales, and Cathy "Carmen" Fiorello

49

want to be Homecoming Queen. Cheer up, sleepy Jean, it's still possible to be a daydream believer.

Whatever the pressures it exerts collectively on its citizens and whatever the residues of suspicion elsewhere, the small town as exemplified by California, Pennsylvania, can be friendly enough. Stores in Pennsylvania do not sell beer. Tall cabinets in the bars display the national brand leaders, as well as quarts of the local Pittsburgh brew.

"Where you heading?" ask the local drinkers. "California? Some trip!"

Like so many clichés about the habits of foreign nationals the image of the jet-setting American flipping from coast to coast is one founded on the day to day experience of the few, not the majority. America's very space still remains daunting. To drive New York–Denver–San Francisco today is still something of an adventure. In the late forties it must have seemed like an expedition, the new postwar mobility awesomely seized for the first time. Little wonder that reading about it a decade later, with the stamp of its daring imprinted upon it, filled younger heads with a new realization. On both sides of the Atlantic: Christ, you can do that, you can just get up and go!

California, Pennsylvania, with its wooden houses and quiet tree-lined avenues with parking restrictions and husbands sent to the market with clipped coupons, seems a typical small American town. Kids hop rides on the running boards of small trucks, the one bar open on a Sunday is wary after a recent bust for serving minors. The local "character" sits disconsolate, dreaming of past glories. The latest in an unending stream of pennants is being contested on the TV over the bar. The jukebox is loud. The ephemeras of American popular culture are everywhere. This is some of the roaring world Kerouac dreamed of returning to from his mountaintop, the American reality he always missed when on expedition down among the fellaheen. In the age of the freeway, the cross-country traveler does not roll through a hundred little towns like this in the way the great trips of *On the Road* and *Visions of Cody* do.

Speed and momentum, by the very fact of their existence, treat with a measure of contempt the lives of people spent in one place. The real-life freneticism of Cassady's driving could scarcely have allowed the experience of too many smalltown bars and citizens. It was on his hitchhiking adventures, stopping but never stopping too long, that Kerouac confronted Main Street, U.S.A. A community like California, Pennsylvania, encapsulates those American values and experiences, valuable in their very familiarity, their universality, which he saw in "Saturday night all over America" – all the boys in pick-up trucks with six-packs going to collect a girl from a porch in the soft evening light.

It is here that Arthur Knight, aided by collaborator and wife Kit, produces *the unspeakable visions of the individual* (named from Kerouac's *Essentials for Spontaneous Prose*), a series of eccentric volumes chock full of esoteric Beat material, contemporary interviews, disinterred letters, resurrected photos from the forties and fifties, a labor of love and a cornucopia for the connoisseur, a house journal for a vanished race and an attraction that draws strangers to California, Pennsylvania.

Buffalo Bill's defunct

In the Ohiopyle State Park, where the Youghiogheny River boils white for a seven-mile stretch and famous falls tip out into space off a ledge of rock as sharp as a hatchet, I buy a hat. The big country store is crammed with everything from pizzas to pool. Even the ice machine gives trading stamps. On impulse I pick up the hat and perch it on my head. It's a big black Stetson-style with a braided leather band and four bright feathers in a cluster. A real bad guy's hat. To my surprise it fits. I can never get a hat to fit. The label says "EL." Sixteen dollars. Sixteen scarce gas-and-Budweiser greenbacks. Oh, well.

As the kid said to Freewheelin' Franklin: "Aren't you too old to be wearing a cowboy costume, mister?"

*Can you hear me, Dr. Benway, are you really just a
shadow of the man that I once knew?*

Of the original Beats the one the impartial observer might have
least expected to survive was Burroughs. Increasingly photographed since he became a fully-fledged media celebrity, the
images show *El Hombre Invisible* is slowing up at last. Nearly
septuagenarian, mentor to the young lions of Columbia in the
forties – age is beginning to do what all the years of needles and
staring at the toe of his shoe never could. Weapons freak all his
life, Burroughs walks the streets of SoHo now with an anti-
mugger kit which includes a can of Mace, a Cobra (a steel and
leather zap that extends when put to use) and, pointedly, a
heavy walking cane. The pistol that was a constant in Mexico
(and which was to cost Joan Vollmer her life) has given way to
the symbolic walking stick. The famous long face is on the way
to being gaunt. The lines from foreign sun and cynicism are the
cracks now of passing time.

Yet it is Burroughs who best personifies the changes which
there have been in the public image of the original Beats. When
the National Endowment for the Arts gives Orlovsky ten grand
the *National Enquirer* still rails about "taxpayers' money for
obscene poetry." That sort of sniping is directed at the radical
Ferlinghetti, the queer eco-freak Ginsberg and the druggie
Corso, yet Burroughs has sailed onto a wave of international
prestige of the kind that shuts up the hayseed critics at home like
nothing else. If European opinion says Burroughs is a genius,
home opinion is chary of refusing to see the Emperor's togs.
Like all the others, Burroughs started out condemned for the
frankness of his approach to his materials (it was as frank as any).
Naked Lunch, like *Howl*, had its day in court. Typically,
Ginsberg went, Burroughs didn't. Burroughs shifted ground
then, explicated the cutups and foldins to a point where any
reasonably literate person could see there was a serious purpose
there, not just a lazy man's way of writing a book.

Now, as he himself admits, Burroughs is in show-biz – the

readings, the interviews, the book signings. The serious purpose – the one-man battle against the control systems (like a consumptive gunslinger taking on the whole town because he has nothing to lose, old junkie as Gary Cooper) – is once more in danger. From the media blitz this time.

Burroughs' concerns tend to reveal themselves to those who associate with him, in person or in literature. When Victor Bockris was compiling his book of interviews with Burroughs he saw in his sleep a lady he had fancied for some time and his body started to make the appropriate responses. What might otherwise have been put down as a particularly vivid wet dream became, under Burroughs' tutelage, a visit from a succubus. It is impossible to tell, given Bockris' handling of the event, whether Bill was having him on. It *is* possible to tell that the thought never crossed Bockris' mind.

Just straying into Burroughs' territory makes you vulnerable to that eerie blend of prophecy and coincidence.

On the sixth floor of the unaccustomed luxury of the Marriott Hotel on the outskirts of St. Louis (the airport is opposite and the place is popular with pilots), awaiting room service's real tea and burned muffins, the universally bad color of American TV flickers across the midmorning educational shows. A film about one of Burroughs' fixations, the Mayan Codices, viewed in his home town. Come in, Captain Clark.

Jay Landesman, founder of *Neurotica* and another native of St. Louis, made this trip partly possible when he bought the outline of a book. When I leave St. Louis I will drive to Kansas City, where the Dean of Graduate Studies at the University of Missouri lives and he will present me with its arts journal, which will contain John Clellon Holmes' "Exile's London," the prize-winning essay on his visit to Landesman in 1968. It will also contain a piece on Harvey Matusow who lived in my home town, in the house where Burroughs' *Book of Breeething* was first published. Ground control to Inspector Lee. It is hard not to see the synchronicity in all this.

Rona, the disillusioned activist in *Kennedy's Children*, charting her progress from 1960 Freedom Rides to 1974 heroin, recalled distinguished visitors to the Democratic Convention at Chicago in 1968.

"Burroughs," she said, "who I thought was a god."

People who scarcely open a book declare Burroughs a genius, *Lunch* the greatest book ever. It is the anarchy. It is the sense that his work exudes of having gone beyond any rules except those that he makes for himself. To live outside the law you must be honest. Burroughs grimly pounding the jungle path with rifle and solar topee, hunting jaguars and ahahuasca. Burroughs on Houston Street, leaning on his cane, Cobra, steel and leather in the hip pocket, Mace can under his coat. Sufficient, as always, unto himself.

Willy Lee call Dr. Benway, Hôtel Rue Git Le Coeur . . . what you need to know, the only thing you can ever learn . . . Mr. Bradley, Mr. Martin, call Gysin at the Villa Mouneria, Tangier . . .there must be a room free, someone on the beach. . .what are you telling me? *Quien sabe*, masked man? Where is the Tangier whiff of 1956? Queersville-on-Sea not what it was, street boys gone calculating my dear . . . Billy Bradshinkel got such a nuisance he had to be killed off. . . You go up in the air and you hang around for a while and when you come down it is another country, another. . .spectral images floating off down the newsreel alleys. Oh fader, Inspector Lee gone among the streets of SoHo with a steel Cobra. The only thing you have to learn is what you already know. Breeething in a large quiet house with sawed-down pianos rusting in the mossy grounds. Listen, my little brothers. . .the only thing is what you know already. Do you know the warm progress under the stars? Do you know the control systems survive on a lack of communication? (Dr. Benway, call Mr. Bradley, Mr. Martin –) Information belongs to those who can use it. Mayan codices in a St. Louis hotel . . . Duke Street, St. James's, a stone's throw from the Queen's grocers, what an irony my dear . . . Old Bull Lee, call Sal in paradise, drinking sherbet from a golden cup. . . They were sweet little critters, I might be there yet. . . Information belonging to Duluoz before the senses at the moment in time what you already know belongs to those who can be bothered to use it. . . Flapping images in the gritty wind of the alleys of 1956 Tangier. . . We'll cross the Sahara and never come back. . . Call Times Square, 1944. . . A finkish world. . . Will Dennison in the brown Derby of forgotten images. . . Ti Jean, call the Beat Generation at the Cedar Bar. . . Winter wartime uniform drifting smoke down empty alleys of flapping broken film memory fading in the spectral green Pokerino light. . .

What is that feeling?

> I looked back to watch Tim Gray recede on the plain. That strange guy stood there for a full two minutes watching us go away and thinking God knows what sorrowful thoughts. He grew smaller and smaller, and still he stood motionless with one hand on a washline, like a captain, and I was twisted around to see more of Tim Gray till there was nothing but a growing absence in space, and the space was the eastward view toward Kansas that led all the way back to my home in Atlantis.
>
> (*On the Road*)

Down by that stretch of the Mississippi between two bridges where there is a floating MacDonald's you can park at night and watch the jellied lights throbbing on the water and their cousins hightailing it, blurry, across the cloverleaf. On a lovingly restored riverboat a three-piece jazz band works out to a scant audience, and a waitress in fishnet stockings and the fully flounced petticoats of the dance-hall girl looks wryly at her tip as the group of tourist matrons waddle out and says: "Thank you, ma'am. Y'all come *back*, now, y'hear?" On the river's cobbled bank, carloads of black and white kids split six-packs and pass joints to the music of their car radios.

Whichever way I stand, wherever I look, I am conscious of it, looming over my shoulder or rearing up before me, even in the darkness. Finally I realize I'm not going to get any peace until I confront the damn thing. I start up the grassy slopes leading to it. Noises of carnal commerce come out of the bushes and the dew flecks the pointed toes of my boots.

Out of the concrete slabs it goes up, above, forever. If you hit it with your fist there is a slight metallic *dong!* To raise your eyes to follow its sheer parabolic passage into the sky is to risk vertigo. Stainless steel that picks up the starlight: the idea of actually working on the damn thing, as the spidermen must have done, makes your head hurt. Up close, you can see that it is indeed big enough to house the elevator shafts which take visitors up.

For the first time since I landed I understand again what Andrew Sinclair was saying in *The Hallelujah Bum*. "Only three things made by men make me want to fall down and pray. Bridges, cranes, highways. All straight, all clean, all clear purpose. No frill, just the plain struts of beauty and use."

The arch at St. Louis, gateway to the West, where the wagon trains started from, highest unsupported structure in the U.S. of A., perched on the banks of the world's greatest river, soars up into space and whispers of space: all that space in between two oceans.

I can claim some experience and skill in the scrivener's trade

Burroughs, of course, denied specifically to interviewer Daniel Odier that he even was a member of the Beat Generation.

D.O.: What is your relation to the Beat movement, with which you associate yourself? What is the literary importance of this movement?

W.B.: I don't associate myself with it at all, and never have, either with their objectives or their literary style. I have some close personal friends among the Beat movement: Jack Kerouac and Allen Ginsberg and Gregory Corso are all close personal friends of many years' standing but we're not doing at all the same thing, either in writing or in outlook. (*The Job*)

But as sure as the movement had a social as well as a literary influence, Burroughs' antagonism towards postwar America typified and activated much of the Beat sensibility. His early works bear the Beats' stamp – the characteristic literary experiments were of a later vintage. His New York role was as elder statesman. He did the classic Beat tour of various methods of employment.

"But what was your last job?" I ask.
   "Bartender in Newark."
   "Before that?"
   "Exterminator in Chicago. Of bed bugs, that is."
   "Just came to se ya," he says "to find out how to get papers, to ship out." (*Vanity of Duluoz*)

Burroughs was called Will Hubbard in that book, Bull Hubbard in *Desolation Angels* and *Book of Dreams*, both written long before he got interested in L. Ron Hubbard's money-spinning Church of Scientology and came to challenge its founder. Just another of the coincidences.

He had found college less traumatic than either Ginsberg or Kerouac and it may have been the shaping discipline of academic training that made him such an influence (Holmes excepted) on the New York group.

Even Corso, a juvenile delinquent about to go down the river when the Beats first formed, who only met Burroughs in 1953, responded as positively as Jack or Neal Cassady had done. Here is Gregory writing Bill on that favorite source topic, the dream life.

Dear Bill, my dearest and smartest and goodest man in my eyes in the whole world. . . I then told you, "Bill, you are going to be the great writer of this age; you will write a great book; . . . I am telling you that you [sic] will be the great writer of the age. . . I always sometimes when I hold your word to be THE WORD I see the image of willie the weasel, I think you recall me calling you that, that I suspect you to be not this godly being, but a con man – well all that is gone now, that dream did it, yr voice and face was god-made, no doubt about that, and by god I mean what you mean by it. (*The Beat Diary*)

Though he was older, it was significant to Kerouac that this did not seem to matter. "He was nine years older than me but I never noticed it." (*Vanity of Duluoz*) He reacted to Burroughs' fund of stories and personal philosophy with an absorption bordering on the apostolic. A quarter of a century later he was still awed.

But I bite my lips when I hear the word "marvel" and I shudder with excitement when I hear Will say "marvelous," because when he says it, it really's bound to be truly marvelous. "I just saw a *marvelous* scene in a movie this afternoon," with his face all flushed, exalted, rosy, fresh from wind or rain where he walked. His glasses a little wet or smoky from the heat of his enthused eye, "this character in this awful beat movie about sex downtown, you see him with a great horse serum injector giving himself a big bang of dope then he rushes up and grabs this blonde in his arms and lifts her up and goes rushing off into a dark field going 'Yip Yip Yipp ee!'" (*Vanity of Duluoz*)

In 1952, at Rocky Mount, Neal Cassady conceived a work on a grand scale. Just like Jack: use historical fact and the rest flows from that starting point.

Being volatile Neal, of course, it petered out after a page or three of enthusiasm, but most of it was about the man who was the starting point for the "Hip Generation."

BOOK ONE

The Hip Generation went on Strike Against Man.

1

William Hubbard was born in St. Louis in 1917 an heir to the Hubbard Typewriter; he never had to worry about money the rest of his life.

By sixteen he was as high-horse as a Governor in the Colonies, as nasty as an old Aunt, and as queer as the day is long. (*The First Third*)

Burroughs, like the rest of the gang, drew on the raw material around, in the unpublished *Queer*, in *Junkie*, in the epistolic *Yage Letters*. It was the really Beat that fascinated him, authenticating the nice raw snap of decay, crime, and addiction with which he was so often concerned. Mostly his serious purpose has been obscured, in critical reaction, by shock and affected disgust. Under the sensationalism, anyone capable of reading can discern an anti-authoritarian voice so articulate and vicious that his continued survival seems to prove that the CIA cannot read.

Cutups first surfaced with *Naked Lunch*. They have been seen both as an attempt to "liberate man from the traumas of early verbalization" and the evasion of authorial responsibility. To Eric Mottram he has always been a satirist of the order of Goya, Daumier, or George Grosz.

The violence of his vision has caused his books to be feared and banned. . . He creates conflict through opposition to authority, and this includes the authority of established method of plot, time and space in novels and the readers' response to them. . .of authoritatively accepted literary forms. (*Snack*)

Like Allen and Jack, the dream material: that involuntary nightly trawl through the painful silt of consciousness. Freedom from practical constraints and a different logic.

W.B. : A great many of my characters, sets, and situations I get in dreams. I'd say a good 50%.

G.M.: Do you have a certain technique for notating dreams?

W.B.: Well, yeah, I keep a pencil and paper by my bed. . . I just make a few brief notes; that's all that's necessary. If you even have two words they can bring it back. Then I'll expand them into dream-scenes. If they're particularly interesting or important to one that might be usable in a fictional context I'll make a longer typewritten account. . . I get long sequential narrative dreams and some of these have gone almost verbatim into my work. (*The Beat Book*, interviewer Gerard Malanga)

If one wishes to describe drug experiences, the subconscious flow and the hallucinatory are valuable tools. In its abrupt alteration of direction and tone, cutup is dream. A police stenographer sat by Dutch Schultz's deathbed and wrote down all 2,000 words. Bootlegger's delirium with no exit but death. Vivid and unconnected and impacted without the constraints of logical progression. A boy has never wept nor dashed a thousand kim.

Joyce wrote it and let it stand, but Burroughs, in *The Job*, gave a handle to his name, a glance at a manifesto. Ostensibly a long interview, it is really a series of dialogue-connected essays, "answers" carefully and painstakingly argued. Ironically, perhaps, given the confusion that his work often creates, his conventional prose is lucid to the point of being mandarin.

Cutups and foldins, far from being a refuge from a paucity of talent, are the weapons in the fight that the Beat Generation started somewhere in Times Square in 1943. "What we see now is power exercised for purely destructive purposes. Whether they know it or not, the present controllers are bent on annihilation." (*The Job*)

Whither goest thou, America, in thy shiny car in the night?

What is that feeling when you're driving away from people and they recede on the plain till you see their specks dispersing? – it's the too-huge world vaulting us, and it's goodbye. But we lean forward to the next crazy venture beneath the skies.   (*On the Road*)

American literature is the literature of search. Search for personal identity, for the American Dream, for a lost father. Travel has always been the major theme. All the attractions, to the writer, of the picaresque – a strong story line with the opportunity to bring on a fresh character, a new situation at any point – and a continent full of stories. To settled Europe, America was at first an ideal as much as a physical entity. Charles Olson's *Call Me Ishmael* illuminates the search genre in its understanding of *Moby Dick*.

I take SPACE to be the central fact to man born in America, from Folsom cave to now. I spell it large because it comes large here. Large, and without mercy.

It is geography at bottom, a belt of a wide land from the beginning. That made the first American story (Parkman's): exploration.

Something else than a stretch of earth-seas on both sides, no barriers to contain as restless a thing as Western man was becoming in Columbus' day. That made Melville's story (part of it).

PLUS a harshness we still perpetuate, a sun like a tomahawk, small earthquakes but big tornadoes and hurrikans (sic), a river north and south in the middle of the land running out the blood.

The fulcrum of America is the Plains, half sea half land, a high sun as metal and obdurate as the iron horizon, and a man's job to square the circle.

All that raw land, said Kerouac, all that road going. That immensity is not inherently understood by Europeans but the inner search is international. David Widgery caught it in his obituary for the Kerouac lost by those who were young and English in the sixties.

Everyone I know remembers where they were when they read "On the Road". . .because of the sudden sense of infinite possibility. You could, just like that, get off out of it into infinite hitchhiking futures. Armed only with a duffle coat you could be listening to wild jazz on the banks of the Tyne or travelling east–west, across the Pennines. Mostly we never actually went, or the beer wore off by Baldock High Street and you were sober and so cold. But we were able to recognize each other by that fine, wild, windy prose and the running away motif that made so much sense. (*Oz* magazine)

American writers have always faced the vastness of their land: Chingachgook and Uncas padding easily, day after day through virgin forest; Huck and Nigger Jim rolling South under the stars on a great natural waterway; Melville's sailors, white and black and red, establishing the Pacific as the furthest reach of America's boundaries. The Beats followed the tradition but on a scale made possible by postwar technology: the Conestoga, raft, and sailing ship gave way to the Greyhound, the automobile, the aircraft. The need to communicate the awe remains. In Holmes' *Get Home Free* May and Verger return to their roots. The physical distances they travel from New York, to the deep South, and New England respectively, equate with the psychic distance from the experiences of their adolescence. Ginsberg's *The Fall of America* is virtually a travel book. Written during, and about, his incessant journeys back and forth, its poems' titles an itinerary, it attempts to assess the state of the nation.

The minutiae of travel observation – the advertizing slogans, hoardings, news items – are interspersed with reflections on the military-industrial complex, the war, pollution.

HIWAY POESY LA-ALBUQUERQUE TEXAS–WICHITA
Up up and away!
we're off, Thru America –

Heading East to San Berdoo
as West did, Nathaniel,
California Radio Lady's voice
Talking about Viet Cong –
Oh what a beautiful morning
Sung for us by Nelson Eddy

Two trailor trucks, Sunkist oranges/bright colored
    piled over the sides
  rolling on the road –
Grey hulk of Mt. Baldy under
  white misted skies
Red Square signs unfold, Texaco Shell
  Harvey House tilted over the superhighway –

Afternoon Light
  Children in back of a car
  with Bubblegum
a flight of birds out of a dry field like mosquitos

". . . several battalions of U.S. troops in a search and destroy
operation in the Coastal plain near Bong Son, 300 mi.
Northeast of Saigon. Thus far the fighting has been a series of
small clashes. In a related action 25 miles to the South,
Korean troops killed 35 Vietcong near Coastal Highway
Number One. . . "

Empire State's orange shoulders lifted above the Hell,
New York City buildings glitter
    visible over Palisades' trees
  2 Guys From War put tiger in yr Tank –
  Radio crawling with Rockmusic youngsters,
          STOP – PAY TOLL.
  let the hitchhiker off in the acrid Mist –
Blue uniformed attendants rocking in their heels in green
  booths,
  Light parade everywhere
    Motel Hotel
    Lincoln Tunnel
    Pittsburg Shitsburg
    Seagram's A Sure One
      Macdaniels vast parkinglot –
Cliff rooms, balconies and giant nineteenth century schools,
  reptilian trucks on Jersey roads
Manhattan star-spread behind Ft. Lee cliffside

> Evening lights reflected across Hudson water –
> brilliant diamond-lantern'd Tunnel
>> Whizz of bus-trucks shimmer in Ear over red brick
>> under Whitmanic Yawp Harbor here
>>> roll into Man city, my city, Mannahatta
>>> Lower East Side ghosted &
>> grimed with Heroin, shit-black from Edison towers
>> on East River's rib –

Ferlinghetti used exactly the same technique (though he claims to disagree with Ginsberg on "poetics") in his most consistent book, *Starting from San Francisco*. The poet is a solitary traveler, the whole work a search for the self and for mystic America. Naturally enough this quest is scarcely noticeable in work done in exile or closely following it. Paris, Haarlem, Berlin, Italy, Greece, England, and Egypt are all settings for Corso poems: between 1962 and 1968 Ginsberg wrote poems about England, Wales, Czechoslovakia, Cuba, Indo-China, Japan, and India. Burroughs, the long-term expatriate, is the explorer of inner space, but even he harks back to his American roots.

> After a parenthesis of more than 40 years I met my old neighbor, Rives Skinker Mathews, in Tangier. I was born 4664 Berlin Avenue changed it to Pershing during the war. The Mathews family lived next door at 4660 – red brick three-story houses separated by a gangway large back yard where I could generally see a rat one time or another from my bedroom window on the top floor. (*Paris Review*, 35)

Corso's first published book, *Vestal Lady on Brattle*, was written in Cambridge, Massachusetts, between 1954 and 1955. It could scarcely have been written anywhere else.

> The old bastard lied that told me Melville
>> visioned loss of times while walking
>> in the early morning,
>> separate from the carpets and parade, on Brattle.

I've walked Brattle lots these days,
   and not once did I catch from out the fark
   a line of light
He said: – Walk, man, walk that crazy Revolutionary
   road, old Brattle;
You'll dig the greatest visions ever;
Man, like Melville visioned Moby Dick on Brattle!
Right in the middle of the street!

Kerouac enjoyed the drive a lot more than the driving. His travel pieces show the greatest sense of relaxation and enjoyment when a trusted friend was at the wheel and he was free to look around him and swig from his bottle.

So there's old Willie waiting for us down on the street parked across from the little pleasant Japanese liquor store where as usual, according to our ritual, I run and get Pernod or Scotch or anything good while Dave wheels around to pick me up at the store door, and I get in the front seat right at Dave's right where I belong all the time like old Honored Samuel Johnson while everybody else that wants to come along has to scrabble back there on the mattress (a full mattress, the seats are out) and squat there or lie down there and also generally keep silent because when Dave's got the wheel of Willie in his hand and I've got the bottle in mine and we're off on a trip the talking all comes from the front seat – (*Big Sur*)

Neal Cassady's prowess at the wheel – "the greater driver" – was simply a legend during the man's own lifetime. The skill seems to have stayed with him even up to the awful, jangled end of his life, when the pills had set his wheels in the downhill ruts of martyrdom to speed. He was synonymous with the wheel as Kerouac was with the road (Tom Wolfe gets its tone exactly in *Acid Test*) and Charles Bukowski recognized the stubborn, driven nature of a kindred spirit in *Notes of a Dirty Old Man*: "Neal would just go on driving, either grim or happy or sardonic, just there – doing the movements. I understood. It was necessary.

It was his bull ring, his racetrack. It was holy and necessary."

During the years of Kerouac's deepest fascination with Cassady's personality, when they "rode around the country free as a bee," a long car journey with Neal at the wheel captured, for Jack, the essence of travel as freedom and escape – as pushing *on* – familiar to him from American classics. Melville's Ishmael, in *Moby Dick*, goes to sea when the pressures of life on land – society – start winding him up to the point of decidedly anti-social behaviour.

James Fenimore Cooper's noble savages are less in need of a safety valve as they are of simply keeping out of the way of the beginnings of American civilization, already corrupted by the greed and treachery of the Old World. In the forest or on the lakes they still have virgin wilderness.

Hester Prynne and Arthur Dimmesdale can only express their love for each other in the forest, not in the settlement, and it is their failure to leave it, to seize the moment and take off through the forest or over the ocean, breaking with society, that leads to their final tragedy.

Huck and Jim live an idyllic existence on the river, true freedom only touched by greed and viciousness when they touch the shore, with its blood feuds, lynching mobs and murders. On the river Huck comes to relate to the runaway slave as another human being and attains real manhood (when he apologizes to Jim – "humbles himself to the nigger"), uncorrupted by the warped values of the violent bigots on shore.

. . .and whilst I eat my supper we talked, and had a good time. I was powerful glad to get away from the feuds, and so was Jim to get away from the swamp. We said there warn't no home like a raft, after all. Other places do seem so cramped up and smothery, but a raft don't. You feel mighty free and easy and comfortable on a raft. (*The Adventures of Huckleberry Finn*)

A similar isolation and self-sufficiency grows up in the community inside a moving car. Albert Saijo, speeding along with Lew and Jack in *Trip Trap*, became part of such a community.

> We sped along. The country slipped by. We were provisioned with blankets and bags, spare tire, extra fuel, booze, peanut butter, bread, fig newtons, lettuce, jam, cigarettes, and milk.
>
> There was diverse and sundry talk about politics and politicians, intricate crimes, talk of wars and panics, food, drink, clothes, beds, flowers, talk of women, relatives, home-towns, travel, foreign cities, talk about movies and movie stars, about sports and champions of sport, gossip of the literary life, ghost stories, fables, riddles, jokes, talk of grammar, of origins, about what's real and what isn't, and plain swap talk. . .
>
> The moods a long car ride can put you through! Buttes and mesas. Telephone poles whipping past. (*Trip Trap*)

In such a unit, isolated from the world flowing past the car windows, Kerouac's characters explore their memories, the intricacies of their feelings, and, having created their own conformity and their own state, abide by its rules and set out to get to know each other in depth.

> We all decided to tell our stories, but one by one, and Stan first. "We've got a long way to go," preambled Dean, "and so you must take every indulgence and deal with every single detail you can bring to mind – and still it won't all be told. Easy, easy," he cautioned Stan, who began telling his story, "you've got to relax too." Stan swung into his life story as we shot across the dark. He started with his experiences in France but to round out ever-growing difficulties he came back and started at the beginning with his boyhood in Denver. . .
>
> Then I began talking; I never talked so much in all my life. I told Dean that when I was a kid and rode in cars I used to imagine I held a big scythe in my hand and cut down all the trees and posts and even slived every hill that zoomed past the window. "Yes! Yes!" yelled Dean. "I used to do it too only

different scythe – tell you why. Driving across the West with the long stretches my scythe had to be immeasurably longer and it had to curve over distant mountains, slicing off their tops, and reach another level to get at further mountains and at the same time clip off every post along the road, regular throbbing poles. For this reason – O man I have to tell you. NOW, I have IT – I have to tell you the time my father and I and a pisspoor bum from Larimer Street took a trip to Nebraska in the middle of the depression to sell fly-swatters. (*On the Road*)

The sharing of geographical locations gave the movement another area of common ground. The lopsided triangle of New York and San Francisco, which both had bohemian communities, and Denver, where Cassady and his original henchmen came from, were the main U.S. cities. Outside the States it was Mexico City, Paris, and Tangier. North Beach and Greenwich Village had traditions since the twenties on which to build and after the Beats began to attract a following, circa 1957, new hip communities, now accessible to each other and able to cross-pollinate as never before, mushroomed.

"The Plains are about 300 miles west of here, the most goddam desolate country I've ever seen, not a tree in any direction. God, it's ghastly."

Lord God, Billy Bob, this is ridiculous. It's a bit like walking along underwater must be, a slow move through sensory deprivation. When there *is* a town it's precisely like the last one. A continuation of flat treelessness that makes the Fens seem like undulating copse country. There's supposed to be one surviving rock station in Wichita but I'm darned if I can find it. Out here they don't even share the American airwaves' taste for round-the-clock Beatles. C & W; local politics; bargains at the store;

C & W. A record about every fifteen minutes and they're so bad you can't wait for the adverts. Heather's gone to sleep and it'd be criminal to wake her to this. Half the problem is this 55 m.p.h. law on highways built for gas guzzlers at a hundred-plus. Signs on the side of the road warning of helicopter speed patrols. Push on, like everyone else, at a steady seventy (honoring the law in the breach as the natives do) and speed up in the wake of any truck that sails past, in the theory that his CB will have told him if there's a bear in the air.

A little yellow scrub along the roadside and occasionally a stretch of fence posts (where did they get the timber?) and the long continuous white line reeling up under the left front tire. No telegraph poles for Jack and Neal's imagined childhood scythes to lop down. Low-lying cloud and the earth looking bare and raked. In the days before car radios no wonder they told each other their life stories on hurtles across the country like this. What traveling across it on horseback – dogging cattle or hunting buffalo – must have been like is enough to bring a shudder.

It is late afternoon in Kansas and I have to reach Denver, Colorado, tonight and if I make it I will make it in the dark and I will not see the Rockies rise out of the flatlands. They used to call the brothers Dalton, Younger and James, "Long Riders" because they went over such prodigious distances in this country in order to rob banks or trains outside the area where they were known. No wonder they needed a gunfight when they got there.

". . .no, Sagamore, not alone."

Many of the themes which concerned the Beats had concerned American writers since the birth of the nation. Acknowledging the importance of its predecessors, the Beat movement was neither an aberration nor simply an opposition to the literary status quo, but a further progression of American letters. Asked

69

to write an article on whether writers were born or made, Kerouac's mind spontaneously came up with three *American* examples. "Writers are made for anybody who isn't illiterate can write; but geniuses of the writing art like Melville, Whitman or Thoreau are born." (*Writers Digest*, vol. XLII, no. 1) The "know-nothing Bohemians" instinctively identified with America's finest writers. Holmes' *The Horn* borrows its structure from jazz – eight choruses, six riffs, and a coda. The two prefatory quotes are from Charlie Parker and Herman Melville. The choruses are prefaced by Thoreau, Melville, Emily Dickinson, Whitman, Poe, Hawthorn, and Twain.

Ferlinghetti peppers his poems with literary references and quotations. A *Coney Island of the Mind* takes its title from Henry Miller and tips its hat to Hemingway: "or the Sun Also Rises which begins Robert Cohn was/middleweight boxing champion of his class." Ferlinghetti's *Starting from San Francisco* refers to Whitman's line of a century before. "Starting from fish-shape Paumanok where I was born." Whitman is the dedicatee of Ginsberg's *The Fall of America* and two passages from his *Domocratic Vistas* preface it. There is a couplet from "Song of Myself" on the title page of the indefatigable *Howl*. "Unscrew the locks from the doors/Unscrew the doors themselves from their jambs!" Clearly, this sort of careful quotation is meant to identify with the original sentiment and set the new work in its existing tradition.

Besides Whitman, most of the Beats had a special regard for Emerson, Thoreau, Hawthorne, Melville, Thomas Wolfe, Pound, William Carlos Williams, and Hemingway, and it is references to them that are the most frequently made.

When living in Paterson, New Jersey, in 1947, Allen Ginsberg managed to get the local paper to send him to interview William Carlos Williams. Two years later Ginsberg wrote the older poet a letter which is reproduced in Ginsberg's *The Gates of Wrath*, published in 1972. Williams took an interest in Ginsberg's work (Ginsberg is the "young poet" referred to in *Paterson*) and wrote introductions to both *Empty Mirror* (1952, although the book was not published until 1961), which also has a prefatory quotation from Melville, and *Howl*. "Hold back the edges of your gowns, Ladies,/we are going through hell." (*William Carlos Williams*)

Williams' work is a major influence on Ginsberg, another is Whitman, who is imagined, reincarnated, wandering bemused around a "neon fruit supermarket."

> I saw you, Walt Whitman, childless lonely old grubber,
> poking among the meats in the refrigerator and eyeing
> the grocery boys.
>
> I heard you asking questions of each:
> Who killed the pork chops? What price bananas?
> Are you my Angel?
> "A Supermarket in California",   *Howl*

Whitman's philosophy is in many respects identical with that of the mature Ginsberg. Partly this is due to the similarity of their sexual orientation, but the "Intense and loving comradeship, the personal and passionate attachment of man to man" which was Whitman's ideal became increasingly important to Ginsberg as he grew older, a fact which he clearly wishes to indicate by quoting this passage as preface to *The Fall of America* in 1972. It is this book that contains the elegies to Neal Cassady, a symbol of comradeship for the Beats, whether their attachment to him was sexual (as in Ginsberg's case) or non-sexual (as with Kerouac). When Neal Cassady perished by the railroad track at San Miguel Allende, whether from exposure, heart failure, or the effects of alcohol with barbiturates, the Beat Generation symbolically died. Ginsberg also sees his relationship with Cassady as part of a direct link with Walt Whitman. "Edward Carpenter slept with Walt Whitman. Gavin Arthur (the grandson of Chester Alan Arthur, the twenty-first President) slept with Edward Carpenter. Neal Cassady slept with Gavin Arthur. And *I* slept with Neal Cassady." (*Esquire*, vol. LXXIX, no. 4)

As Jack Kerouac noticed, those qualities about Peter Orlovsky

71

(once described in *Who's Who* as being married to Ginsberg)
which recall the Whitman who became a Civil War nurse were
part of the reason Ginsberg was so attracted to him.

> – And strange too, that Simon's jobs have all been Whitman-
> like, nursing, he'd shaved old psychopaths in hospitals, nursed
> the sick and dying, and now as ambulance driver for a small
> hospital he was batting around San Fran all day picking up
> the insulted and injured in stretches (horrible places where
> they were found, little back rooms), the blood and the sorrow,
> Simon not really the mad Russian but Simon the Nurse –
> Never could harm a hair of anybody's head if he tried –
> (*Desolation Angels*)

In his role as public figure Ginsberg has perhaps come closer
to Whitman's conception of the poet as a powerful force for
social change (an ideal endorsed by the Beat Generation in
general) than any other American writer, and his continued
efforts to expose the evils of the military/industrial complex is
directly in line with Whitman's ideas on the development of
democracy.

Kerouac frequently pointed out how the mystique of writers'
lives and personalities fueled his own ambitions.

> . . .read the life of Jack London at age 18 and decided also to
> be an adventurer, a lonesome traveler; early literary influences
> Saroyan and Hemingway; later Wolfe (after I had broken leg
> in Freshman football at Columbia read Tom Wolfe and
> roamed his New York on crutches). . . (*Lonesome Traveler*)

Kerouac's time at the slightly posh Horace Mann prep school
in New York and the period at Columbia which followed are
dealt with in the final volume of the Duluoz Legend (paradoxically
harking back to the beginning of his adult life). Over and over
again Kerouac in his forties recalls the Kerouac in his teens with
a headful of dreams of American scribes.

. . .I just sat in the grass in back of the gym and read Walt Whitman with a leaf of grass in my mouth. . .

. . .reading Jack London's life. . .start writing my own brand of serious "Hemingway" stories, later . . .

. . .putting men now in the mind of what Thoreau said about the little blisters that appear on good autumn pears when you look at em close with a magnifying glass: he said the blisters: "they whisper of the happy stars," whilst russet red McIntosh apples only yell of the sun and its redness. (*Vanity of Duluoz*)

A common love of books is shared with "Sabbas Savakis," a pseudonym for Sammy Sampas, brother of Stella, Kerouac's third wife, referred to in *Lonesome Traveler* as "Sebastian Sampas, local young poet who later died on Anzio beach head."

"Do you read Saroyan?" he says. "Thomas Wolfe?"

"No, who are they?" ". . .Have you been reading, what do you read?"

"Well, I've been reading Hardy, Thoreau, Emily Dickinson, Whitman. . ."

Sabby: "Pretty solid so far." (*Vanity of Duluoz*)

Kerouac's first attempts at writing he recalled as a pastiche of those writers he admired as he sought to develop his own style.

"I was happy in my room at writing 'Atop an Underwood', stories in the Saroyan–Hemingway–Wolfe style as best I could figure at age nineteen. . ." (*Vanity of Duluoz*)

Interviewed in Lowell, he amplified on this.

As for Soroyan, yet I loved him as a teenager, he really got me out of the 19th century rut I was trying to study, not only his funny tone but his neat American poetic I don't know what. . . he just got me. . .Hemingway was fascinating, the pearls of words on a white page giving you an exact picture. . . but Wolfe was a torrent of American heaven and hell that opened my eyes to America as a subject in itself. (*Paris Review*, 43)

What the Beats were in revolt against was what they saw as the sterility which held sway in the fifties, not the themes and progression of American literature as a whole. The Concord and the Merrimac Rivers feature in the work of both Henry David Thoreau and Jean Louis Lebris de Kerouac. They were both born in Massachusetts and both had French ancestry. That much is coincidence. That they both experienced the real freedom of life in solitude close to nature and then felt the need to communicate the experience in books is a phenomenon arising out of being born in America, a country where freedom is both prized and elusive.

This argument applies to other writers associated with the Beats besides the main figures. Gary Snyder's *Riprap*, and Lew Welch's *Hermit Poems*, for instance, both reveal an attitude of mind in revolt against materialistic values, in search of a natural simplicity, and an awareness of nature similar to that of Thoreau. Welch appears in *Big Sur* as Dave Wain, the "red head Welch-man" and co-authored *Trip Trap* (named after Snyder's *Riprap*) with Kerouac and Dave Saijo. The Four Seasons edition of *Riprap & Cold Mountain Poem* has a photograph of the author, as the frontispiece, on Sourdough Mountain in the summer of 1953. Snyder's *Back Country* contains poems on the lookouts and the mountains. It was as a direct result of meeting Snyder that Kerouac spent the summer of 1956 as a lookout on Desolation Peak, the experience recounted in *The Dharma Bums*, *Desolation Angels*, and *Lonesome Traveler*. Poet Philip Whalen, who was roommate to both Snyder and Welch at Reed College, Oregon, and who appeared in *The Dharma Bums* as Warren Coughlin and in *Desolation Angels* and *Big Sur* as Ben Fagan, had also been a lookout.

Personal freedom and the right to the pursuit of happiness is a theme constantly explored in American literature, and the Beats' work is no exception. The image of a nation founded by seekers of religious tolerance and fighting its war of independence over the issue of personal liberty, however inaccurate, is one still cherished. Though it never started out that way, the Civil War is presented as the war to end slavery. The free and fearless spirit has been an American archetype since James Fenimore Cooper wrote *The Leatherstocking Tales*. To the Beats, however, the need of the settled society to reject the outsider, the outlaw, was at odds with this ideal. Their lives and work have that in common. Drink, drugs, and sexual freedom gave them notoriety. Their non-discriminatory attitude to junkies, blacks, homosexuals, and criminals was a sincere rebellion against the conventions of the times. In the mid-fifties they used terms about themselves held to be obscene. Shig Murao and Lawrence Ferlinghetti were handcuffed, imprisoned, fingerprinted, all before being released (on bail) charged with publishing or selling obscene writing. The writing in question was *Howl*. The Beats definitely set out to change that sort of thinking.

Describing the historic 1956 Gallery Six reading, Kerouac wrote, "Fuck you! sang Coyote, and ran away" read Japhy to the distinguished audience, making them all howl with joy, it was so pure, fuck being a dirty word that comes out clean. (*The Dharma Bums*)

Hopefully, Burroughs is correct when he expresses the opinion that that particular battle is well and truly won.

> J.T.: Michael McClure once wrote that his intention was "to free the word fuck from its chains." Has that happened?
> W.B.: It has: there are no chains there.
> J.T.: And no future possibility of chains?
> W.B.: I doubt it, unless something drastic happens. (*The Beat Diary*)

No beer to go in Colorado

Denver is another spread of city lights sprawled as far as the eye can see in every direction. Impossible to tell where the suburbs and where downtown. The traffic unwinds in the darkness on both sides in the same direction, in front and behind. The feeling that it is impossible to get off this freeway, that I'll roll relentlessly on at 55 m.p.h. in the urban night forever, trapped. The left front headlight on the LTD is out, giving the impression that cars veering in from that side are farther or closer than they really are. Tension knots in back of the neck and eyeballs aching. Heather asleep with her head on my accelerator leg, cramped from holding a constant speed and not wanting to wake her. Car horns through the rain, straining to read the overhead road signs in time to get in lane, one headlight reflecting back off the rain-slicked tarmac.

Thirty miles from the Denver sprawl driving past the campus of the University of Colorado in Boulder, sign too late to get in lane and the turnoff whipping by, impossibly, the other side of two lanes of traffic. Up ahead a left turn: illegal. Eight hours' driving, half of it in the dark with one beam gone. The screech of the tires in this tight circle and the wail of some bastard's klaxon as he comes, almost alone, down the other side of the highway but chooses to jam on his brakes and scream his horn sooner than shift into the empty lane beside him. To hell with him. Ignore him and make a turn here and also here and into this mall parking lot to find a phone. Ease this sleeping blond head off a leg long gone to sleep. Pins and needles shooting up the thigh. Howl of tortured rubber and slamming back of car doors and very rude remarks hurtling across the car park in advance of this large and incensed gent with so few manners who does not understand that my eyes are scorched and my back is aching and I am a little thirsty, tired, and that my nerves are a little, well, raw, and that I am in no mood for discourtesy from someone fortunate enough to have just witnessed some inspired built-up area driving, British style.

Moved very slightly back and forth in the hand, the chrome wrench throws back flashes of light from neon signs outside stores. Very quietly now, the large gent gets back in his car and drives away.

A bar the best bet. There, with a sleepy and acquiescent Alsatian at the door (a German shepherd I suppose I should think) looks a likely spot.

76

Holy film set, what is this? I wanted a bar and I've got a bank. And not just any bank, an 1890s frontier model. Vaults, safes, big and iron and black with painted gold trim, period furniture and decor, the lot. Like Butch Cassidy said, the old bank was so *pretty*. But there's a counter, and there're bottles behind it, and a friendly lady with a ready smile, who reels off the list of beers slowly so that a stranger can take it in.

"Well I'll have a draft Coors please, as I'm in Colorado. You have coffee? A coffee and a cognac too. The lady'll be in in a moment."

Heather comes in, looks around, blinks. The last she saw of the world before she crashed out was the endless plains of Kansas, those achingly lonely, tightly clenched little towns along the ribbon of Interstate 70 that you hurtle past somehow slighting the people who spend whole lifetimes in them. Now she's in a scenario that only needs Holden, Borgnine, Warren Oates, and Ben Johnson to walk in tooled up to the teeth to make it perfect. She sits down and drinks her coffee. I ask the lady behind the bar.

"You have a phone?"

"Sure. You British? On a vacation?"

"That's right. Writing a book, too."

She has on a checked shirt and jeans. Western barmaid in the rocks of the Rocky Mountains.

"Thank you, miss. How much do I owe you?"

She smiles widely and takes the glass cloth off her shoulder. "That's OK. That's your 'welcome to Boulder' present."

"Why thank you."

"You're welcome."

After my customary tussle with American pay phones I hear a ringing tone and a familiar voice telling me the number. I tell the voice who I am and it relays the information to a silent Peter and then asks where I'm calling from and do I want to stay? It then gives me directions and house numbers.

A couple of beers and a visit to a supermarket later ("Sorry," explains my cowgirl barlady, "no beer to go in bars in Colorado.") I drive up a quiet, tree-lined street where each house is set in a nice-sized piece of land so that you can see your neighbors but don't have to share their quarrels. On top of a slope to the right, the Rockies brooding quietly in the moonlight over to the left, is a white, two-story wooden house with a deep porch. I go up the stone steps and ring the doorbell. Allen Ginsberg answers the door and gives me a hug.

A *touch of mutability in the mountains*

In Boulder the four-man road crew tearing up the pavement outside a store with shovels and rakes and implements of destruction wear big boots and tarred jeans, the uniform of manual workers the Western world over. The fact that each of them wears a rope of hair down between his shoulder blades seems not the least bit incongruous. Boulder can be neatly encapsulated by such images. Heterosexual English writers get winked at by two very non-fey gays (one black, one white) in a hundred yards. A young woman with a plait to her waist, boots and a long skirt, comes out of her wooden house, with the squirrels bobbing in the yard, and gets into a Volkswagen bug. The mountains hang blue, visible out beyond the edge of town. Boulder, Easterners will say, somewhat disparagingly, is a hippie town.

Not really. Or rather, not just. The enthusiastic music which draws passers-by to the square where the girls in their tiny flared skirts and little cloaks lift their knees and toss their batons while the boys *oompah* away – both sexes in uniform, glittering helmets bought army surplus from Ming the Merciless – reminds one of the other essential ingredient of Boulder, the University of Colorado. A short drive from Aspen, where Doonesbury's characters take John Denver's name in vain, where celebrity singers bump off the latest ski bum when he tarnishes their reputations, and of which Hunter S. Thompson came within an ace of being elected sheriff, Boulder has long been in a neighbor-

78

hood that has a certain appeal to the well-heeled young American WASP as a good place to go to school. What with Suzy Chaffee making something of a habit of being photographed on her skis wearing helmet, goggles, boots, and nothing else, and the fact that the first Orcan to visit Earth is resident there, Boulder is now hipper than ever. The bars tend to be old buildings refurbished with a theme or to feature live bands. (The Boulderado Hotel, where Burroughs stays when he's there, one of the town's oldest buildings, is a warren of old staircases and cellars decked out with thirties B-movie posters.) No one on the street is over twenty-five, and they come up and talk to strangers driving cars with New Jersey or New York plates, just to keep in touch with home. Boulder has something of the atmosphere that Brighton, Norwich, or Colchester had in the sixties (being the towns with the liveliest universities). It is a relaxed place to live. Good grass is not hard to get. The fringe occupations and entrepreneurial endeavors can flourish. And, just as on those British campuses of dear dead recall, one rubbed shoulders with the earnestly bearded Anglican, the muscular Catholic, the Sufi, the TM merchant, or the Little Fat Guru's devotee, so, in Boulder, there are the Buddhists.

Affectionately jeered at (they were named "pods" after the film *Invasion of the Body Snatchers* appeared) by those whose tastes in the spiritual run more to a six-pack of Coors and the desire for a Porsche, the Buddhists are there because of a Tibetan expatriate called Chogyam Trungpa Rinpoche whose Naropa Institute is located on Grant Street. Some of them are also there because of an "elect of the American Institute of Arts and Letters" called Allen Ginsberg.

The Jack Kerouac School of Disembodied Poetics is the logical extension of what Ginsberg has been achieving in that area which Americans called "poetics" – a sort of hinterland to the actual process of writing the stuff – ever since the publication of *Howl*. Ginsberg's own Buddhism (as well as that of those other poets closely associated with the Disembodied School, like Ginsberg's roommate of a quarter century, Peter Orlovsky, and his co-director, Anne Waldman, the original Fast-Speaking Woman), which he has practiced since the fifties, finally led him to seek out Trungpa, a younger man, to be his guru. Ironic that the poet with perhaps the most passionate personal number of disciples and adherents of all should seek enlightenment from a man who tells him to cut his hair and wear white shirts instead of black ones. Ginsberg's involvement with the Naropa Institute and the development of the Disembodied School have run concurrently. Boulder is central and easily reached in the days of domestic jets. In a university town it is not difficult, especially if running summer schools, to find accommodation for lectures and students. In places, the two institutions overlap, sometimes uneasily. Writer Tom Clark reported that Corso wrecked his room when told that he had "donated" his fee to Trungpa after teaching a course at the Disembodied School, and Ed Sanders' group, who chose the Halloween party incident when Trungpa's henchmen forcibly stripped W. S. Merwin and his Hawaiian lady, Dana Raone, as the practical for their course in "Investigative Poetics" seem to have divided poets into two camps as far away as San Francisco. Ginsberg, first on a purely personal basis, and then through Committee on Poetry, has always poured a personal, administrative, practical, organizational energy into his role as a writer. It was never confined to his own writing, it spread out to include all that he considered good – from his early, Pound-like efforts with the manuscripts of Kerouac and Burroughs, the support that his works have been to City Lights (and consequently other less well-known poets), through his political and ecological activism, the financial support of the walking wounded, Ginsberg has refined his techniques of support for art and artists. As Ed Sanders said, if they're not writing Ph.D.s about the Disembodied School yet, they soon will be.

The day has a blue haze. It is October, Kerouac's month. The squirrels are hopping in prehibernation business. Jack would have tossed them some nuts, if he had some. The leaves are turning and there is frost seeping down from the blue mountains these clear mornings. In the concrete at the back of the wooden house (which has grids in the floors so that the heat from the basement boiler may rise through the whole dwelling space) words were written when the mixture was wet.

On 9 September 1942, with America in a war that was far away from the snowy mountains of the west, a boy called Phillip Wickstrom wrote his name in the concrete at the rear of a house in a quiet tree-lined street in Boulder, Colorado. Kerouac would have been twenty, Cassady, in reform school or a Denver flophouse, sixteen. Forty years later, Allen Ginsberg and Peter Orlovsky, having outlived Neal and Jack, share the house on Bluff Street and no one, despite his proud and sad youthful attempt at immortality, knows who, or where, is Phillip Wickstrom.

I don't expect to speak of my contemporaries as a distinct and separate group again

One theory has a general feeling of isolation making strange bedfellows of American writers, who form literary groups whose members have little in common. Certainly John Clellon Holmes, a horn-rimmed professor who put down his roots early, is far from the popular conception of the frenetic Beat writer. Nevertheless, he has concerned himself with the central Beat themes and is fully a part of the cross-pollination of ideas.

In answer to your queries: everyone (it seems) has their own conception of what the Beat Generation was and where it originated, etc. I happen to agree with yours – it was the New York group which catalyzed most of the others that were springing up in San Francisco, Black Mountain, etc. But then I was part of that group, and gave it the earliest attention in print. I still think that Kerouac, Ginsberg, and Burroughs will prove to be the most lasting writers to emerge from the

81

whole "movement," but that opinion, too, is perhaps biased by personal acquaintance and preference.

Yes, shared experiences, rather than literary tendencies, tied us all together as friends. After all, none of us had published anything when we met (except for some poems of mine), and our affection was based on being together, and making similar life-discoveries in each other's company. We continued to be friends, I suppose, because the friends of one's rash and eager youth seem to be the ones that last the longest. The shaping experiences of the late forties and early fifties became the well out of which our later writings came, and that's why we all appear and reappear in each other's books. We gave support to each other because we each believed the others were on to something important, something the critical establishment of the time scorned and ridiculed, but which we felt was going to be crucial to the future. (Unpublished letter to the author)

Holmes used the characteristic device of the recognizable pseudonym from the first. Go features the full cast list. Some of them later appear, in the first person instead of the third, in Get Home Free (Holmes' best book, in Kerouac's opinion). The Horn, a favorite novel among jazz men, contains the most arcane example, when the dying saxophonist sees two young, white jazz aficionados, a dark one, and Paul, who wears glasses, excitedly listening in the street to a tenor sax player on the outside speaker of a record store.

You're right about that bit from The Horn: that's Jack and me (Paul and Gene from Go), and you're the first person who's ever picked it up. Also, I refer to Dennison in Go (who's the Dennison – Bill Burroughs – from Jack's Town and City), a sort of inside-reference that no one has noticed. There are undoubtedly others. Insofar as Jack and I both wrote versions of roman-à-clef, it was inevitable that our material would overlap continuously. In fact, I once got a letter from a reader of Go that stated that the writer was certain Kerouac had written the book under a pseudonym, and who was I trying to kid? Doesn't speak well for that writer's reading of either Jack or *Go*. (Unpublished letter to the author)

Paul Hobbes, the protagonist of *Go*, crops up in *Get Home Free* like a Somerset Maugham colonial gone native. May, the returning prodigal coquette, persuades her escort to take her to Fats', the Negro jazz joint, where the "white trash" in filthy sneakers, cut-offs, and a khaki shirt black with sweat, laboring over the piano, turns out to be Hobbes.

In both *Get Home Free* and *The Horn* Holmes tackled the task of creating credible black characters, virtually the only Beat writer to take on that particular American challenge. Kerouac's attempt at such a projection, talking in *On the Road* of "happy, true-hearted, ecstatic Negroes of America" seems hopelessly sentimental, even for the time. *Pic* didn't really come off, either.

Holmes' archetypes in *The Horn* are reminiscent of legendary jazz figures. Geordie, the beauty with a different "Ofay" escort every night, recalling, at thirty-five, her entry into the world of neon and needles and of finally tying herself to her bed to go cold turkey. Edgar, "The Horn" who drives himself to his end with heroin and booze, dying in a night club, revered, ruined, mourned. Like Lester Young (who originally had the line about there being a lot of *paper* at a big band session), he was a tenor player. Like Bird, he was self-destructive and soon resurrected.

I will go home tonight, and chalk upon the unfeeling iron of the subway wall, "The Horn still blows,". . . . He will join the others who obsess us still. Bessie moaning in her blood as they carted her crosstown; King puttering away his days forgotten in Savannah; Bix coughing in his horn or glass; old Fats gone finally to sleep in the ultimate lower berths; young black Fats grown pale and thin; Wardell killed down hard in a snarling bar; Bank finding he could still pick cotton; Tesche dead in an auto crash; Brownie dead in an auto crash; Bird dead, Horn dead – tuberculosis, narcosis, arteriosclerosis, neurosis – It does not matter what carried them off. Once they blew the truth. (*The Horn*)

Anticipating attempts at identification, Holmes added a disclaimer to his book, wishing it to be seen as something more than a piece of early "faction."

The incidents in this book are not intended to reflect the factual history of jazz music during the 1930s and 40's; nor are the characters intended to depict the actual men and women who made that history.

The book, like the music that it celebrates, is a collective improvisation on an American theme; and if there are truths here, they are poet's truths. (*The Horn*)

Holmes achieves his authenticity through the use of a milieu with which he was thoroughly familiar – the night world of the "vest pocket clubs of Fifty Second Street." His flashbacks are of a different order, an existential leap at conveying the black man's experience. His character Edgar Pool, reflecting on the rebel path he has followed, the sharp edge of what he might expect and endure as the result of a black skin compounding the hardship, universalizes the pointlessness of the work lives of most men: ". . .to escape, finally and worst of all, the knowledge. . .that this was the best you could hope for. . ." (*The Horn*)

Having tried in *The Horn* to project black experience, in *Get Home Free* Holmes takes on that other risky job, writing in the first person as a woman:

He looked at me, wary, lidded, curious, angry and I suddenly realized what he saw – a tipsy, reckless white girl in a sexy dress and a man's large raincoat, who had stepped across a line no one stepped across in his experience, except for certain dark and dangerous reasons. And how could he know my motives? Or fail to wonder about them? I was panicked by what he might be thinking. He's from Detroit, I don't know Detroit, maybe Detroit Negroes are different – that approximates my thoughts. "I'd better get some cigarettes," I murmured, and fled after Hobbes. (*Get Home Free*)

Holmes' first published novel centers on the disintegrating marriage of Paul and Kathryn Hobbes, who have been married for six years, since he was nineteen and she was twenty-one. Kathryn goes out to work each day while her husband, with little experience of the world apart from Columbia and his wartime service in the Navy, sits struggling with his novel. Hobbes, married too young, on impulse and against parental wishes, caught between guilt and his creative impulse, finds release in the heady atmosphere of the streets, the bars, and the lofts of his friends. He is caught up in the energy and appetites of Gene Pasternak (Kerouac), David Stofsky (Ginsberg), Hart Kennedy (Cassady), and Bill Agatson (Cannastra). Kathryn, less captivated than her husband by the lights reflecting off the bottles, is in mature contrast to the group in which Hobbes finds the camaraderie lost to his adolescence by the war. Symbolic of marriage and maturity, Kathryn already possesses the self-knowledge that her husband and his friends seek in their relentless exploration of each other. Agatson's death, a shock almost too great to absorb, shakes each of the book's main characters: Agatson had been extra, vitally alive. Now he is dead and their own mutability is brought home to them. It is the end of their innocence. *Go* ends with the Hobbes reconciled, temporarily at least, gazing over the rail of the New York ferry traveling towards a spiritual and literal dawn.

The death of Agatson and the arrest of Stofsky in *Go* are virtually verbatim reports of actual events. In *Nothing More to Declare* Holmes describes his divorce and remarriage. The hippie Holmes encountered in *Get Home Free* finishes the story: "We split. I heard she got married and happy."

Holmes marked the watershed of his fortieth birthday by assembling the best of his articles and memoir pieces into *Nothing More to Declare.* His essay on Kerouac has the insight and sympathy of a close friend (lacking in full-length works on him) and altruism enough to recognize both the scope of his talent and his human frailties.

I saw a man, often quarrelsome, sometimes prone to silly

class resentments, as defensive as a coyote on the scent, and as intractable as a horse that will not take a saddle; a man who sometimes seemed positively crazed by the upheavals in his own pysche, whose life was painfully wrenched between the desire to know, for once and for all, just who he was, and the equally powerful desire to become immolated in a Reality beyond himself. I saw a man who (for as long as I had known him) had undeviatingly pursued his vision of the dislocations and attritions of his generation's experience "in great America," undeterred by failure or despair, so selflessly enlisted in its service that the man and the vision were inseparable; the process by which one fed the other (and vice versa) too organic and too mysterious to comprehend, and the only word inclusive enough to contain the full range of all the gifts, and all the flaws, that vague word, "genius." Looking at Kerouac, I realized he was the single writer I had ever known for whom no other word would do.

Many anthologies representative of Beat writing ignore John Clellon Holmes (his work is not included, for instance, in Thomas Parkinson's *Casebook on the Beat* or Leroi Jones' *The Moderns*). Bruce Cook's *The Beat Generation*, which discusses in some depth the contribution to the phenomenon made by Norman Mailer and Robert Duncan (both peripheral figures), mentions Holmes briefly but enthusiastically: "John Clellon Holmes' excellent novel, *Go* [is] filled with the pulse and drive that can be sensed in all the best Beat writing." Holmes wrote the first book wholly concerned with the Beat scene. It has been described by Ann Charters as "the first to describe Ginsberg, Kerouac and Cassady," which it wasn't.

The Town and the City was. Through Peter Martin's involvement with the junkies, hustlers, and thieves of Times Square he meets Leon Levinsky (Ginsberg) and Will Dennison (Burroughs). *On the Road*, published in 1957, but begun as early as 1948, brought them the notoriety but it was Holmes who first published a whole work built around their attitude, lifestyle, and philosophy.

Various reasons have been advanced to account for the critical and popular success of *On the Road*, while *Go*, initially at least, was a profitable failure. (The novel sold 2,000 in hardback and the paperback rights were sold, but no paperback appeared: Holmes made about $10 for every $3.50 book sold.) Whether it was the mood of the times or Kerouac's dark quarterback's good looks, *On the Road* took off and *Go* didn't. Though the two books have common ground, one is set wholly in New York and one is a picaresque flinging out all over North America and Mexico. John Montgomery, the original of the rapping mountaineer Henry Morley in *The Dharma Bums*, once made an absurd charge of plagiarism:

> . . .John Clellon Holmes, a plagiarist of Jack's. Incidentally, Jack was sad about Holmes as after reading Jack's Ms., ON THE ROAD, he quickly pounded out what Jack called an imitation called GO and immediately sold it while Jack had to wait seven years while Cowley and Viking Press attorneys sat on waivers from all the people who were the basis and got up courage to release it. (*Jack Kerouac – a Memoir*)

Published correspondence between the two points not to plagiarism but to mutual supportiveness typical of the Beat coterie. Holmes has written that *Go* was half-finished in December 1950: "I was 24 when I wrote the second letter, and my novel, GO, was about half-completed. Jack had been having trouble for months with the start of ON THE ROAD, and the letter was an attempt to be of some help." (*The Beat Diary*)

Kerouac would often send the only copy of a new manuscript to Holmes through the post. This had a profound early influence on the younger man. "But if my writing was under his spell in those days (the four years' difference in our ages put me four years behind him in experience and skill)." (*Nothing More to Declare*) Towards the end of his life, asked if he corresponded with other writers, Holmes' was the only name Jack Kerouac mentioned. In "The Great Rememberer" Holmes gives a realistic assessment of his friendship with Kerouac, owning up to the inevitable moments of conflict in a long and close relationship. One paragraph sums up not only the closeness of their association but also the fascination that the essence of their group held for them all as writers.

> He has awed me with his talents, enraged me with his stubbornness, educated me in my craft, hurt me through indifference, dogged my imagination, upset most of my notions, and generally enlarged me as a writer more than anyone else I know. We have wrangled, and yelled, and boozed, and disliked, and been fond of one another for almost twenty years. He has figured in my books, sometimes directly on the page, but most often standing just off it; and I appear here and there in his, under various names, though usually as a snide, more fortunate, migraine-headache intellectual, who borrows his ideas, makes money from his perceptions, and is always trying to involve him in stifling ego dramas. And yet only one part of his complicated nature thinks of me this way. For the rest of it, we are curiously close. We represent something to one another: everything we are not ourselves. (*Nothing More to Declare*)

Too much for my mirror

In a vast, looping rest stop in West Virginia, where the traveler may park and picnic and wash and shave in warm water in the brick bunker of the comfort station (but may not sleep) the dawn wind whispers through a field of maize high as a pachyderm's eye and stretching out in a swimming ripple over the mellow horizon. The enormous trash can is labeled with a stern admonishment against putting trash in it. It contains a sole beer can with the admirably direct decoration: "BEER"–logo the same in New York or the Midwest. In Kansas City, Missouri, it is explained to me, by Herwig G. Zauchenberger, who was in a

Displaced Persons camp in Austria in 1945 and who is now Dean of Graduate Studies at the University of Missouri, that everything packaged in this stark black-and-white livery is a "generic" product. Costs cut by doing away with frills and packaging. In Allen's house in Boulder the toothpaste tube, all colors and none, carries the legend that the carton had been eliminated to save expense. On the radio in the rainy night in Kansas came a little psychodrama with a husband who staggers, presumably by mistake, into the kitchen and finds it stocked with the unfamiliar, non-rainbow packages, cans and tubes.

"That stuff'll *taste* funny," he whines.

"But dear," placates Mrs. Middle America, her gingham apron almost audible on the airwaves. "You've been eating generic products for months now."

"I have?" says the stunned Dagwood. "Well, they *coulda* tasted funny."

Thus does American consumerism take a body blow. In answer to the excess of florid packaging, point-of-sale punchlines, and the vast sums spent on brand loyalty development and identification, some enterprising body brings out cheap and anonymous comestibles. And then has to counter the American matron's induced fear of seeming parsimonious: by advertizing.

> ". . .& the trouble with these creeps is they wouldn't know poetry if it came up and buggered them in broad daylight." (Allen Ginsberg, Notes on Finally Recording Howl)
> "Having reviled his times and been honored for it, the poet had raged out of his dark strangeness and become attractive." (The Secret Swinger)

Allen Ginsberg is immensely prolific. His bibliographer, George Dowden, emphasizes that his volume is incomplete, that he had particular difficulty in tracing foreign items (there are no entries for Cuba or Czechoslovakia, both countries from which the poet was expelled). Covering the years from 1943 to 1967 only, the bibliography still runs to 324 pages. "Anyone who asked for poems I sent them," wrote Ginsberg in the prefatory acknowledgements to *Reality Sandwiches*. Through his policy of wide dissemination many obscure publications have been able to publish America's best-known living poet without paying a fee. He makes constant demands on his fees and royalties to subsidize events like the Kerouac Conference at Boulder in 1982. In 1973 an *Esquire* article estimated his income: "Ginsberg's various activities bring in almost $32,000, about $20,000 of which goes to a private foundation for the support of poets and poetry. If he decided to keep all of the money for himself, however, he could move to a luxury high-rise, buy a Porsche, and spend his summers in Southampton."

The voluminous output, the approachable nature, and a reputation which ensures that editors clamor for even slight fragments of verse have meant that a great deal of indifferent material has found its way into print. Ginsberg's finest poetic achievements are sometimes in danger of being obscured by the second-rate, a fact of which he is aware:

> Because I've finished putting together all my poetry from 1955 to 1971; and I found that I'd written an enormous amount of poetry – so much that it was almost more than enough than I could bear to edit for people to read. That it was boring – that it went on and on and on, it was all about the war, it had no backbone, no structure. It had great brilliant improvised moments, there were some classic moments within it. But I found that I had written a big, long poem, with very loose forms. . .(*Melody Maker*, 15 March 1972)

The English poet whose name is most synonymous with brevity and the paring down of poems has been of some influence in countering Ginsberg's natural verbosity. Basil Bunting seems to have begun to affect the American's work in 1965, and Ginsberg wrote a poem in imitation of Bunting ("Studying the Signs," *Planet News*) in June of that year. In 1973 he said that he had been reconsidering his output: ". . .The teacher I've been working with in this area – the guru here for me – is Basil Bunting. . . I once met Bunting in England and I read through all of my poetry. At the end he said: 'Too many words.'"

Ginsberg's verse in many ways typifies Beat poetry; occasionally brilliant, with form and content sometimes perfectly matched, it is flawed by sentimentality, often over-reliant on vulgarity, and lacks the discipline to reject spontaneity when this is unsuccessful.

In such a vast body of work it would be strange if there were no references to close friends, but mention of the names of the original Beats, as well as later associates like Michael McClure and Gary Snyder, occurs regularly in Ginsberg's writing through-out his continuing development. Ginsberg has a special place in the group's generation. His enthusiasm and simple confidence in their genius encouraged the others. Names and titles were taken from his letters and conversations. Much of the activity which made postwar New York the Beat Golden Age was Ginsberg's.

In March 1957, part of the second printing of the City Lights edition of *Howl and Other Poems* was stopped by customs in San Francisco. The subsequent trial made the book a bestseller, obscuring later, better poems like "Kaddish."

Ginsberg's first attempts were influenced by Wordsworth and Shelley, Emily Dickinson and Poe, as well as by the poems of his father, Louis Ginsberg. ". . .When I began writing I was writing rhymed verse, stanzaic forms that I derived from my father's practice." (*New York Quarterly*, 6, Spring 1971) Because of his fame and the factors mentioned earlier, much of this juvenilia has actually been published, none of it greatly adding to his reputation.

Ginsberg's strength and resilience as a personality, which dictates so much of his public stand as both poet and protester, comes from facing and overcoming the traumas of his childhood and adolescence. Being treated as mad, struggling with his sexual inclinations, and memories of his mother's illness were the shaping forces. Naomi Ginsberg's madness dictated his attitude towards the female. "Mescaline" indicates that the traditional possessiveness of the Jewish mother, combined with the hallucinations and incontinence he witnessed during puberty, were the main factors in his sexual orientation.

> Yes, I should be good, I should get married
> find out what it's all about
> but ' can't stand these women all over me
> smell of Naomi
> erk, I'm stuck with this familiar rotting ginsberg
>
> *Kaddish*

When Ginsberg was eighteen he was suspended from Columbia, either for allowing Kerouac to sleep in his room, or for writing "Fuck the Jews" on his window, or a combination of both. His last letter from his mother, which arrived two days after her death, contained the sort of injunction which Ginsberg was more used to from other members of his family: "Get married Allen don't take drugs." Stofsky, the character in John Clellon Holmes' *Go*, is very closely based on Ginsberg. Holmes was evidently a careful listener: his account of Stofsky's visions and of hearing the voice of Blake corresponds to Ginsberg's in minute detail. Stofsky has a mother in a madhouse and a father who pressures him over his lack of conventionality.

The dramatic series of events which culminated in Ginsberg's arrest and detention is described in several books, fictionally in *Go*, more factually in the biography *Kerouac* by Ann Charters. He was kept out of prison by being sent, first, to the then Columbia University Hospital for observation in May 1949, and was finally released in March 1950. In *Kaddish* he speaks of "the bug house that year eight months" and in the preface to the reconstituted 1977 edition of *Junky* he states, "I was rusticating . . .after 8 months in mental hospital as result of hippie contretemps with law." Out of this period of self-examination he gained both the insight and the courage to confront the realities of his existence and his past. It is in *Howl*, *Kaddish*, and *Reality Sandwiches* that Mailer's accolade "the bravest man in America is most deserved. As William Carlos Williams wrote in the preface to *Howl*, "Literally he has, from all the evidence, been through hell."

Addressed to Carl Solomon, in its sexual imagery and its drug-induced or mad visions *Howl* reveals what Robert Duncan and Ruth Witt-Diamant described as ". . .all of life, especially the elements of suffering and dismay from which the voice of desire arises. . . The poet gives us the most painful details; he moves us toward a statement of experience that is challenging and finally noble." ("Horn on *Howl*," *Casebook on the Beat*)

Much of *Howl*'s impact comes from Ginsberg's "Hebraic-Melvillian bardic breath." Each long line is one breath unit, partly inspired by the rhythms of the Old Testament and the cantors of the synagogue. The coincidence of publication at the same time as the San Francisco Poetry Renaissance (the two fueling each other) provided the atmosphere where the shocking rolling lines could be declaimed to maximum effect.

> Who howled on their knees in the subway and
> were dragged off the roof waving genitals
> and manuscripts,
> Who let themselves be fucked in the ass by
> saintly motorcyclists, and screamed with
> joy,
> Who blew and were blown by those human sera-
> phim, the sailors, caresses of Atlantic and
> Caribbean love,
> Who balled in the morning in the evenings in
> rosegardens and the grass of public parks and
> cemeteries scattering their semen freely to
> whomever come who may,
> Who hiccupped endlessly trying to giggle but
> wound up with a sob behind a partition in a
> Turkish Bath when the blonde and naked angel
> came to pierce them with a sword,

Who lost their loveboys to the three old shrews
    of fate the one-eyed shrew of the heterosexual
    dollar the one-eyed shrew that winks out
    of the womb and the one-eyed shrew that does
    nothing but sit on her ass and snip the
    intellectual golden threads of the craftsman's
    loom. . .

Kerouac's *The Dharma Bums* contains a description of the effect the reading of the poem "Howl" had on the audience at the Gallery Six.

Everyone was there. It was a mad night. . .by eleven o'clock when Alvah Goldbook was reading his, wailing his poem "Wail" drunk with arms outspread everybody was yelling "Go! Go! Go!" (like a jam session). . .

In a poem written before "Kaddish" but published later, Ginsberg details his growing confidence and maturity. Addressed to Kerouac, who disapproved of Ginsberg's homosexual practices, the poet is able to confront his old friend with an honest appraisal of his emotional position, risking rejection, accepting the inevitable lack of sympathy.

MALEST CORNIFICI TUO CATULLO

I'm happy, Kerouac, your madman Allen's
finally made it: discovered a new young cat,
and my imagination of an eternal boy
walks on the streets of San Francisco,
handsome, and meets me in cafeterias
and loves me. Ah don't think I'm sickening.
You're angry at me. For all of my lovers?
It's hard to eat shit, without having visions;
when they have eyes for me it's like Heaven.
                                  Reality Sandwiches

In *Desolation Angels* Duluoz muses over the great scatological manuscript of "Nude Supper" asking Old Bull the point of it all.

Ginsberg seems to have shared Bull's attitude. "But where'll all this shit get us?"/"Simply get us rid of shit, really Jack." Rather than sublimate the trauma, Ginsberg confronted it. In "Kaddish," the cathartic outpouring of all the pain stored up from his mother's illness, he reached his most intense and complete poetic achievement. Naomi Ginsberg died in 1956; "Kaddish," dated 1959, is Ginsberg's farewell to her and his cauterization of the wounds her illness inflicted upon him. The *kaddish* is part of the daily ritual of the synagogue, composed of thanksgiving and praise, ending with a prayer for universal peace. It was especially recited by orphan mourners. In using the word (instead of, say, elegy or threnody) Ginsberg acknowledges his heritage. The poem is divided into six sections: "Poem," "Narrative," "Hymmnn," "Lament," "Litany" and "Fugue." Its structure is reminiscent of an orchestral work and it builds to a powerful climax. "Poem" is the poet's immediate reactions, sorrow and relief and self-comfort, to his loss. "There, rest. No more suffering for you./I know where you've gone, it's good." "Narrative" is the history of Naomi's life in America. After emigration from Russia, marriage, and two sons, paranoia over Hitler worsens into madness and public hysteria, wrenching visits in hospital.

> Naomi, Naomi – sweating, bulge-eyed, fat,
> the dress unbuttoned at one side – hair over
> brow, her stocking hanging evilly on her legs –
> screaming for a blood transfusion – one right-
> eous hand upraised – a shoe in it – barefoot
> in the pharmacy –
>
> "Are you a spy?" I sat at the sour table, eyes
> filling with tears – "Who are you? Did Louis send
> you? – The wires –"
>
> in her hair, as she beat on her head – "I'm not
> a bad girl – don't murder me! – I hear the ceiling –
> I raised two children –"

Two years since I'd been there – I started to
cry – She stared – nurse broke up the meeting a
moment – I went into the bathroom to hide, against
the toilet white walls

"Hymmnn" praises the deity and calls for his blessings on
Naomi. "Lament" grieves for the loss of her memories, the
collection of perceptions and feelings which made her an
individual human being. By "Litany" Ginsberg has gone through a
transformation. The action of re-creating the suffering in poetry
has given back to him the person the years had taken away.
Once again he may address her as "mother."

> O mother
> what have I left out
> O mother
> what have I forgotten
> O mother
> farewell
> with a long black shoe
> farewell
> with six dark hairs on the wen of your breast
> farewell
> with your old dress and long black beard around
>   the vagina
> farewell

The poem closes with a short section entitled "Fugue" which
would seem to be informed by the Jewish tradition of visiting a
grave after the actual funeral for the custom of setting the stone.
The poet is in the graveyard, silent except for the cries of the
black-plumed crows. The sun strikes the headstones and the
awful mystery of mutability lies before him, too large to be
grasped. The repetition of the name of the deity is echoed by the
harsh sounds of the crow. The mind, in its sharpened state,
cannot help but take in the little distractions around it as the past
jostles for position and it recoils from the inevitability of death

and the paradox of existence. It is a powerful ending to a major
poem.

> Caw caw caw crows shriek in the white sun over
>   grave stones in Long Island
> Lord Lord Lord Naomi underneath this grass my
>   halflife and my own as hers
> caw caw my eye be buried in the same Ground where
>   I stand in Angel
> Lord Lord great Eye that stares on All and moves
>   in a black cloud
> caw caw strange cry of Beings flung up into sky
>   over the waving trees
> Lord Lord O Grinder of giant Beyonds my voice
>   in a boundless field in Sheol
> Caw caw the call of Time rent out of foot and
>   wind an instant in the universe
> Lord Lord an echo in the sky the wind through
>   ragged leaves the roar of memory
> caw caw all years my birth a dream caw caw New
>   York the bus the broken shoe the vast highschool
>   caw caw all Visions of the Lord
> Lord Lord Lord caw caw caw Lord Lord Lord caw
>   caw caw Lord

When Ginsberg lost his job the long line of "Howl" found the
time to get born: ". . .I suddenly turned aside in San Francisco,
unemployment compensation leisure, to follow my romantic
inspiration – " (Notes on Finally Recording *Howl*)

Another change in his personal fortunes had a major effect on
his poetry. When *Howl*, through notoriety as well as merit,
became a bestseller, he was able to indulge in a taste for foreign
travel which he had previously had to gratify by enlisting in the
merchant marine. The experience of other cultures and climates
increasingly informs the writing of the late fifties, and early
sixties, most notably in such works as *Ankor Wat* and *Indian
Journals*. From the time of his first political stand in 1963

97

against a visit by Madame Nhu, both the travels and the poetry and prose became increasingly concerned with the causes Ginsberg has publicly espoused; the impersonal evils of America. His beliefs have led him, by a very different route, to a stance very similar to that of William S. Burroughs. Both of them attended the Democratic Convention in Chicago in 1968, where the full force of the American police mentality was demonstrated. Ginsberg himself was gassed. Norman Mailer was characteristically graphic:

> So Allen Ginsberg was speaking now to them. The police looking through the plexiglass face shields they had flipped down from their helmets were then obliged to watch the poet with his bald head, soft eyes magnified by horn-rimmed eyeglasses, and massive dark beard, utter his words in a croaking speech. He had been gassed Monday night and Tuesday night, and had gone to the beach at dawn to read Hindu Tantras to some of the Yippies, the combination of the chants and the gassings had all but burned out his voice, his beautiful speaking voice, one of the most powerful and hypnotic instruments of the Western world was down to the scrapings of the throat now, raw as flesh after a curettage. (*Miami & the Siege of Chicago*)

The concord of opinion between two of the original Beats is seen in certain passages from Burroughs' *The Job*, and articles such as Ginsberg's "The Great Marijuana Hoax – First Manifesto to end the Bringdown." Both see the American drug-enforcement agencies following Parkinson's Law and perpetuating drug abuse in order to ensure their continued existence.

Some time around 1971, convinced that his personal appearance was a factor working against his causes, Ginsberg cut his hair and beard, a response to the sort of attitudes exemplified in his poem "Uptown," published in *Planet News*.

"If I had my way I'd cut off your hair and
   send you to Vietnam" –
"Bless you then" I replied to a hatted thin
   citizen hurrying to the barroom door
upon wet dark Amsterdam Avenue decades later –
"And if I couldn't do that I'd cut your throat"
   he snarled farewell,
and "Bless you sir" I added as he went to his
   fate in the rain, dapper Irishman.

This action was consistent with the attitude noticed, years
earlier, by Walter Gutman, the financial journalist who had
raised the money for the film of *Pull My Daisy*. Ginsberg took
such projects as seriously as he did the business of poetry. At
Bankers Club meetings he was eager and sartorially elegant.

In the late sixties and early seventies Ginsberg's poetry is
marked by more introspection. He seems to have felt the passage
of the years. In 1968 he suffered a broken leg and ribs in a car
crash, in contrast to the time in 1949 when he walked away,
unharmed, from an overturned vehicle. In 1974 he was attacked
and robbed in the street. These events are treated philosophically,
but with a certain regret.

   . . . a steaming auto with broken nose –
   Unstable place to be, an easy way out
   by metal crash instead of mind cancer.
                The Fall of America

as I went down shouting Om Ah Hum to gangs of
   lovers on the stoop watching
slowly appreciating, why this is a raid, these
   strangers mean strange business . . .
                 Mind Breaths

With the ending of admitted American involvement in Vietnam, more of Ginsberg's energies are directed into teaching and
music. *Allen Verbatim* is a record of lectures given from 1971 to
1973. The Jack Kerouac School of Disembodied Poetics takes

up increasingly more of his time. Both his early interest in Blake and his relationship with Bob Dylan (there is a photograph of him among those on Dylan's 1965 LP *Highway 61 Revisited*) continue. Some of Blake's poems, set to music by Ginsberg, appear in *Allen Verbatim*. At least one LP of this material has been issued. *First Blues – Rags, Ballads & Harmonium Songs 1971–74* contains material set to music. The frontispiece, which shows Dylan and Ginsberg at Kerouac's graveside in Lowell, is from Dylan's film *Renaldo and Clara*, in which Ginsberg once again amputated his beard.

The Beat Generation as a concept and its individual members crop up in Ginsberg's poetry and prose throughout his career. In the love poems of the juvenilia the gender of the love object, Cassady, was obscured. In "Howl," the "secret hero" was identified only by his initials.

> Who sweetened the snatches of a million
>   girls trembling in the sunset, and were
>   red eyed in the morning but prepared to
>   sweeten the snatch of the sunrise, flashing
>   buttocks under barns and naked in the
>   lake,
> Who went out whoring through Colorado in
>   myriad stolen night-cars, N.C., secret
>   hero of these poems, cocksman and Adonis
>   of Denver – joy to the memory of his
>   innumerable lays of girls in empty lots
>   & diner backyards, moviehouses' rickety
>   rows, on mountaintops in caves or with
>   gaunt waitresses in familiar roadside
>   lonely petticoat upliftings & especially
>   secret gas-station solipsisms of johns,
>   & hometown alleys too

In the 1961 volume, *Kaddish*, it is Corso's injunction: "Be a Star-screwer!" that precedes "Poem Rocket." *Reality Sandwiches* is dedicated to him. This volume contains the 1954 poem "On

Burroughs' Work" in which there is an allegory of the title of Burroughs' best-known book.

> A naked lunch is natural to us,
>   we eat reality sandwiches.
> But allegories are so much lettuce.
>   Don't hide the madness.

Ginsberg's respect for Burroughs and his work is clear in the first book compiled from their half-lost correspondence, published in 1963, *The Yage Letters*.

When *The Yage Letters* was published, Ginsberg was abroad with Peter Orlovsky. Steeped in a foreign culture and experimenting with many drugs on a rough charpoy in Jaipur, India, he finds the companions of his youth constantly in his thoughts: "At least I'm down in possessions to Peter & a knapsack. I still am loaded with Karma of many letters & unfinished correspondence . . . is Jack drunk? Is Neal aware of me? Gregory yakking? Bill mad at me? Am I even here to myself?" (*Indian Journals*)

Planet News, published in 1968, continues this tradition. The two quotes in the dedication are from *Reality Sandwiches* and *Howl* respectively.

> Acknowledgement Addenda. . . friend
> poet Lawrence Ferlinghetti encouraged
> book to finish, suggested additions & style
>   edited Planet News.

> Dedicated
> to
> Neal Cassady
> again
> Spirit to Spirit
> February 8, 1925 – February 4, 1968
> 'The greater driver
> secret hero of these poems'

In "WHY IS GOD LOVE, JACK?" he confessed his continuing "ashamed desire" for Kerouac.

In that most nostalgic and melancholy phase of his work, after the deaths of Cassady and Kerouac, Ginsberg's poetry continues to refer to his friends, but with the sadness of a man whose own mortality presses in on him through the fates of his contemporaries.

> I threw a kissed handful of damp earth
>> down on the stone lid
>>> & sighed
>> looking in Creeley's one eye,
> Peter sweet holding a flower
>> Gregory toothless bending his
>>> knuckle to Cinema machine –
> and that's the end of the drabble tongued
>> Poet who sounded his Kock-rup
>>> throughout the Northwest Passage.
>>> *The Fall of America*

For the most part, it is the Beat novelists who use recognizable pseudonyms. The poets use the original name or make unidentified references, as Ginsberg did in his early love poetry. In a poem written in 1949, however, Ginsberg did use the device, and in a way which is unique: writing about a character from a book (*The Town and the City*) who is based on himself.

> Sweet Levinsky in the night
> Sweet Levinsky in the light
> do you giggle out of spite,
> or are you laughing in delight
> sweet Levinsky, sweet Levinsky?
>> "The Gates of Wrath"

The reading of each other's manuscripts and the sympathetic appraisal of their aims was a widespread and necessary method of maintaining creative confidence. While some could be vague ("verry innaresting"), Ginsberg seems to have been consistent in

102

his encouragement. Kerouac's portrayals of Ginsberg, however, could sometimes be a little cruel. "Moorad" in *The Subterraneans* is an intrusive character with "an evil smile," but Charters contends that Kerouac was not above exploiting his loyalty:

> After Allen had sold *Junkie* for Burroughs, Jack encouraged him to think of himself as the New York agent for the whole crowd of them scattered across the country writing. Jack had sent Allen the retyped 530-page manuscript of *On the Road* before either Neal or Bill could read it. He said they hadn't had any time. (*Kerouac*, Charters)

In his introduction to *Junky* Ginsberg recalls his own ambitions at the time of Burroughs' genesis as a writer:

> . . .I became more bold. . . encouraged him to write more prose. By then Kerouac and I considered ourselves poet/writers in Destiny, and Bill was too diffident to make such extravagant theater of self. In any case he responded to my letters with chapters of *Junky*, I think begun as curious sketching but soon conceived on his part – to my thrilled surprise – as continuing workmanlike fragments of a book, narrative on a subject. So the bulk of the Ms. arrived sequentially in the mail. . . and was the method whereby we assembled books not only of *Junky* but also *Yage Letters*, *Queer* (as yet unpublished) and much of *Naked Lunch*. . . Once the manuscript was complete, I began taking it around to various classmates, in college or mental hospital who had succeeded in establishing themselves in Publishing – an ambition which was mine also, frustrated. . . I conceived of myself as a secret literary Agent. . . That season I was also carrying around Kerouac's Proustian chapters from *Visions of Cody* that later developed into the vision of *On the Road*.

If anything, Ginsberg has gone too far down that road, and realizes it. "He's not in the publishing business," says Ferlinghetti. "Don't send him manuscripts."

Like Kerouac, Ginsberg provided snippets which the others

adopted. The narrator of *On the Road*, Sal Paradise, takes his name from an early Ginsberg line, "Sad Paradise it is I imitate." *Naked Lunch* is supposedly Ginsberg's reading of "Naked Lust" in Burroughs' handwriting. Naomi's meeting with God in *Kaddish* is strikingly similar to the passage in *Go* in which David Stofsky, the young Ginsberg as he might be played by Woody Allen, meets the deity.

> Yesterday I saw God. What did he look like?
> . . . He was a lonely old man with a white beard. . .
>
> I told him, look at all those fightings
> and killings down there, What's the matter?
> Why don't you put a stop to it?
>
> I try, he said – That's all he could do,
> he looked tired. He's a bachelor so long,
> and he likes lentil soup.
>
> *Kaddish*

Nor was he surprised by the throne at one end of it, a throne that was not surrounded by an ambient light, or even very clean and polished, but still somehow regal and entirely proper to the figure sitting there: an aging man of once powerful physique, now vaguely weary, His untrimmed beard fanned out in white folds upon His chest, His eyes shining with muted brightness as only an old man's eyes can shine out of the limpid stillness of an old face. God.(*Go*)

Stofsky dares to address Him.

God's face grew dim and drawn, as though the question gave Him pain. He knew there was no sense to feel, but pain He took upon Himself in spite of that. He seemed for that moment a majestic and lonely man in His rented hall, on His dusty throne, who had received too many petitioners, too long, and understood too much to speak anything but the truth, even though it could not help.

"I try," he replied simply. "I do all I can."

Then Stofsky woke, and it was still dark. He could remember most of it, as though it had just happened, and felt a kind of heavy peace. But very soon he fell off to sleep again, and dreamt no more, and had forgotten when the morning came. (Go)

Not even in *Howl*, his first book, would Ginsberg enjoy the limelight by himself; he was bound to use the chance to advertize that there were a few other books around that could do with similar, earthly, publication.

DEDICATION
To

Jack Kerouac, new Buddha of American
prose, who spit forth intelligence into
eleven books written in half the number
of years (1951–1956) – *On the Road,
Visions of Neal, Dr. Sax, Springtime
Mary, The Subterraneans, San Francisco
Blues, Some of the Dharma, Book of
Dreams, Wake Up, Mexico City Blues,*
and *Visions of Gerard* – creating a spon-
taneous bop prosody and original classic
literature. Several phrases and the title of
Howl are taken from him.
William Seward Burroughs, author of
Naked Lunch, an endless novel which
will drive everybody mad.
Neal Cassady, author of *The First
Third,* an autobiography (1949) which
enlightened Buddha.
All these books are published in
Heaven.

The nice twist of course, is that it was Kerouac himself who had named the poem. "I mailed him a copy just after I wrote it," Ginsberg told Al Aronowitz, who wrote it up for Seymour

Krim's *Nugget* (an early *Playboy* imitator), " – it was still untitled – and he wrote back, 'I got your howl. . . ' "

Down in Denver, down in Denver all I did was die

Thirty miles and a world away in Boulder the beautiful WASP young dress *après* ski or as urban cowboys. Down in Denver's skid row the desperate, the damned, and the dying stand up when a patrol car goes by, propping their aching limbs against the wall while the Mexican bars spill *mariachi* music and the pawn shop clerks haggle over a leather coat, a cassette recorder, or a gun.

They started to knock down Curtis Street in 1967. Neal Cassady's son by Diana Hansen was named Curtis. Now all that remains of Neal's old stamping ground is two buildings either side of a parking lot, a little jobbing printer's and the Old Curtis Street bar.

In the Old Curtis Street Bar five good ole boys with flushed faces and shirt tails askew are talking loudly in a booth, now into their fifth hour of drinking. A wizened little man with the long angular sideburns of the snowy West, a cowboy hat and a pencil moustache, is eating Mexican food at the bar. The Oly is cold enough to make your eyeballs ache.

On the way to the men's room, back of the bar, is a sight straight out of *Visions of Cody*. Under six lampshades made of metal and red glass and advertizing Colorado's own Coors beer, are three pool tables. The room, empty and lit in slabs of dusty light that begin halfway down from the ceiling – light on the baize only – contains the smaller, coin-operated tables now but is still what Kerouac saw when ducked into the Denver billiard halls with a door open at each end in the perspiring night, "a solid block of poolroom."

Walking over to Larimer Street down 21st you realize how the American language is shaped by its environment. It's not possible

106

to imagine going "three blocks down and two over" in Brighton or "cutting down the street" in Harlow New Town. The telegraph poles in this part of town still cluster away into the perspective down the worn streets like futuristic black Christmas trees and the occasional, totally out of it, Mexican lies face down in the October sun on the sidewalk. Kerouac walked the "Denver colored section" sighing through rose-tinted soul glasses for that spiritual youth he felt that the black man possessed and he had forever lost. It was that loss that stuck him with the awful compulsion of the *driven* drunk. That yearning for *all* experience which is so much in evidence in the early books; the black world would have fulfilled it no better than the white. He must have come to understand that as he grew older and that was when the character of the drinking must have changed, from celebration to desperation. Kerouac wanted to experience the whole world, taste the very essence of the human condition and then put it all in a book, all he could carry back from the world as he had proudly carried back the trophies of track and football field to Papa and Memere. Drearily just being a white man in that vital dawn seemed just not enough. He would have had to have had the Wart's education from Merlin, transmogrification and all, before he could have closed his hand on it without it getting away. So, while he kept on seeing it all, he dreamed of getting it all down in microcosmic masterwork (as Joyce had done with one day in the life of a Dublin Jew), one man's unique vision accessible to all. A tool for the chest. With *On the Road* he almost did it, too. Then he found he had still more to say, so the Duluoz Legend began to emerge. Then, somehow, twixt cup and lip or because of all the vitriol critics poured on his beloved books, or because you "had to be an athlete" and because we grow old, he lost that lovely clear overview and started saying things twice; or sloppily. So, when he walked the streets of skid row Denver "wishing I were a Negro or even a poor overworked Jap" it was not because of naive notions of a glamorous existence, but simply that he wanted to experience *everything*.

Most of Denver's famous Larimer Street is now gone. Below

20th Street though, as if isolated by an invisible Berlin Wall, it remains – the skid row of guarded stores, dim bars, and fat Mexican ladies. The poor are with you always: Jesus. You got to legalize the fellaheen: Duluoz.

Down Larimer below 20th the saddles outside the pawn shops are chained in place. The city fathers must have decided they needed to keep a little of the old Larimer, the Larimer of the Salvation Army hostel and the Goodwill Industries store and the Negra Bar and the Chihuahua Club. In one of the little bars a beer is cheap and served by one of those fleshy Mexican bartenders that have no facial hair and talk in two languages and won't cash a traveler's check. At three in the afternoon, outside, some poor soul in green checked trousers and the foetal position is passed out on the hard and greasy pavement as a black cop in a skintight green shirt, nightstick and holster even blacker than his skin, the tight black curls bristling on his bare head, ducks into a supermarket that gives, somehow, the impression of being *armored*.

When he came West looking for Cassady and courting rejection, Ginsberg lived on a sleazy Denver street called Grant. When he wrote *Visions of the Great Rememberer* to preface *Visions of Cody* he was up in the air-conditioned comfort of the Denver Hilton and it was thirty years on and he was bald and famous. Kerouac was ten years dead but the bums were still there. The poet addresses himself to the timeless things.

Outside another bar, on a corner, there is a fracas. Four white longhairs, two or three blacks, a white girl bobbing in and out. A dispute over the ownership of coat or watch. Not divided along racial lines. A Mexican in a baseball cap sits gazing eagerly across the street.

"You waitin' to see the fight, mon? I like to see it. You doing OK? You want some grass, mon? Joost a leetle?"

In the air-conditioned bus station a black woman is saying: "Eff ah doan get to Oklahoma City t'nite ah'm goan plumb *crazy*." And there is a hippie cop. Hair to his shoulders, dapper Zappa moustache and lip dab, beads at his throat. Twice while I

108

watch, as he courteously answers requests for directions, he approaches characters and throws them out of the bus station. One is sitting chatting to a blond girl and the second is sitting by himself when the hippie cop says to him: "Can I see your bus ticket, please? Right, well. I see you hangin' around here all the time. Go on now." ·

A warm, well-lighted place with young women and ill-attended luggage and nice people who would sooner shell out a buck than be harassed. Every street hustler's dream. Without a patroling rentacop the edgy craziness of Grand Central Station is at the foot of the slippery slope. So, with his long hair and his nightstick and his beads and his walnut-butted .38 Police Special, into the Denver bus station rides the legendary figure of the hippie cop. In the original city of the Western Beats, 1968 straps on a gun to ride herd on what has become of the eighties.

The pits of the earth

The men's room graffiti across the Midwest have dubbed it Lost Wages. Sardonic blue-collar philosophy in the face of the ultimate glittering rip-off. For every genuine *mafioso*, Maverick-hero, or adrenalized high-roller riding the glittering honed edge of his luck (Mailer's Rojack in *An American Dream*; Farina's Gnossos in *Been Down So Long It Looks Like Up To Me*), there are a thousand paychecks and retirement pensions disappearing across the baize into the pouches of the keno girls, in their heels and leotards and tights, or into the metal entrails of the bandits. Built on vices which the rest of America tries to ignore, or at least to suppress (the blazing streets are lined with vending machines selling for 50 or 75 cents, sheets which are two half-assed articles; a thousand ads for massage parlors, outcalls, dominatrices or submissives, black girls or golden girls, and five hundred photographs of Hollywood models, in garter belts and boots, shot in studios a long, long way away), Las Vegas is a phoney destination. No conventional reason to found a city there exists. No commercial or trade routes; no center of scattered population; no natural resources. Just the imported commodities of the loss of money in an adrenal rush and the illicit thrill of a secret, commercial, vacation blow job. There is no reason for Las Vegas to exist – in the middle of the inhospitable desert – except man's inexhaustible need to con himself, to fork over his lucre to the artificial lusts which he created out of his own natural urges. As such, it assaults the senses in a particularly sinister way. To arrive in the tawdry façades of Las Vegas in the heat of the Nevada noon, out of a landscape better suited to a Peckinpah movie than to the New World's version of the Golden Mile, is to comprehend, in a flash, why Hunter S. Thompson was compelled to gulp such vast quantities of pharmaceuticals in order to cope with the town.

Just as the Beats harkened back to their American literary forebears in their themes of travel and search, of quest for identity and redemption, so the books which catch what seems to be the essence of the American Dream today consist of simultaneous journeyings – inside and out – and use the tools available to them now. (The old chest is full, now, of obsolete adzes and awls.) If Hawkeye were to ride the prairie or stalk the forest with the Sagamore, it would be to shoot it out not with Magua and the Hurons but with the FBI. The Army of the Republic would politely direct Nurse Whitman to the Peace Corps. Woody Guthrie might find it impractical to hop Amtrak. Ishmael and Queequeg would sail on *Greenpeace VII* with Ferlinghetti, and Ahab would take Japanese citizenship. To find himself in America now the American needs the technology and spirituality of the second half of the twentieth century. Pirsig rides his BMW equipped, like Kerouac and Ginsberg and Snyder, with his koans but never short of a good conversation now that psychotherapy has identified his Classic/Romantic schizophrenia. Tom Robbins' heroines hasten by automobile or by jet towards death, disaster, or at least bereavement, armed with their newly liberated sexuality and weighted to the page with large helpings of post "God is Dead" mysticism and pantheism. Raoul Duke and the Brown Buffalo sail the deserts and their inner seas in giant cars named for the most glamorous of sea monsters (the White Whale, the Red Shark), jammed up to the eyeballs with coke, acid, tequila, and reds, searching for the mythical extract of the human pineal gland and the American Dream.

The American Dream. Strange how the phrase returns, again and again. Ask an American what it means and, if he can formulate an answer at all, it will usually be along the lines of a chicken in every pot. Prosperity and a vote and apple pie and the schoolhouse and Andy Hardy and Jimmy Stewart for President. An American Dream. The definite or the indefinite makes a difference. "Can't the bastards read?" asked Anthony Burgess, when critics attacked something which they called *"The" Clockwork Orange*. No they can't and that's the trouble.

The phrase was not new to American letters when Mailer adopted it for the living symbol of his own American dream – Cherry, the blond *chanteuse* first seen by Rojak singing over his shoulder in a nightclub, an image central to the legend of that human American dream Mailer was later to write about so extensively, Marilyn Monroe. When Raoul Duke and Oscar Zeta Acosta were maybe roaming the sinister East Side of Las Vegas, tape recorder turning and all the chromosomes dancing down the methedrine river, every place they asked thought the American Dream was a defunct nightclub. Vegas. So fearful and loathsome you think you must be dreaming.

Some things are too good and they go

"I'm not sure about the Spandex disco trousers," I say. "You know what this town goes in for, apart from gambling."

"If you can get away with that cowboy hat, I can get away with the shiny pants," Heather says, screwing the cap on her lipstick.

111

"You are going to get me involved in some ritual of machismo with some vacationing redneck on a fifty of Old Grandad and a hard-on that just *won't* go down. You never see these things coming," I grumble.

"Yes dear." She shuts the inevitable, crammed cornucopia that passes for a handbag. "Shall we go?"

I put on my ten-dollar River Rat shades – purchased this morning in blazing baked Mormon Utah, lock up the LTD, and we head into Las Vegas.

Vegas in sunlight can give a whole new meaning to words like lurid or garish. Or phrases like "questionable taste." A Mississippi paddle steamer welded into the sidewalk outside the Holiday Inn with a Cadillac Seville – top slot machine prize – tilted on a rack outside it. The city block that is the Flamingo – all in dentures-plastic pink – is set behind a row of palms pruned into celery stalks. Opposite Ye Olde Lobster House and Le Petit Mozart, the desert strays a little close to the Strip. It looks bemused, somehow. The tall neon signposts outside the Dunes or the Aladdin are a constant delight, "Double Odds On Craps," "World's Most Liberal Slots." You get so used to *double entendre* that "Eddie Rabbitt and the Pointer Sisters" outside MGM's strikes as being more suitable for Copenhagen.

"What are you staring at?" she asks.

"'Conventions: Welcome American Society of Bariatric Physicians.' What on earth is a bariatric physician? What do they *do* when they convene? Spoon barium meals into each other in some bizarre rite? Why in the middle of the desert? How *does* this place make everything seem sinister? No wonder Raoul Duke got edgy. My nerves are like piano wire already."

"Let's eat, shall we? You can get in the casinos very cheaply because they're all trying to get people in to gamble. I'm starving."

Inside the casino the bootheels sink into the heavy-duty nylon shagpile and the lights over the baize blaze and it could be noon or night. Heather precedes me across the floor, stopping a uniformed flunky in his tracks.

112

"How'd *she* get in here?" he mutters.

"With me, creep," I whisper. He turns, looks up, and I pass on.

The food is served cafeteria-style: standard price and help yourself from hot trays constantly replenished by men in chefs' hats. The waitress only clears dishes and takes drink orders. As madam returns to the table with her second plate of chicken and steak a busboy stops by the table and points at the disco pants.

"Hey," he says. "I really *like* those! They're really sexy, y'know! Really sexy, I mean." There is a small patch of acne by the left side of his mouth. I put down my knife and fork and extract a five-dollar bill from my wallet and hand it to him.

"Gee, thanks. What can I do for you?"

"That is for you to buy yourself a copy of *Playboy* and a packet of Kleenex. At home this lady makes more in a day striding down a catwalk than you make in a week. And you think she cares if some tray-carrying asshole thinks her outfit is 'sexy.' Now clear off before I call for the manager." My knuckles are curiously bone-colored.

"Darling," says Heather, gently brushing back my hair, with just that solicitude with which you soothe a disgruntled old watchdog. "I don't think Las Vegas is actually bringing out the best in you. . . "

The dust blows forward and the dust blows back

"What're you thinking about?"

"Tangier."

"Oh." She starts to talk, casually at first, but with a growing vivacity. She knows that when I think about Tangier, about the Mouneria and the Calle Larache, the lottery building, the Socco Grande, the Socco Chico, and the sad green cannon on the hill – all the landmarks of Beat Africa – then my thoughts usually lead down the coast to El Jadida.

El Jadida still has the harbor walls from its days as a Portuguese fort. It has a solitary British resident and one liquor shop – not run by a Moslem – to its 20,000 populace. On Throne Day, a public festival, the town is crowded with people from the country celebrating Hassan's coronation and the drums beat all night and the soldiers carry their sub-machine guns on their hips and a crowd forms in a moment. When I think about that night I get very angry because I still haven't come to terms with what happened and so, though I know why she is talking so brightly, I allow the fact of her trying to be a salve on that particular wound and I keep my Africa reverie firmly in Tangier.

The poor are with you always

On the way back to the hotel a burly street boy falls into step and begins an insistence for money.

"L'argent! Vous n'comprends pas l'argent?" As we pass a half-built, breezeblock structure he tries to shove me inside. I hit him hard enough under the ribs to make him less brave and then stand not upon the order of my going. Before his friends in the shadows can materialize. One story not to tell in the *souk* the next day: punched out by a Ruomi. Allah never made Christians for that.

In Kerouac's old room the bed is neat and clean and is telling no tales. On top of the wardrobe some previous tenant had left a small-bowled pipe and a piece of *kif* the size of a cob nut. Sometimes the sound of Hunnish activities can be heard through the wall from the engineer from Libya's room. Down below in the cellar bar Heather is drinking Tangerina cocktails with the British expatriates, listening to the stories they know from each other by heart. Downstairs, when I tell one or two myself, I will be given the enthusiastic attention afforded the stranger with a tale not heard before. Now I stand at the French doors opening out on to the tiled terrace, the harbor down to my left, the beach stretching away on the right and, across the straits, the light blinking on the tip of Europe, flashing silently away through the night at Africa. Later, I will go downstairs and lend my Swedish leather coat to the shivering Arab who sits guarding the bar door throughout the dark hours and he will dip his head in uncalled-for gratitude. The next day, I knew, I was going to put on a worn djellaba and *barboushes* and walk among the hustlers and pimps to the Socco Chico or the Socco Grande and drink mint tea and I knew, whether or not the rubia accompanied me (they use the Spanish word), that because I was a Roman and because I was not El Hombre Invisible, that the street boys and "guides" and thieves would gravitate to me like gold prospectors to a rumor, despite my disguise. As Duluoz said, you got to legalize the fellaheen.

To die alone under a frozen Mexican moon

Neal Cassady's charisma caught the spirit of his times. A handsome, sexy anti-hero. Brando, laconic in his leathers, leaning on the handlebars of a Harley. The rebel without a cause crucified on his Winchester. Naming his most famous character, Dean Moriarty, Kerouac fused the method actor whose love of fast driving was to kill him with the alter ego of fiction's most famous detective.

The persona first appears in print as Hart Kennedy in *Go*. He is protagonist of both *On the Road* and *Visions of Cody* and appears in *The Dharma Bums, Desolation Angels, Big Sur, Book of Dreams* and *Scattered Poems*. He is mentioned in *The Subterraneans*, is the "secret hero" of *Planet News*, is eulogized in *The Fall of America*, and is the subject of songs by the Grateful Dead, the Doobie Brothers, and the engagingly named Aztec Two-Step, among others. After the famous "two sticks" bust he became the "greater driver" for Ken Kesey's Prankster bus, Further. He seems to have possessed exceptional personal magnetism right up to the time of his death.

I met Kerouac's boy Neal C. shortly before he went down to
lay along those Mexican railroad tracks to die. . . he never sat
down, he kept moving around the floor. he was a little
punchy with the action, the eternal light, but there wasn't any
hatred in him. you liked him even though you didn't want to
because Kerouac had set him up for the sucker punch and
Neal had bit, kept biting, but you know Neal was o.k. and
another way of looking at it, Jack had only written the book,
he wasn't Neal's mother. just his destructor, deliberate or
otherwise. (*Notes of a Dirty Old Man*)

In the epilogue to his book on the Merry Pranksters, *The
Electric Kool-Aid Acid Test*, Tom Wolfe gives a journalist's
account of Cassady's death.

In February, Neal Cassady's body was found beside a railroad
track outside the town of San Miguel de Allende, in Mexico.
Some local American said he had been going at top speed for
two weeks and had headed off down the railroad track one
night and his heart just gave out. Others said he had been
despondent, and felt that he was growing old, and had been
on a long downer and had made the mistake of drinking
alcohol on top of barbiturates. His body was cremated.

Kerouac heard the news from Carolyn. When it sank in he
did not want to believe it. Allen got it from Huncke's boy, who
was ignorant of who Neal even was. "I got up and answered the
'phone. There was a foreign operator asking if this was the
residence of Mr. Allen Ginsberg and that the 'Senoir Neal
Cassady was passed away.' I said 'Who is Neal Cassady, Allen,
do you know Neal Cassady?'" (*The Beat Diary*)

Do you know Neal Cassady, Allen? Jesus.

Chiefly at Kerouac's urging, Neal made attempts to write. He
lacked the application to complete full-scale projects and much
of what is in print is fragmented, often letters and transcripts of
tape recordings or raps. "Drive Five" is the soundtrack of Kesey's
home movie, *Neal Cassady in the Backhouse* and "Neal Telling

Story Fall '63" is included in *The First Third*, having been saved from loss forever by being "taken down handwrit" by Allen. The best of his output, credited as the inspiration for Kerouac's spontaneous style, white-hot prose according to those who read it, *is* apparently lost for ever.

> I got the idea for the spontaneous style of *On the Road* from seeing how good old Neal Cassady wrote his letters to me, all first person, fast, mad, confessional, completely serious, all detailed, with real names in his case however (being letters). The letter he sent me is erroneously reported to be a 13,000 word letter. . . no, the 13,000 word piece was his novel *The First Third*, which he kept in his possession. The letter, the main letter I mean, was 40,000 words long, mind you, a whole short novel. It was the greatest piece of writing I ever saw, better'n anybody in America, or at least enough to make Melville, Twain, Dreiser, Wolfe, I dunno who, spin in their graves. Allen Ginsberg asked me to lend him this vast letter so he could read it. He read it, then loaned it to a guy called Gerd Stern who lived on a houseboat in Sausalito California, in 1955, and this fellow lost the letter: overboard I presume.
> Neal and I called it, for convenience, the Joan Anderson Letter. . .all about a Christmas weekend in the poolhalls, hotel rooms and jails of Denver, so Allen shouldn't have been so careless with it, nor the guy on the houseboat. If we can unearth this entire 40,000 word letter Neal shall be justified. We also did so much fast talking between the two of us, on tape recorders, way back in 1952, and listened to them so much, we both got the secret of Lingo in telling a tale and figured that was the only way to express the speed and tension and ecstatic tomfoolery of the age. . .Is that enough? (*Paris Review*, 43)

It is this original which probably most closely informs *Visions of Cody*: exhaustive detail, arbitrary points for the beginning and end of narrative, a deliberate break with the unities of time and space. Whoever was to blame for the loss of the Joan Anderson letter, both of Cassady's friends understood its influence on Kerouac's "spontaneous" style.

> So what he did was try to write it all out, as fast as it came to his mind, all the associations; the style being as if he were telling a tale, excitedly, all night long, staying up all night with his best friend. The prose style being modeled on two buddies telling each other their most intimate secrets excitedly, the long confessional of everything that happened, meeting and recognizing each other like Dostoyevsky characters and telling each other the tale of their childhood. . . (*Allen Verbatim*)

The original *The First Third* details, in its first eighty pages, Cassady's childhood with his father, "the Barber," among the bums of "lower downtown Denver" where he became "the unnatural son of a few score beaten men." It is detailed and loosely structured in a manner common to untutored autobiographers but it does evoke the America of the time.

> Balcony-nestled amid lowerclass couples and their whimpering offspring, self-engrossed lovers, noisy young toughs whistling to fluster timid girls bunched in giggling ascent of the stairway, and all the varieties of midnight showgoers, Father would contentedly nip his wine chased by salted peanuts. To me, beside him, these hours contained only continuously unfolding thrills.

The subsequent edition restored by his widow, published in 1982, includes family history from before the birth of young Neal. The book's second section is fragmentary and includes Cassady's contribution to the chronicles of the Columbia campus and Times Square where the Beat Generation came together. "One night in the summer of 1945. . . First meeting with Jack Kerouac and Allen Ginsberg at Columbia University."

In the letters to Kerouac and Kesey which round off Neal's sole volume all the energy and exuberance which so captivated people, the freedom and spontaneity which Kerouac refined and developed, but which Neal could not match in formal writing – only in the unrestrained form of a letter to a close friend – are in evidence.

She (her name Patricia) got on the bus at 8 PM (Dark!) I didn't speak until 10 PM – in the intervening 2 hours I not only of course, determined to make her, but how to DO IT.

I naturally can't quote the conversation verbally, however, I shall attempt to give you the gist of it from 10 PM to 2 AM.

Without the slightest preliminaries of objective remarks (What's your name? Where are you going? etc.) I plunged into a completely knowing, completely subjective, personal & so to speak "penetrating her core" way of speech; to be shorter, (since I'm getting unable to write) by 2 AM I had her swearing eternal love, complete subjectivity to me & immediate satisfaction. I, anticipating even more pleasure, wouldn't allow her to blow me on the bus, instead we played, as they say, with each other.

Cassady's unique contribution to American literature is not his small body of published work but the important part he played in the work of the writers who were his friends. Ginsberg refers to him in both verse and prose, exuberantly in early poems like "The Green Automobile," in sentimental terms in the elegies.

> I'd honk my horn at his manly gate,
>   inside his wife and three
>   children sprawl naked
>   on the living room floor.
>
> He'd come running out
>   to my car full of heroic beer
>   and jump screaming at the wheel
>   for he is the greater driver
>   *Reality Sandwiches*

119

After friendship fades from flesh forms –
heavy happiness hangs in heart,
I could talk to you forever,
the pleasure inexhaustible,
discourse of spirit to spirit,
O Spirit.

The Fall of America

Cassady is frequently libeled by critics who never met him and who seem incapable of grasping the poetic truth about the man. He is variously described as psychopathic, alienated, in violation of every moral tenet, a barbarian, and, in one memorable phrase, "degenerate and deformed." But the man was forgiven, supported, protected, and cherished by talented and intelligent men and women all his life, even when the awful abuse to which he subjected his athletic frame had taken its vicious and dreary toll. Writers from Charles Bukowski to Kenneth Tynan were so impressed by the man in the flesh, even after one meeting, that he became the subject of even more pen portraiture.

We faced each other across a broad table, beside a window that overlooked the Bay. He was healthily handsome, with fair, close-cropped hair: "the Johnny Appleseed of marijuana," somebody once called him. He spoke freely about his life and his many wives, using no hipster idioms and no obscenities, but falling at times into oddly old-fashioned forms of speech, among them a trick of always referring to women by their full names.

No swell of emotion disturbed the flow of talk. (*Tynan, Right and Left*)

The practical problems of life with such a Dionysian character are seldom mentioned by his admirers, but are explored in the writings of his former wife, Carolyn Cassady (Camille in *On the Road* and Evelyn in Kerouac's *Big Sur*).

Late afternoon we drove home, sunburned and sandy but refreshed. Entering the silent empty house we were confronted

with a macabre version of Goldilocks and the Three Bears.
The living room gave no particular hint, but my bedroom,
John's room and the patio provided a series of sickening jolts.
My bed was stripped of bedding, the blankets in a heap on the
floor. The missing sheets were soon found, stuffed loosely in
the washer and splotched with blood. John's room resembled
the aftermath of a cyclone.

Neal had been given an intricate and expensive racing-car
outfit that he had proudly and ceremoniously presented to
John, spending many gleeful hours with him in its installation
and operation. What remained was a mass of twisted metal,
scattered and broken cars.

The patio was strewn with paper, garbage, overturned
chairs, and the pool held a multitude of soggy toys, some of
the racing cars and any other object an unattended child
would be happy to pitch in. There was no sign of Neal and no
note. I had heard his newest mistress had a two-year-old son.
The explanation dawned. I did not reveal it to the children.
("Coming Down," *The Beat Book*)

The complex and charismatic personality indicated by such a
variety of interpretation is most fully realized in Kerouac's
portrayals. Dean Moriarty is encountered in moments of reflec-
tion, of exuberance, of manic activity.

The girls yammered around the car. One particularly soulful
child gripped at Dean's sweaty arm. She yammered in Indian.
"Ah yes, ah yes, dear one," said Dean tenderly and almost
sadly. He got out of the car and went fishing around in the
battered trunk in the back – the same old tortured American
trunk – and pulled out a wristwatch. The others crowded
around with amazement. Then Dean poked in the little girl's
hand for "the sweetest and purest and smallest crystal she has
personally picked from the mountain for me." He found one
no bigger than a berry. And he handed her the wristwatch
dangling. Their mouths rounded like the mouths of chorister
children. The lucky little girl squeezed it to her ragged

121

breastrobes. They stroked Dean and thanked him. He stood among them with his ragged face to the sky, looking for the next and highest and final pass, and seemed like the Prophet that had come to them. He got back in the car. (*On the Road*)

Moriarty is an attractive and successful character. Kerouac draws the reader to him despite the selfish and careless traits in his creation's personality.

When I got better I realized what a rat he was, but then I had to understand the impossible complexity of his life, how he had to leave me there, sick, to get on with his wives and woes. "Okay, old Dean, I'll say nothing." (*On the Road*)

As early as New York Cassady, through raw energy and charisma, was the center of any group he was in. By the time of *Big Sur* fame and affluence had shifted the emphasis to Kerouac, who relieved Cassady of his latest mistress simply through celebrity: she had read his books.

Allen, once the eager quaint "character" (as Ringo to the Beatles), the Jewish kid with the jug ears, on the periphery of the handsome and physical football heroes, became, with fame and notoriety, the powerful personality which he now is. Cassady, in his decline, the energy now chemically fueled, the desperation sometimes showing, came to sit at the feet of another prime mover, also charismatic, also possessing money and success: all the Pranksters called Kesey chief.

Dean Moriarty and Sal Paradise were not carbons of Neal Cassady and Jack Kerouac. Real people and many real events were used as the basis for a novel about a man who encounters the other side of his personality, living and acting out some of his most vivid dreams and ambitions. Kerouac and Cassady were of similar age, build and coloring. Both were Roman Catholics, basically heterosexual, with strong sensual appetites. In the car-stealing, irresponsible delinquent with his Casanova conquests, Sal Paradise is able to cast off the social, conventional, and familial constraints that bound the real Kerouac. Circumstances cut Neal's umbilical cord at an early age. Jack never cut his. The wanderings of Sal and Dean are romantically represented as a search for the old lost father (who existed all the while, and was found with comparative ease when the Cassadys put their minds to it). Whatever excitement he generates, it is clearly impossible to live any kind of a normal life with a Dean Moriarty. Carolyn Cassady's writings endorse this: there was always another frenetic jaunt, a gambling jag, a new drug, another arrest, yet another mistress. Cassady's charisma survived his death. Elegized, his ashes were carried back to his true wife by his last mistress. His bigamous third wife sought a tithe of them and wracked her brains for an appropriate resting place.

finally she called and said she'd phoned Stella Kerouac, Jack's widow, in Florida, who'd never heard of her, and asked if she'd let her bury the ashes on Jack's heart. That was it. So Stella told her that when she sold the house in Florida she and Jack's mother were going back to Lowell and that she hadn't got Jack a proper headstone yet and when she did she'd meet her there and they could dig up the grave. (*Rolling Stone*, 119)

III   The West Coast

Heather wants to go to the sea

Coming out of Nevada under cover of dark and the California customs checking and inspecting trucks to detect fruit-fly smugglers. The darkness around the pool of light which is the truck stop and filling station reminiscent of Hopper's paintings: clarity by contrast. Inside, the wall is covered with Polaroids of good ole boys who stop here and get their vacuum flasks filled with coffee for free. Nicotine, caffeine, and benzedrine, the truckers' friends. Eat here and support your independent operator.

In the motel room one of the queen-size beds is still made up and she's asleep in the crook of my shoulder and I'm watching, insomniac, an old Anthony Perkins movie on the TV, high on the wall. As usual the reception makes it all but incomprehensible. The first color TV system in the world and they get lumbered with a standard of picture so bad they have to invent cable to get anything watchable. I wish I had the book Helmut Newton shot in American motels, just to substantiate my reality: a real naked lady in rooms that cease to exist once they are left behind. Tomorrow I will go over to the little beat diner – because motels serve no food – and the coffee machine will be busted and I will head out on Route 40 towards Barstow (on the edge of the desert, where the drugs started to get aholt of Raoul Duke and the Brown Buffalo), past all those great stretches of desert (well away from the prying highways), that the military industrial complex uses for war games: Fort Irwin, Twentynine Palms, China Lake Naval Weapons Center. Submarines in the middle of the desert? The ocean as a desert with its life underground?

Then I shall head on down the highway past Edwards Air Force Base towards Bakersfield, where Jagger met the girl with the Faraway Eyes, and into the San Joaquin Valley, where so much of *On the Road* takes place, and down through southern California, where Sal Paradise lived with Terri ("The Mexican Girl" – the first part of *On the Road* to get into print), whose sort of itinerant workers, living out their casual nomadic amours in the shacks and tents at the edges of the fields, are largely gone. Between the fields and the highway the packed white blocks will stand, caged down into oblong slabs, covered in sheets of glossy blue or black plastic, looking for all the world like giant tin loaves. There, where a TV series called *Route 66* was filmed, all about two cute boys in a Chevrolet Corvette (if memory serves), one of them with those dark good looks so reminiscent of the young Kerouac, some hip and friendly radio station will play me Jefferson Starship along the last few hundred miles of driving the big magenta LTD and towards my meeting, at last, with the mistress and muse of the Beat Generation, Carolyn Cassady.

> "'Now chillun, here's the pad,' turning into a narrow country road, and another, and into a driveway and a garage – 'There's the Spanish Mansion Pad and first thing is sleep.'" (*Desolation Angels*)

The sides of the LTD are streaked with the rain, dust, mud, and grit of three thousand miles of city, mountain, desert, and plain. The stacked hulks of the scrapyard tower over it like menhirs to the machine age – steelyard blues. Acres of built-in obsolescence rusting away under the California sun, but no, they don't have a hubcap for an LTD.

In her sunglasses and the shawl that has been to Africa and Asia and now America (worn today like a Mexican serape), sun glinting on the fall of hair, dust coating the thongs of her Indian sandals, Heather has bought a bagful of big, bright-skinned oranges and is studying the hundred-yard stack of Halloween pumpkins.

"That one looks the most sincere," I say.

"Oh, hi. Did they have one?"

"No, they didn't."

"Do you think it was nicked?" she asks, putting her purchases in the car.

"I think if Dion and the Belmonts had snuck into the parking lot they'd have taken all four. No, I reckon it went that time I drove all night through Indiana and that guy drove me off the road coming along on the wrong side."

"Probably you going back to driving on the left."

"*You* didn't even wake up."

"Anyway," she says, getting in and smoothing down her skirts. "I don't see what you're bothered about. It's only a hubcap."

"I am bothered because I signed for four. It's on the agreement. Just below the part that says 'No unlicensed firearms,' see?"

"I remember: you asked the chap if that meant you could take a Carl Gustav and a General Purpose Machine Gun if they were licensed and he said sure."

I wheel the big car out onto the road and we roll down the sticky tarmac lanes in the heat haze, air-conditioning on.

"You know, I know Israel is a client state and all, but I still don't understand why they named all these freeways after Begin."

"I wish we could find out who this mysterious Oriental guy is whose name's painted on the road so often. Who is 'Xing Ped'?"

"Probably some legacy from Vietnam. Could you light me up a Primo del Rey?"

"You're out of those. Will a King Edward Invincible do?"

"Even better." She puffs the cigar alight and puts it between my teeth.

"You know," I continue, "if you try to drive onto a freeway down one of the exit turnoffs there are signs saying 'Stop. You Are Going the Wrong Way.' Kesey made that the slogan for the end of the sixties."

"Really? What *are* you doing? We're on a freeway! You can't park here!"

When I sprint back to the car and drive away again, after a hairy little trip on foot down the nearside lane, I have a hubcap. You sometimes see one, lost and unheeded, at the roadside. Outside a bar I hammer it on (it's not the right size of course)

129

while she goes in and calls Carolyn's number for directions. I go in and order a beer and give her the keys.

"You drive. I've gone nervous all of a sudden."

So, through the urban freeways, checking the office where the LTD has to be surrendered tomorrow, to stopping at a carwash to jet-hose the travel off him. Then under the baked hills, past the San Jose Airport, where Cassady's ashes arrived in the States, and out to the pleasant little town of Los Gatos, where Georgie Best used to tour the bars when he played for the San Jose Earthquakes, up the highway signed for Saratoga, which was countryside when Neal's railroad broken leg compensation money bought the house, suburb now, and turning into a narrow country road, and another, and into a driveway at the end of which there is a mailbox on a post and it is labeled "Cassady."

If Neal and Jack were a Beat Hope and Crosby in a real-life road movie (Road to Mexico? Road to Denver? Road to California?) then Carolyn Cassady was Dorothy Lamour. The eternal spice of friendly rivalry in the American buddy system.

As Camille in *On the Road* she appears only fleetingly and has little depth compared to even minor male characters. Ed Dunkel or Carlo Marx remain in the memory as the loping laconic Westerner or the young Jewish intellectual with the burning eyes, while Camille is little more than a stereotyped deserted wife. The lady herself feels that the name indicates the way she was at the time – with "Dean" buzzing energetically between her and "Marylou" and his other women, "Sal" looking on in admiration and scarcely admitting that such behaviour has the potential for causing misery. Carolyn Cassady's autobiography (the full, as yet unpublished, 625-page book, of which *Heart Beat* is but an excerpt) exhaustively catalogues the disillusionment of this time. Almost penniless, abandoned with a tiny child, Helen Hinkle (Galatea Dunkel) her only friend and confidant, the menfolk off on something like a superannuated schoolboy jape. *On the Road* deals with her feelings briefly but vividly. Camille appears, tear-stained, to scream, "Liar, liar,

130

liar!" at a retreating Dean, and Sal, with a poet's pang, sees a painting of Galatea done from life (and in reality the product of many long and penurious hours) and realizes that the two women have sat, and surely talked just as deeply as he and Dean have, without having "adventures." This fits neatly into his pre-conceived, idealized image of homemaking womanhood (absorbed from the dutiful, powerful, Catholic matriarchies in which he was brought up, in which the women won their power by making themselves indispensable). Men might goof but women looked after babies. Later, with age and hindsight and the experience of a love affair with her, he was to see Carolyn's position with a greater awareness.

There has been, inevitably, questioning of the role of women in Kerouac's books, in the whole catalogue of Beat writings, in the Beat Generation itself. Knowing how Jack felt about the hippies one should be able to predict the degree of unease with which he would have confronted a certain kind of eighties feminist. The defenses, in his later books, about "living with his mother" are the forced and slightly shrill tones of the man who knows he's on shaky ground. Memere affected all his relation-ships with women – from telling her not to read certain parts of the early books to paying, with marriage, for a nurse for her. It comes as no surprise that the love affairs he celebrated in literature all ended in sorrow. Perhaps because of the central place that homosexual men had in the Beat group it is some-times seen as being "anti-women." In reality, the Beat Generation socially was a bit of a bohemian boys' club and the girls who were welcomed into it, and felt at home there, were the ones who were capable of being one of the boys. Lenore Kandel striding around in her purple panties; Joanna McClure writing, like Lenore, sexy poems about women's eroticism; Diane DiPrima cheerfully rolling around in between Jack and Allen and putting it all down in *Memoirs of a Beatnik*; Anne Waldman bare-breasted on her Himalayan postcards; Joyce Glassman pretty and attentive in the Cedar. Beat literature reflected the attitudes of Greenwich Village and North Beach, of American Bohemia. A chick was decorative in leotards. If she smoked a joint it established her status. She made her own decisions about her sexual nature and activity. Being quiet while the men argued, though, was still a highly desirable quality.

Do you know the way to San Jose?

The highway on the outskirts of San Jose was concrete and hot and wide and cared little for those who traveled on foot. By the small shop selling motorcycle accessories and black, logoed T-shirts for men bikers and black, logoed singlets, with a suggestion of black lace, for girl bikers, the little creek ran in a shadowy, sheltered bed. It was crossed by a small, concrete-cast bridge with a city reference number and name etched into it.

The interior of the noonday bar was black as sin and twice as chilly. A gossiping bartender left the only other customer, a middle-aged woman.

"What can I get you?"

"I'd like to have a beer, please."

"Bottle or draft?"

"A bottle please. A Bud will be fine."

"One Bud. Wanna glass?"

"Yes, I want a glass. Thanks."

"That's a buck. Have a nice day."

"You have a nice day too."

Perched on the tall stool, alone in the cool dark, he unzipped his boots, slipped them off and let the aching feet cool on the floor. When he went to the john the bartender stared, sure that he had been taller.

Out on the sidewalk the proprietors of the bikers' shop were checking a consignment. Sweet smoke edged out of their doorway. They looked up as his shadow darkened it.

"Hi, bro."

"Hello there."

"Toke?"

"Yr OK, pal."

Down the long highway into San Jose cars were traveling through heat and smog, miles away in the impossible distance.

He took off his leather jacket and slung it over his shoulder, shifting the camera so that it hung under his arm. Interlinked wire fences sagged away to his right. Behind them were stretches of settling land, clumped with grass and scattered with rusted beer cans. Notices sternly forbade the stealing of the fence.

The gun shop was empty except for the dozing and dusty head of a mature, male moose. The plate-glass windows were streaked and dirty.

He stopped and looked down from the bridge over the narrow and silted river. It was in a cleft that was in verdant contrast to the dry and dusty hinterland of the highway that led into the outskirts of San Jose. Flat-bladed things grew in the shallows and the banks were green and mossy. From beneath the bridge, a man appeared. He was about thirty, bearded, dark, with a knife holster at his belt.

After a few moments another man followed him out from under the bridge and, without saying anything, shinnied sideways across the waste pipe which spanned it. The second man was losing his hair. He was wearing trousers that bagged out at the backside and a belt that was not looped through the belt loops of his baggy trousers. On the belt was a sheath with a non-folding knife in it. Behind them all, the traffic, uncaring, went along into San Jose and out of San Jose. Above them the sun of the early afternoon was hot. Down river a little way there were trees which shaded the banks of the river. Now, on either side of the river, the two men were scanning its banks, carefully and systematically.

On the surface of the river was the straight shadow of the bridge. On the hot concrete highway he was the only pedestrian. The man who was losing his hair saw the shadow on the water and looked up at the bridge. Then he hissed quietly across the river. His companion looked up at him and then he looked up at the bridge and then he looked scared.

The two men started to move back up towards either side of the bridge. They moved swiftly towards the slopes which led up to the highway where the cars went by at a pace towards and away from San Jose.

He took the leather jacket off his shoulder and twirled it like a matador's cape and then used its momentum to wrap it around his left forearm. He tucked the coat's hem in on itself. He lifted his own sheath knife out of the back pocket of his jeans and pulled the sheath around to his right hip and rested the heel of his right hand on the haft, pulling it out against the leather of the sheath, and stared down at the water as the two men were climbing up on either side of him.

The man on his right, the one who was losing his hair, stopped moving. He looked up at the bridge, with the shadows of the cars sluicing by behind it and he took his hand off the knife on his belt.

"Where you from?" he demanded.

"I'm from England," said the man on the bridge.

The man who was losing his hair said, scornfully, "You didn't learn that in England." He shaded his eyes, squinting. "Where'd you learn that?"

"That's just something I learned over in England," said the man on the bridge.

All the stories that were told

It is morning over the big wooden bungalow off the Saratoga and the sun is pouring down into the porch where Kerouac dossed down in his sleeping bag until a spaniel called Cayce started to pester him and he was obliged to move out into the sleepy meadow behind the house and slumber among the clumps of grass. Out by the little blue pool a long slender blond in a black string bikini is painting her toenails. She looks up after thirty seconds in response to my gaze and flutters her fingers languidly at me. Carolyn, glass of California Chablis in hand, walks out to join her. I return my attentions to the electric Olympia 65C.

"Evelyn is all radiant blond in the morning," Jack said in *Desolation Angels*. "She's a very pretty little woman and a top-notch mother —" The way he saw her in the sunny West. That knack of finding a characteristic in a model to make the fictional creation come alive.

The back room of the house is the study. Bookshelves, filing cabinets, the typewriter on a desk built on uprights of ornamental breezeblock. Under the sloping roof are a collection of framed photographs: Allen eating cereal and Jack brooding in a freight yard, (both in color); Gavin Arthur looking benign; Jami, the younger daughter, in a leotard during her ballet days; formal studio portraits of some of the cast of *Heart Beat*; she and Sissy Spacek together; Neal and Al Hinkle and another conductor, all smart in their uniforms, standing by a train; a back-lit biker with waist length hair; Heather and I in Watermelon Sugar. Pride of place — over the open dictionary on its stand — goes to the 1948 shot of the Cassadys taken arm in arm on the street in San Francisco a few weeks before they were married. Neal in a suit, coat and wide trousers, Carolyn in a skirt and heels, a young Monroe. Below is the biggest print in the collection, the one Carolyn took across the street from 29, Russell (because the sun was on that side of the street), of Jack and Neal — the cover of *The First Third*.

I have been installed here, with Michelob and a supply of seventy-cent Primo del Reys, since shortly after our arrival. It is an archive full of strange and wondrous things: the copy of Saroyan's *My Name is Aram* which Kerouac read, containing the story "The Summer of the Beautiful White Horse" which he mentioned to Aram Saroyan (son of William) during the *Paris Review* interview. The other boy in the story is called Moorad. Kerouac called Ginsberg Adam Moorad in *The Subterraneans*. Synchronicity again.

Now and again I leave the sanctum to drive over the hills above Santa Cruz, where the Doobie Brothers sang about Neal, and feed the sealions or shoot in the galleries or listen to jazz outside the Cooper House or eat in the Sirloin and Brew (all the wine, beer, or California champagne you want with your meal, says the Vietnamese waiter). Most of the time I work.

"This cabinet drawer has all the reviews and publicity on the film. This one is clippings on Jack's books and this file is on Neal and up there are the copies of Jack and Allen's books that they gave me. And these" (handing me a thick buff folder) "though only copies, I'm afraid, because the originals are with the University of Texas, are all Jack's letters."

Cook me a pizza!

Throughout the fifties the letters reflect the restless rovings: Rocky Mount; Tangier (with the Queen's head on the sixpenny stamp); Northport; Orizaba 210; Mexico City (from which he wrote under the pseudonym of Jean Levesque); Richmond Hill; the S.S. *William Carruth*.

They were written in the true confessional mode, with absolutely *no* revision – private material never conceived for public ink. There is an oddly touching little vulnerability about them – he constantly spells "goofing" as "goffing" – little gauchenesses edited out by proofreaders. The poetry of the letters is punctuated by awkward raw patches of his real soul. The yearnings, obsessions, and insecurities show through. He was always on about Carolyn's pizzas. In '55 and '56 he was all Buddhism. The little jealousies surface in this trusted security. Allen and Holmes are tiresome, though they think themselves very interesting. Brass-necked people are ripping him off.

"The nerve of that Solomon proposing that Neal turn himself into a A.A. Wyn slave and let his children starve while he turns out 'Mickey Spillane'. . . "

"(Holmes has started publishing jazz stories THAT I MYSELF TOLD HIM imagine the gall)"

136

Mexico City July 3

Dear Neal & Carolyn,

Just to let you know I'm leaving
Mexico City and going to live, write and
till my special soils in a small shack
type made of dobe bricks in the country
not far from here, in a valley...for pract-
ically & eventually nothing—— don't know
for how long— will be my headquarters.
Won't write for a long time because want
to sink into natural oblivion with myself,
dog, indians, beattiful & sad indians
&——— Let my mail dust under a floorboard,
see you on some spectral New Years Eve.
Love & dumb kisses.

My Ma all set at sister's now *South Carolina*

J.

p.s. Eventually I want to go to Ecuador
where the mangos, orchids & wives grow
wild, no want, no phoney hassels, no anger
and all that kind of shit ad infinitum..

Any important messages for me send to Allen,)
who will undoubtedly relay them by telepathy

KKK's to you & children
Old 2695 . (*Write Neal Fury Third — Five C. sentimentally*)

+ visit me on a burro

"(Holmes made $20,000 on *Go*) (will inherit 8,000 from Family)"

Poor loyal old Jack – the hopeless envy in the letter of 11 February 1953. How he'd have loved a house like Holmes', a family like Neal's – rootless and restless and longing for a mansion, a family, a home.

The dreams are constant: always he will return to California, work on the railroad again, earn the stake, buy the shack, the cabin, the ranch, go to South America, be a rancher.

They are always a *fait accompli* when they're written down. So are the books, which are always due to be finished in a fortnight. He thought aloud in the letters to the matron Muse: once it was all dreamt up it was as good as done.

Charlie Chaplin on Columbus

When Lawrence Ferlinghetti was reading for his doctorate at the Sorbonne in postwar Paris he met another expatriate who lived the bohemian life and was mad about books. In the early fifties both men started bookshops. The Mistral in Paris and City Lights, the first ever paperback bookshop in America. In the sixties, George Whitman found a tradition lying around on the Left Bank that no one was using and re-named his shop. Nowadays, City Lights stocks the postcards of its "sister" bookshop, on the rue de la Bucherie, Shakespeare & Co.

Closer to a *bibliothèque* than any American conception of a bookshop, City Lights is still open until midnight seven nights a week. Clerks do not hover menacingly while the customer sits at the tables and samples the goods before buying. The sign advising that "all shoplifters will cheerfully be beaten to a pulp" is so high it may only be seen from the balcony office.

It was also European tradition which prompted Ferlinghetti to become a publisher as well as a bookseller. City Lights publications gave up its separate premises a few years back but continues to bring out six or eight books a year.

The basement, a bare brick cavern, is entirely given over to poetry. The giants of the Beat Generation and the outlaws of North Beach – Corso, Ginsberg, Kerouac, Kaufman, Micheline, and Hirschman, are here with the European they all acknowledge – Apollinaire, Rimbaud, Verlaine, Baudelaire.

Live readings are held, the survivors invested with the new aura accorded living legends. Signings feature writers who might otherwise be shy of such events. Brautigan will stride loftily in: El Hombre Invisible has been known to materialize. Window displays – books once banned or writers born in November, have a snap of originality. The 1982 calendar was literary lovers – Lawrence and Frieda, Hem and the original of Catharine Barkley. The provincial Compendiums of Britain bear witness to the spread of the idea. The actual name has been pirated in Ontario and Sydney.

BOOK BUYERS' GUIDE

1. Is it literature by any stretch of the imagination?
2. Is it politically or sociologically important, whether Left or Right?
3. Is it a basic text or a classic in a particular field?
4. Is it counter culture of any particular significance? Far out or Far in in some not mindless way?
5. If it has porno characteristics, does it have any "redeeming social significance" (legal criterion)?
6. Is it by a local author?
7. Is it slick, is it schlock, is the price too high?
8. *Is it schmaltz?*
9. *Does it bounce?*
10. *Will it sell?*
11. *Is it circumcised?*

> (Sign on City Lights office wall, the last four penciled in different hands.)

. . .poor Monsanto a man of letters. With his husky shoulders,
big blue eyes, twinkling rosy skin, that perpetual smile of his
that earned him the name Smiler in college and a smile you
often wondered "Is it real?" until you realized if Monsanto
should ever stop using that smile how could the world go on
anyway – *Big Sur*)

Born in 1919, Lawrence Ferlinghetti was older than all the Beat
writers except Burroughs. Playwright, poet, novelist, essayist,
travel writer, painter, bookseller, and publisher his range of
creative activity is unique within the group. His traditionally
mysterious personal history was only breached in 1981 by the
biographer, Neeli Cherkowski. It plays comparatively little part in
his work. Based in San Francisco after his sojourn in France, he
did not share the formative New York traumas. On the other hand,
he appears in the others' books and they crop up constantly in his
own work. Also, his City Lights bookshop and publishing house
were of unique importance: there would have been no manifestation of the Beat Generation on the West Coast without him.

His experience of France, to which he sailed in 1947 after
receiving his M.A. from Columbia, was crucial. He had already
encountered Prévert, whose *Paroles* he translated. His novel,
Her, was published in France in 1961, as *La Quatrième Personne
du Singulier*, to enthusiastic, if somewhat inflated, praise.
". . .the confirmation of a great American writer who, in the
hall of American literary glories, takes the place left vacant by
the death of Hemingway." (Pierre Lapape – dust jacket quote)

Though it is far from being his favorite role, Ferlinghetti's
function as the Beats' Sylvia Beach, sympathetic and involved
publisher, can scarcely be overrated.

His prosecution and defense of *Howl* enhanced the dignity
and reputations of both publisher and poet and brought the
movement squarely to the attention of the West Coast media
and its intellectuals. The heavy-handed attitude of the authorities
could not fail to secure bestseller status once the book was
cleared and available. An obscure San Francisco cop called

Captain Hanrahan launched Allen Ginsberg as a media star – ironically the exact opposite of what the policeman wished. Besides his writing, publishing, and painting Ferlinghetti has been film-maker and playwright. Along with Lawrence Lipton and Kenneth Rexroth he was closely identified with the short-lived "poetry and jazz" facet of the San Francisco Renaissance. His publishing list reflects a very personal taste and the circles in which Ferlinghetti moves. The lions of the Beat Generation are mostly all there – Burroughs, Cassady, Corso, Ferlinghetti himself, Ginsberg, and Kerouac, beside the less well-known or peripheral Beats – Paul Bowles, Bob Kaufman, Philip Lamantia, Michael McClure, Carl Solomon.

Evergreen Review had given the Beats a showcase on the Eastern seaboard since 1957. In 1963 and 1964 the spasmodic *City Lights Journal* provided the same thing on the West Coast. Number one, with Ginsberg on the cover wrapped in a blanket against Himalayan chills and snapped by Snyder, had Kerouac among the Iroquois, Harold Norse elegizing the Beat Hotel, a flash of Burroughs, Ted Joans in Africa, Ferlinghetti in Mexico, Brautigan in a trout stream, Michaux on mescalin and Mayakovsky about to die. Number Four, published fifteen years later and edited by "Mendes Monsanto," has the cosmopolitan mix as before. Kerouac (this time dreaming bilingually in 1955 Berkeley), his daughter in El Salvador and Costa Rica, Norse ("Bastard Angel") on his childhood, Ferlinghetti's second manifesto, Apollinaire, Blaise Cendrars, Pablo Neruda, and Mohammed Mrabet. Fraternal considerations are not allowed to adulterate the quality of Ferlinghetti's list.

However important his enterprise and acumen have been to the Beat movement Ferlinghetti would insist that his own poetry be considered as his main contribution. Whatever its faults it appeals directly to people not automatically among poetry audiences. One of the main planks in his platform is his use of literary references. His degree of learning shapes and colors his work in ways not always immediately apparent. Thomas Parkinson is critical.

141

"One of my main objections to Lawrence Ferlinghetti is that he is much too literary in tone and reference. He writes for the man in the street, but he chooses a street full of *Nation* subscribers and junior-college graduates." (*Casebook on the Beat*)

Ferlinghetti's themes, his personal and political attitudes, have remained more or less constant. A painter himself, the immediacy of his response to paintings by Goya, Monet, or Klimt are the inspiration for poems. Well known canvases by Whistler, Picasso, Chagall, or da Vinci are mentioned in his works. His early poems, when irreverent or sexually explicit, were taken as typical of Beat poets.

> and the sweet semen rivulets
> and limp buried peckers
> in the sand's soft flesh
>
> * * *
>
> Sometime during eternity
> some guys show up
> and one of them
> who shows up real late
> is a kind of carpenter
> from some square-type place
> like Galilee
> *A Coney Island of the Mind*

He is more political than most of his contemporaries.

> And after it became obvious that the strange rain
> would never stop and that Old Soldiers never drown
> and that roses in the rain had forgotten the word
> for bloom and that perverted pollen blown on sunless
> seas was eaten by irradiated fish who spawned up
> cloudleaf streams and fell on to our dinnerplates.
> *Starting from San Francisco*

His most individual trait is his extensive use of quotation. He scorns quotation marks and there is no guarantee that his readers have read the same books he has, yet acknowledgement of his sources (Henry Miller for the title of A *Coney Island of the Mind*, Walt Whitman for *Starting from San Francisco*), are the exception. It's a lot of fun spotting the quotes, but relying on them is cheating a bit.

> If I were you I'd keep aside
> an oversize pair of winter underwear
> Do not go naked in to that good night
> And in the meantime
> keep calm and warm and dry
> No use stirring ourselves up prematurely
> "over Nothing"
> Move forward with dignity
> hand in vest
> Don't get emotional
> And death shall have no dominion
> There's plenty of time my darling
> Are we not still young and easy
> Don't shout

> White lilacs last in the dooryard bloom, Fidel
> > *A Coney Island of the Mind*

> > I had not known
> > life had undone so many
> > Inside Woolworth's sweet machine
> > > *Starting from San Francisco*

> at the very top
> where surely a terrible beauty is born

> There's breathless hush on the freeway tonight
> > *Who Are We Now?*

The list could be extended. Dylan Thomas, Walt Whitman, T.S. Eliot, and W.B. Yeats should be familiar to those who read books of poetry, but the nineteenth printing of A *Coney Island of*

143

the Mind claimed a half million copies in print. It is surely unlikely all its purchasers are conversant with the writings of Sir Henry Newbolt. It is possible, of course, that the poet really does imagine that his audience – does consist of *"Nation* subscribers and junior-college graduates" but in an unguarded moment he is not above confusing sources himself.

> FERLINGHETTI: The poet has to be involved with life in all its aspects. If he is a liberal or a humanitarian he must be very aware and sensitive to the world's problems, no matter where he goes. Blake said it: "For whom the bells toll, they toll for thee." (*Penthouse*, vol. 1, no. 4)

Hemingway's readers will be familiar with Donne's sermon. Ferlinghetti has both bootlegged Hemingway (*Collected Poems*) and passed judgement on him ("intellectually bankrupt long before A *Moveable Feast*") and so has really little excuse. The reader is left to wonder whether a nice turn of phrase is "borrowed" without its origins being clear to the borrower. If so, the reader is in danger of imparting a meaning to it that is possibly not intended. Excessive use of quotation leaves a poem's claims to originality open to question. A case in point is "Junkman's Obbligato," written to be read to jazz and relying heavily on lines from other works, it leaves itself open to being seen as a pastiche of Eliot's "Prufrock" and "The Waste Land" and Yeats's "The Lake Isle of Innisfree." This makes the identification of common ground with his fellow Beats problematical. "Kaddish" draws much of its final power from the cawing of the graveyard crows, the repetition of the cry "Lord Lord Lord." Ferlinghetti has written poems with these refrains.

> Even as a crowd of huge defiant
> > upstart crows
> sets up a ravening raucous
> > caw! caw! caw!

Who Are We Now?

144

They are burning them
lord lord

the same leaves born
lord lord
in a red field
a white stallion stands
and pees his oblivion
upon those leaves

Lord lord never returning
the youth years fallen
away back then
Under the Linden trees in Boston Common
Lord Lord
Trees think

Lord Lord Lord
every bush burns

Lord Lord Lord Lord
Small nuts fall
Mine too.

Starting from San Francisco

Derivation aside there are pointers in Ferlinghetti's work which mark him out as a member of the Beat Generation. The tell-tale references to fellow members are there. In the first Populist Manifesto he directly addresses both Ginsberg and Snyder.

All you masters of the saw mill haiku

No more chanting Hare Krishna
while Rome burns,

The hour of oming is over

Who Are We Now?

For the former he reserves special praise. "Allen Ginsberg is no doubt the greatest American poet since Whitman," said *Penthouse*. Reference to Ginsberg's expulsion from Czechoslovakia (after he had lost a notebook which was found by a secret policeman who could read English) is made in *Starting from San Francisco* – the Comrades are too puritanical. "He" is dedicated to his friend.

> with a long head and a foolscap face
> and the long made hair of death
> of which nobody speaks
> And he speaks of himself and he speaks of the dead
> of his dead mother and his dead Aunt Rose
> with their long hair and their long nails
> that grow and grow
> and they come back in his speech without
> a manicure
> *Starting from San Francisco*

Dylan and Kerouac also feature in his cast of characters. The clearest tip of the Ferlinghetti hat to the Beat ideal, however, is in the surreal novel, *Her*, in which the habitués of the Beat Hotel in rue Git le Coeur, birthplace of *Naked Lunch*, declare the final messianic revolution of poetry.

> . . .a wailing wild ragged band of American poets from the Rue Git-le-Coeur rushed out of a side street into the middle of the boulevard and fell into the winding land, jumping onto the shoulders of the dancers and hanging onto the necks of the women, singing and shouting that the Poetry Police were coming to save them, the Poetry Police were coming to save them all from death, Captain Poetry was coming to save the world from itself, to make the world safe for beauty and love. . .

"The Howling Dogs of Poetry"

My mental picture of Lawrence Ferlinghetti has always been of a tall, grizzled man in an unusual hat, sloping through San Francisco, usually with a dog at his heels, thinking poetry. Just the way he appears, picking his way over the Band's cables, to deliver his anthem from the stage in *The Last Waltz*. I had had the impression that he was a slightly prickly character. Like so many pre-formed notions this all turns out to be absolutely accurate.

"What's your book going to be called?" he says. "Call it 'The Howling Dogs of Poetry.'" Two minutes I've known him and he's naming my book for me. An unraveling skein of gray wool loosely made up to resemble a dog nuzzles affectionately around his ankles. He is the successor to the legendary Homer, and he, at least, seems disinclined to howl.

Like Allen when you first meet him, Ferlinghetti gives the initial impression of being more concerned to talk than to listen, to launch into an account rather than respond to a line of questioning. Getting to know either a little better you realize that this is just a response to being misquoted and misrepresented so often. Mention of his profile in *People* is greeted with a snort.

"Full of misinformation. . .still trying to correct the impression left by the damn thing."

Once perceiving some glimmer of knowledge or intelligence in an interlocutor, Ferlinghetti will move from harangue to conversation, but he remains very conscious of his place, his literary stature, his body of work, and his achievement. The slight wariness does not evaporate.

"I thought you'd have a tape recorder. These are all important little points and they're being lost. They come pretty small these days." He exudes a slightly peeved air.

"I don't like them. You stick a microphone under somebody's nose and it's very inhibiting. I make notes and my memory's adequate." Leaning on the balcony looking down into City Lights, Heather giggles, as she always does when someone causes me to sound British and pompous.

147

Ferlinghetti leans back in the swivel chair in front of the roll-top desk (its roll top no longer actually in evidence) Kerouac recalled in *Big Sur*. Established elder of poetry and publishing, receiving an acolyte from across the sea. The casual chaos of the City Lights office, with the poster of Chaplin and the bowler hat and cane hanging over the desk, are at odds with this. Today's *chapeau* is a black, spaghetti Western number. He growls his answers with a mixture of humor and impatience, exploding at the mention of the word coterie, an image so far removed from his howling dogs. Yes, he says, what Allen says is correct, the more successful City Lights authors subsidize the works by less famous writers. The familiar little black and white Pocket Poets Series (probably the most pocketed poetry volumes in the world, in both senses), reached its fortieth with Ginsberg's *Plutonian Ode*. But he seems either bored or restless talking about the publishing side. I remember Allen telling me that he did nothing to promote *Howl* after the bust, when most publishers would have promoted it for all its worth. It begins to dawn on me that he really *is* a reluctant businessman, determined to remain surreal in the world of Mammon. Yes, he says, it's true he didn't like the portrait Kerouac put of the genial literary businessman in *Big Sur*. "I was older than most of those guys. I didn't know Kerouac very well," he says, as if, had they been closer, Jack would never have presented him as he did.

"I'm an artist." Certainly the bookshop seems to be run by Joe Wolberg as, presumably, it was by Shig Murao before his departure.

Let's get some common ground here if we can, I decide.

"Was your Ph.D. thesis written in French? What was it on?"

"Yes it was. It was on the influence of the *pissoir* in French literature."

"The what?"

"The *pissoir*."

Now I've heard that one before and I'm not sure if he's serious but let it go.

"Far from being 'know-nothing bohemians' it seems to me

that most of the Beats read the European writers avidly and spoke more than one language. Was *Her* written in English or French? Did you translate it yourself?"

"It was written in English and I didn't translate it. I find if I translate I wind up writing another book. You're right about the Beats – I've heard Allen carry on conversations abroad in Italian as well as French and Spanish. At the Chile Conference in 1959 he was communicating more than the entire U.S. embassy. Like Julian Beck and Judith Molina – doing *Antigone* in French for instance – the Beats are heading towards being polyglots of language. They have completely come into ascendancy in Europe. The Amsterdam Festival in 1981 was completely dominated by them, they are the true international poets now, particularly Allen and Gregory. I disagree with Allen sometimes, over poetics, but not as a brother poet."

"Do you or Gregory still have Italian?"

"Not really. We were both disconnected from our fathers at a very early age. When I go to Italy I get the language back some."

"You've been more reticent about your early life than most of your fellows. It seemed sometimes, in the anthologies, that you were being deliberately imprecise: 'he may have been shown in swaddling clothes the coast of –'?"

"Well in those days I considered myself very much a surrealist." He laces his fingers. "I used to write fake surrealist biographies for the anthologies. Why should a surrealist give out a real biography?"

"You don't seem to have done many interviews. There was one in *Penthouse* in '65 and Gavin Selerie's one."

"I don't remember the first one you mention but I like the Selerie one. I did it when I was doing a reading at the Riverside. Pity he can't get it published in a better format, though."

"Well the second one, with Allen, is much better, with good photos. Your first 'Populist Manifesto' was published in Leicester (where there's also a Beacon Hill) in Z *Revue*. Did they pirate it?"

"No, they asked to publish it and I said yes. Can't remember who."

"Would it be Dennis Gould?"

"Dennis Gould, yes!"

"I take it you wanted it read as widely as possible?"

"I wanted to scatter it plentifully about, yes. Where does one get a long poem published in England now that *Encounter*'s gone?"

"One doesn't."

"Who's the new Dylan Thomas? Who's emerged?"

"No one of that stature. The best platform poets are in their forties now. People start a record company, not a magazine. Do you still have a cabin in Raton Canyon?"

"Yes but not the same one. People go up there because of the Kerouac associations. Copy down all the graffiti in the outhouse. BUDDHIST ANARCHIST TEMPLE is the biggest. The Young Museum wanted to take the outhouse and put it on display in San Francisco."

"The only place I've ever seen quite like City Lights is Shakespeare and Co."

"Our sister bookshop! George Whitman and I stole books together, at the Sorbonne, before we *had* bookshops. He started his bookshop '51, '52. We'll be co-publishing a polylingual review, *Polyglot Paris Review*. George is the most eccentric individual I've ever met. He'll give you some room to stay in if he likes you and it'll be full of books. He's a true bibliophile, you can't find any trash – first editions lying around in the open. In Europe booksellers were publishers too so it seemed logical to do the same. George will just leave somebody, usually a girl who's just walked in, in charge of the bookshop, give 'em the keys and go off somewhere. Felicity had a baby when she was twenty-six and she puts it in his arms and there's George with this baby and he doesn't know what to do and he has to change its diapers. One American bookshop you should go to – Gotham – it's good but it has that hard-edged New York aggressive face."

Risking touching on publication again I mention *City Lights Journal*. He agrees on its importance. He concedes that Mendes Monsanto is a name he uses, often when writing to the newspapers. Portuguese-Sephardic, the Monsantos left Portugal during the Inquisition and went to St. Thomas, in the Virgin Islands.

"There is a connection with Pissarro –" he continues.

"The conquistador?"

"No, the painter." He glances at his watch and stands, asking if I would like some review copies – City Lights stuff only, of course. I move along the shelves, my arms becoming full as he urges this Kaufman, that Hirschman on me with great generosity.

"One last question: in *The Mexican Night* you speak of Cassady's 'lost and found manuscreeds.' I take it that *was* the original version of *The First Third*? It wasn't the fabled Joan Anderson letter?"

"No. Gerd Stern, the guy who got the blame for losing that letter, said Allen greatly exaggerated its length. It was nowhere near 40,000 words, only a few pages long."

"Are you still fascinated by Klimt's work?"

"Yes."

"You're doing a lot of painting now, and you've written plays as well as essays, a novel and of course, the poetry. What do you like to be thought of as?" He pauses in the doorway, making sure he understands the question.

"An artist," he says.

OK, not a publisher.

Leather riders selling news

On the bus up into the Haight Ashbury district a black hipster and his stooge start a game of Find the Lady. A white kid with gullibility writ large on his face shows interest. The black driver makes growls and the hipster shuts up like a fan and sits very quietly.

In the Chinese liquor store the lady's cash register keeps adding a six-pack and a bottle of wine up to over ten bucks. It is mightily reviled in Cantonese.

Michael McClure's house is lofty wooden San Francisciana, bought a score of years ago, long before the apotheosis of the Summer of Love. Inside, it is alcoves, paintings, rugs on wooden floors, chairs that invite one to loll. Heather sits back and says little, the blue eyes snapping back and forth between us as if watching an invisible ball game. McClure produces long-stemmed glasses for the Pabst, drinking with the frugality of the fitness fanatic. He runs every morning. Creeley was anxious when McClure invited him to the gym (in which he taught part-time, J.C. Penney's) over possible comparisons of physique. The once-abundant hair is clipped short now, still a full head though steely grey. He is clean-shaven. Of my hirsuteness he says, rather ruefully, "I have been there." Can't risk growing old and looking like Karl Marx. Daughter Jane, he says, is a grown-up young lady now. He is concerned about his smile, dislikes being photographed when speaking. In his youth in the vortex country of Kansas he was self-conscious. Just too good-looking for a place like Wichita. Makes the blue shirts edgy. Kerouac called him the most handsome man he'd ever seen. This is the Pat McLear of 1960, "handsome enough to play Billy the Kid in the movies, that same slightly sliteyed look you expect from the myth appearance of Billy the Kid." (*Big Sur*)

Joanna comes in and says hello on her way to the kitchen. A friendly, pretty, brown-haired American matron she scarcely looks the sort of girl who sent such delicious *frissons* of shock up the colons of her contemporaries by writing very explicit poems about what she and her old man get up to in the sack.

We talk a little about Kerouac, rather a lot about Allen. He too laments Trungpa's influence and the depilated version of Ginsberg. "I think the beard suits Allen."

"Do you have any inside dope on what really happened over W. S. Merwin and his girlfriend? *The Great Naropa Poetry Wars* has Merwin defending the two of them with broken beer bottles until he was finally overpowered and they were forcibly stripped in front of Trungpa by his goons."

"I don't know this book," he says, reaching for a pencil.

152

"Originally published in the *Boulder Monthly* by Ed Sanders and a bunch of people. Tom Clark took off from their research and brought his book out the next year. Apparently he's not very popular in some parts of Boulder now. 'Tibetan guru in a plaid shirt swilling Green Death slobbering over a beautiful Hawaiian girl being denuded along with her distinguished poet lover!' *National Enquirer* stuff. Allen comes out of the whole thing rather well. Lots of dignity."

Like me, he thinks that Allen's interest in this form of paternalistic Buddhism has something to do with his frustrated Jewish family man instincts. The conversation shifts to McClure's own work, particularly the novel, *The Adept*, a personal text for me, nearly as important as *On the Road*. I want to try to tie the author down to something here. I have always sensed an ambiguity about the model for the novel's protagonist, Nicholas, the leonine coke dealer who won't eat the flesh of the beast because it poisons him, but whose leathers and long hair are responsible for spontaneous wet-ons wherever he goes.

In correspondence, I had drawn parallels between Freewheeling Frank (the Frisco Angel whose biographer McClure was), Freewheeling Franklin of the Fabulous Furry Freak Brothers, and Rark, the laconic sidekick in *The Adept*. McClure's reply had not ignored the question completely but had been non-commital: biker, cartoonist, and novelist had all moved in the same circles at the same time. "I think 'Fr. Franklin' is based on Freewheelin'. Shelton was around a lot – probably he met Frank. Certainly he saw him on the scene. Frank's an amazing guy. He's out of the Angels and back in jail right now."

Writers sometimes seem unforthcoming with this sort of information. Perhaps it undermines their own estimate of their creative credibility. Perhaps I just had too much academic training. I want to know, though: when I discern Jim Morrison in Nicholas who's putting him there, McClure or me?

Like Cassady driving both the Hudson and "Further," like Ginsberg in both the forties Pokerino and the sixties antiwar marches, McClure was part of both the Beat and the Hippie

Generations. He once wrote that Dylan's music is important to him the way Kerouac's writing was. He has numbered both among his friends. He had much in common with the Doors' lead singer." When Jim Morrison died *Rolling Stone* rang McClure and asked if they could send Annie Liebowitz over. 'I'd love to have my picture in *Rolling Stone*,' said the poet. 'But not because my friend's just died.'"

In *The Adept*, Nicholas, on a coke-shopping expedition in redneck Texas, kills a mad racist dealer who attacks him in the desert. He then pounds the little skean dhu straight down into the arid earth, hidden forever, and buries the body. Jim Morrison's hitchhiker was picked up by a driver in the desert.

> I was out in the desert for a while
>> Riders on the storm
> Yeah. in the middle of it
>> Riders on the storm
> Right . .
>> into this house we're born
> Hey, listen, man, I've really got a problem.
>> Into this world we're thrown
> When I was out on the desert, ya know,
>> Like a dog without a bone
>> An actor out on loan
> I don't know how to tell you,
>> Riders on the storm
> but, ah, I killed somebody.
>> There's a killer on the road
> No . . .
>> His brain is squirming like a toad
> It's no big deal, ya know,
> I don't think anybody will find out about it, but . .
>> *An American Prayer*

Whither goest thou, America, in thy shiny car in the night?

The Adept exemplifies McClure's creative concerns. The

154

sensual, savage imagery, the nature of man as wild beast, is there from the very start. In the first line Nicholas defines himself as a "healthy full-grown adult male *animal*." He is anarchic as a wild cat, living by a set of self-imposed rules which admit no need of society's laws. While he gets both his living and his kicks selling hash and cocaine in quantity, he will not deal in heroin or speed, the killer drugs. He constantly adopts the gestures and attitudes of a big cat. His Harley-Davidson is a surge of speed and brute power. In the novel this platform of McClure's is perhaps at its most easily assimilated, more so than in the plays and much of the poetry. Many have found the "beast language" incomprehensible.

> HAHHR ROH NORR THAR RAH GRAHG
> ahh thee doohr. Ah we no thap kran moor
> coffee, the fogs arise, drift, frah, nooh too oh
> broo noor grahh. Nooh weep be my skroll thah
> thy oh neen ooh marr dahoww tha neet
> drips teerz ah me zahd. Thee, oh, my Dahoor
> breth. AIEOOO AIEEEE YEEORRR
> GRAHHH!!
> RAGOOOR! GARR! GRAHHH . . .
> Blissfulness hidden by no veils and not there.
> But here, ragoooooor, oh my bleesh.
> THAH OHH OOOH ME
> my ooh mee ole tree meed.

Ghost Tantras

The answer simply (as the notes to *Ghost Tantras* points out) is that, to realize their full potential, the poems in beast language must be read aloud and sung. It is not that McClure finds the English language either unattractive or insufficient (his Naropa lecture, collected in the *Talking Poetics* pair of volumes, took the form of instructions on how to produce a "personal universe deck" of a hundred words meant to encapsulate an individual's personality), though it was necessary to push back its limits in order to express himself fully. The later poems are more accessible.

We try for purity
    but
    still
we're glorious
    blobs of meat.
I worship you
    like blood
or oil or wheat.
         Antechamber and Other Poems

But then, the poet himself, like so many of his contemporaries, is more accessible, relaxed. As McClure supposedly said to one commentator, "We're all nice now. I've only been nice for a couple of years, but Allen's been nice for longer than that." A degree of critical understanding and acceptance has assuaged much of the anger. I don't imagine that, if *The Beard* were to be revived now, the L.A.P.D. would bust the actors for obscenity every time Billy the Kid went down on Jean Harlow.

I've brought along a couple of paperbacks from City Lights and he inscribes them. Care was taken in the layout of the poems, giving them an extra dimension in the clean, black and white New Directions volumes.

"I'd have brought *The Adept* over from England and bugger the extra weight," I tell him. "But I couldn't be sure you'd be around."

Writing, he says, "Are you coming to Old Hippie Day tomorrow? They asked me to read. It's really called All Beings Day. A parade and then a free concert on the hill. I said, 'Oh that's Old Hippie Day. I'll read at that!'"

"Don't tell me Country Joe's playing?"

"Yeah."

"Well I'll be – ! I wouldn't miss that."

We go through into the living room at the front of the house for some last photographs. I pose Heather by the window, Northern California sunshine backlighting the long blond locks, with Michael looking through it. She directs at him the sort of sideways glance patented by Anna Magnani.

As we leave, he ducks out of the room and comes back with a present for me: an inscribed, hardback copy of *The Adept*: "For Chris. We're Instruments That Play Ourselves. Michael." In the bus back downtown I open it up.

Growing hair is a yogic endeavor. It is a test of the will. It is rare now for anyone except a few lumpen workmen to make any comment. I have gone beyond the bounds. I have burgeoned at the last pale! Let future generations who do not know this be aware. . . There are a multitude of states and sub-states that are passed through while growing the hair to an extreme length. Finally the hair becomes a power play. The hair grows so long that it places the grower – whose egostrength has been heightened by the experience – in a position of great power and indifference to social evaluations of himself. Finally, the name-calling and insinuating stares become admiration, at best, and sheer disbelief, at worst.

"What are *you* so pleased about?" asks Heather.

Tellygraft Hill, Tellygraft Hill, knobby old, slobby old, Tellygraft Hill

From the intersection of Columbus and Grant the TransAmerican pyramid resembles a wedge of French jam sponge stood on its end. California sunshine and the fine sense of dottiness around North Beach suggest comparisons like that. We have a hot dog and a Coke in a postage stamp-sized diner on a corner. The local shopkeepers drop in for coffee and scuttlebutt. She takes my arm when we stroll down to Washington Square, three thousand miles away from its namesake in Greenwich Village. Ben Franklin stands on his plinth, apparently none the worse for his scamper at Heathrow. Three winos nip discreetly on their bench. Muscatel, by the look of it. A few brown leaves crunch underfoot.

"Are you nibbling my ear?" she asks.

"Certainly not."

"Well *why* not?"

The heroic statue dedicated to the San Francisco fire brigade is all sinews, boots, and helmets. The lady who paid for it certainly knew what she liked. I wonder if it was she who erected the phallic fire hose which looks out over the bay up on the very dizzy top of Telegraph Hill. Between that lovely, silly pinnacle and the Fisherman's Wharf mooring of the Balcluthla there is concentrated the history of West Coast Bohemianism – North Beach.

She breaks away and does a twirl among the autumn golds. The winos show some signs of animation.

"OK, boss," she says. "Why're we here? What's the Beat angle on Washington Square?"

"The cover for *Trout Fishing in America*, I suppose. And the spinach sandwiches supposedly distributed from that church over there."

"But Brautigan wasn't a Beat, was he?"

"Well, second-generation: *City Lights Journal* published the first chapters of *Trout Fishing*. I wanted to see the place that's on the cover of the novel. When I lived in Pancho Villa with Hermoup and Balfour, which was my own version of the 'regular bachelor nuthouse' that Jack wrote about in *Big Sur*, we'd all read Brautigan and used to quote him all the time. You only had to say, 'What did you frog?' and the place broke up."

"Really? Why?"

"Well, it all has to do with Lee Mellon and Jack mackerel. . . "

The sunlight edges the leaves stirring before the white front of the Italian church. We drift back up the hill.

It's not that they don't have blonds and long-hairs of their own in North Beach, nor that Brits are still a novelty, but within twenty-four hours of arriving I'm getting messages left for me – and delivered – in the stores and bars. The place remains a neighborhood. I really had not thought that spirit of community would have survived all the flak, all the commercialization. "Hey, you're the guy staying with Michael Gallagher? Your old lady said to tell you she's left your other camera with Joe Wolberg while she goes in that dress shop round the corner from the Adler Museum and she'll see you later in Vesuvio's. . . "

The Adler is full of memorabilia – sailing and bohemian twenties and warnings that obscenity-transgressors shall suffer the dreaded Eight-Six. The old Spaghetti Factory is draped with theater stills and plants and elderly bicycles. The Place and the Co-Existence Bagel Shop are long gone. Vesuvio's is something else.

It is possible to fall in love with Vesuvio's – perched on the top of Columbus next to Dr. Ferlinghetti's labyrinthine bookshop – before you get past the door. In the concrete outside are etched the names of the Beat Generation worthies: the mysterious Two-Dollar Burt, the legendary Bomkauf, the usually drunk and increasingly toothless Gregory Corso. (Corso is, nowadays, 86ed.) On the outside wall it says:

> When the shadow of the grasshopper
> Falls across the tail of the field mouse
> On green and slimey grass and the red sun tosses
> Above the western horizon silhouetting
> A gaunt and tautly muscled Indian warrior
> Perched with bow and arrow nocked and aimed
> Straight at you it's time for another Martini.

Inside, it vibrates with paintings and acrylic murals and beautiful illuminated advertizing signs for Anchor Steam Beer, which is darker and fuller-flavored than most American beers and gives you a Shipstone's head and has been brewed in San Francisco since 1896. Both balcony and ground floor have a slide projection of vintage postcards and the waitress glides up the stairs with folded dollar bills sticking out between her fingers like underwater tendrils while Leo, the boss, who used to run the Coffee Gallery, another famous Beat hangout, bangs down the leather dicebox and asks if he's dirty. You can stroll down to Vesuvio's at one-thirty in the morning knowing you have comfortable time for two drinks before the place closes.

America, often only a place in the mind

San Francisco settles into a warm and muggy evening. We eat a subterranean dinner in Chinatown and find a saloon with a pianist. A complicated series of fans, all on one central rod, rotate the thick air above the bar. I have a beer and she orders coffee. The fleet is in the bay and San Francisco is thickly sown with drunken sailors. Three of them are seated at a table. One is nodding, half asleep. One has an arm in a cast. The third, blond and with a fist-kissed nose, very smart in his dress blues, his cap beside him, is talking to Richard Brautigan.

"Either he has a double," I say, "or that is Richard Brautigan."

"How strange," she says. "Everyone says that Enrico's is his hang-out."

Richard Brautigan looks very much like the pictures on the covers of his books. His hair is a little shorter and when he stands up he is taller than he appears in the pictures. Other than that, he looks just like Richard Brautigan, famous writer.

He is drinking a good deal of very pale whiskey from a stemmed glass. When the sailor in the cast gets to his feet, precariously, to pay for some drinks he leans forward and says, "Young man! That's all taken care of!" The sailor in the beautiful dress blues stands up and heads for the john. The other two sailors are all but passed out.

"Excuse me," I find myself saying. "Are you Richard Brautigan?" He looks at me, focuses and nods. He sticks out his hand. He has a firm handshake. "I admire your books a great deal," I say.

Richard Brautigan looks ever so faintly surprised. As if the books were a dripping tap he had been meaning to fix and someone had called him by name and told him that the tap was

160

dripping. "Hey, Richard Brautigan, you need a new washer!" How do *they* know?

"I've just been talking to this very charming naval officer from the 7th Fleet," says Richard Brautigan. "He's going to be in San Diego for a couple of years. I don't know if you know San Diego?"

"No," I say.

"Yes," says Heather, tapping her cigarette.

"And his wife is in Honolulu. I've been telling him he ought to bring her over, near to San Diego. Can you draw maps?"

"Yes," says Heather.

"Could you draw a map, with San Diego, and Cardiff near it?"

I am sure he says Cardiff.

"Oh I couldn't do that," she says. "I couldn't remember it well enough."

I know I should have heard Cabrillo, or Chula Vista, but I am sure he said Cardiff.

The naval officer with the bent nose and the dress blues returns. Richard Brautigan says something to him about San Diego that I do not catch.

"Yes," says the sailor from the 7th Fleet. "I'll have to look into that. Nice to meet you, sir. What was your name again?"

"Brautigan," says Richard Brautigan.

"Burlingame?"

"Brautigan."

"Oh," says the sailor, putting on his cap and raising his companions to their feet. "Well, nice meeting you." The sailors leave, two of them weaving rather.

Heather and I walk up the hill and into City Lights, open and dotted with browsers in the North Beach night. A few moments later Richard Brautigan comes in, tall and striding and bespectacled, and fills his arms with books. He takes three cased sets of his novels and goes over to the cash register and pays the clerk twenty-six dollars and forty-seven cents and goes out of the store. Standing on the sidewalk I see him stride back down the hill and

161

through the door of the bar with the rotating fans. A few moments later he comes out again. He wears a puzzled expression on his face. He crosses the street, three cased sets of his books slipping around in his arms, very tall, quite famous, and probably reasonably rich and starts up a side street lined with topless joints and adult movie theaters. Looking for three sailors on shore leave who have never heard of him.

Even if I kept on running, I'd never get to Orange Street

The next day Dennis McNally, the Kerouac biographer, drives us to Golden Gate Park in a car in a truly heroically rattling condition. Neal would have loved it. We had been to a costume party the previous night and Dennis had suggested taking six-packs of Weinberger along. American beer labels give no information about original gravity and consequently I have a head of truly Brautiganesque proportions, ". . .a classic hangover like feeding time in an anteater grotto and you're it, buster." The only response to feeling like that is to take a good stiff drink, so I find a store and when I walk into the aura of the legendary Hippie Hill I am engaging in the time-honored American custom of brown-bagging.

The crowd is gathered around the stage upon which the various poets and musicians are giving their services for free. Country Joe MacDonald strums. The most famous courtesan in San Francisco raunches on in fur and boots. It is the sort of crowd – hippies, bikers, earth mothers, and people in their teens there for the music – familiar to anyone who ever went to an Albion Fair. I immediately feel so comfortable I disappear. The two different and very American elements are the 'Nam vets and the burnouts. They are all about my age. Their adolescence and the sixties arrived hand in hand like strange bedfellows, and they've all taken too much war or too much acid without the necessary psychic helmet. Sometimes they have taken too much of both but it is usually possible to tell which was the key to their descent: clues in the eyes and the clothing and the way of addressing strangers. It is something that Americans have incorporated into their consciousness so completely that they never point it out to visitors: Southeast Asia will hang round America's neck like a dead crow until all these people, and anybody who ever loved them, are dead. It is only when you see men your own age who are so strung out that their lives are effectively finished that you understand the legacy of Vietnam. If you think this is far out, baby, wait till you see Edge City.

This is the first event of its kind, parade and free concert, since the Haight died in the welter of recrimination and commercialization. Dennis is getting more and more pleased that he's here. His training and bent are towards being a historian, and, as a result of writing *Desolate Angel* he is now doing a history of the Grateful Dead family. His *bijou* residence on Russian Hill accrues data as a magnet draws iron filings. Bob "Ace" Weir's song "Cassidy" was supposedly written while one of the Dead's ladies (Mountain Girl?) was giving birth to a girl baby who was to be called that, so it is partly about her and partly about Neal, even though the spelling's different.

> Ah child of countless dreams
> Ah child of boundless seas
> What you are and what you're meant to be
> Speaks its name when you were born to be
> Born to be Cassidy. . .

(It does not matter whether or not the story is true: the true history of the Beat Generation is a poetry and a legend.)

Dennis is excited. He keeps telling me how glad he is we came because there are so many people here he has to refer to about the Dead odyssey, then belting off to talk to the leading Schumacher exponent in San Francisco or Kush, the Condorman. Heather is surrounded by aspiring Angels who have approached her with the ultimate crown, a white-brimmed, braided Harley-Davidson cap, which they have reverently set upon the golden tresses. I make out a mental note on my H. Rider Haggard file card. McClure waves me over to the roped-off area for the performers behind the stage. He is talking to a gent dressed as some kind of gopher or chipmunk with the appropriate face paint and a silver star which reads "Boss Clown." He has been announcing the performers as they have taken the stage.

"This," says Michael, "is Wavy Gravy."

This seems to me a most amazing fact.

Of a sudden I know exactly how Tom Wolfe felt when he walked into Kesey's domain that first time and saw a man flipping a sledge hammer and knew, beyond all shadow of a doubt, that he was looking at Dean Moriarty. Wavy Gravy: well I'll be Buffalo Bill's uncle. Wavy Gravy, who wrote: "i deny cremation! neal cassady is alive in san diego in a tortoise egg." Wavy Gravy, of the Hog Farm commune, who stood up there with his front teeth gone in front of half a million people at Woodstock and said, "If some of you think that Capitalism isn't *too* weird you might buy a hamburger off him," after the vendor's stand got burned down. Wavy Gravy, who, in an earlier incarnation over in Greenwich Village, was called Hugh Romney and wore a nice striped tie and the regulation hip young Ivy League beard and is pictured on page 129 of Elias Wilentz's *The Beat Scene*.

"Watch this guy," says Michael, poking a fit finger into my chest. "He takes photographs of people with their mouths open." Wavy Gravy has a swig of my Bud.

We are joined by a stout man with a shock of iron gray hair like a grown-out crewcut. He wears a weskit over a shirt and sweater and has a cigarette jutting upwards at the corner of his mouth. He is instantly recognizable from every photo I've ever seen of him: holding Bomkauf around the shoulders, like a kid with a reluctant cat, in 1974; up above City College in 1969. When he brought out his first book, *River of Red Wine*, in 1958, Kerouac wrote the introduction. This is Jack Micheline. Jack

Micheline has a swig of my Bud. When he gets up on stage to perform "Rock Song" the effect is rather like being given a short straight right between the eyes by a good young welterweight. The backs of your arms tingle and the blood goes to your head and your feet are welded to the turf.

He hits the rhythm in one and the guttural drone of his cigarette throat flows out over the crowd like a flung net.

> "its the dead that rule the world
> its the dead that rule the world
> its the dead its the dead
> its the goddamn dead –"
>
> "Rock Song"

And now, they tell me, he is little interested in being a poet. Wants to concentrate on his painting.

The shadows are lengthening over Hippie Hill. The performing is over and the crowd thins out. The chill in the air is undeniable now. I go and collect She and we go back into the city.

The archers fled the trees

Down the street there is a massive demonstration. Serried ranks around a notorious vivisection laboratory. Young women roughly handled by policemen. Not wanting animals tortured to death testing cosmetics or shampoos that sting the eyes anyway is treated as a crime. The officially estimated numbers will be smaller than the reality and the irony of the reinforcements kept in reserve – police horses and police Alsatians – men using animals to defend their oppression of animals, will go unreported.

The large hall packed with people one might otherwise have expected to find on such a demo: vegetarians, self-sufficients, Buddhists, tribalists, all shades of alternative lifestyles represented at the Schumacher conference.

On stage Wendell Berry and Gary Snyder are being introduced

by a little Indian gent with a musical voice. Do we all wish them to speak again or shall they read some poetry and then have a break or do we wish to ask questions or –? The only trouble with congregations of the small and beautiful is that the essential democratic consensus takes forever. Eventually they both read: Berry a long poem of early American exploration, buffalo stampeding when hearing a gun (the thin end of the wedge), for the first time; Snyder some new material, and then make way for another speaker. Snyder comes out into a quiet section of the corridor to answer questions. Eyes pink with exhaustion, he is as jet-lagged as a winter pipe in Oregon, wrapped around with that particular tiredness which comes of long hours of tedium on the road, punctuated by the adrenal rushes of the public platform. In the flesh he is smaller than anticipated, the outdoor lines in the brown face even deeper, the beard a feature of the face not an adornment. The knot of hair at the nape is gone now. He is almost dapper in shirt and tie, though his clothes, tweed and cleated soles, have the practical edge with which the woodsman dresses to go to the city: if the overalls have to be set aside it will be for something rugged and lasting.

Years ago this man's "Hay for the Horses" helped fuel the determination needed to get away from a comfortable but increasingly stultifying desk.

> "I'm sixty-eight," he said,
> "I first bucked hay when I was seventeen.
> I thought, that day I started,
> I sure would hate to do this all my life.
> And dammit, that's just what
> I've gone and done."

> *Riprap*

In June 1956, Snyder sailed for Japan to study in a Zen monastery. Effectively divorced from America for a decade, he missed out on the Beat furor. As the star of *The Dharma Bums*, he would have been a star in that firmament. When he came back, San Francisco was gearing up for the Summer of Love and Snyder's forest and mountain background and ecological concerns made him a natural hero-spokesman for one branch of the hippies, just as Allen and Neal were on other fronts. Articles like "Why Tribe?" appeared in the magazines and papers of the Underground Press Syndicate. From there to pieces like "Earth is Sacred" in the Schumacher Society's *Resurgence*, he has ploughed that same straight furrow: good husbandry. Take from the earth and give back to it. He made provisional his Boulder Kerouac Conference booking and indeed did not, finally, attend because he was "required for Zen building." Like the rest (even though his association with the group was fleeting by comparison), he puts the others in his writing. In "Migration of Birds" (*Riprap*) Kerouac sits reading the Diamond Sutra in the sun. (When Kerouac quoted the poem, in *Bums*, some quirk of modesty made him sit Sean Monahan in his place.) The model for Monahan, Locke McCorkle, is the dedicatee of Snyder's "Bubbs Creek Haircut," a poem in which Ginsberg is also a character.

No, Snyder says, polite and very weary, he does not mind answering personal questions. Yes, he was married to Joanne Kyger once: it's important to get these things right.

His sister, the crazy Rhoda from *Bums*, still has the exuberance which Kerouac depicted. She just celebrated her fiftieth birthday by flying over San Francisco on a light aircraft. Standing on the wing. He is patient and meticulous recording dates and details. Nobody had quite realized how bad Welch had got when he disappeared. He had been drinking heavily and was building a house and not getting the help he needed.

An anxious organizer in a flap sighs with relief on finding him. Interrupted, he rises to return to the stage. Here is his address and I should write if he can be of any more help. He looks forward to seeing my book. A firm handshake and he walks, slightly stooped from tiredness, back to the audience. I never get the chance to tell him about the difference made by "Hay for the Horses."

The Reedie trio

Gary Snyder, Lew Welch, and Philip Whalen roomed together at Reed College, Oregon, the state that prides itself on remaining comparatively rural, in contrast to its noisy neighbor. "Don't Los Angelize Oregon" read the bumper stickers.

Snyder had early experience in the deep woods. Like him, Welch and Whalen were influenced as writers by solitude in the great outdoors. It may have been from Snyder that Welch got his interest in tribalism, Whalen his Buddhism. Certainly it was their common interest that gradually filtered through to Kerouac, getting him into the notion of spending a whole season in a fire lookout, squatting alone on a mountaintop, with nothing but chores to distract them from the meditation of the void. When Jack set off for Desolation Peak Snyder was on a boat for Japan. Years later Whalen was also to commit himself to Buddhism fully, by becoming a Zen monk. It was Whalen who watched over Jack as he slept, strung out on the sweet wine, out on the park grass in 1960, when he was having another try at meditation in the woods but getting claustrophobia in the slit of Raton Canyon. "When I leave town," Whalen is quoted in *Big Sur*, "all my friends go back on the sauce." He lived, at the time, along with Welch and others, in a shared house that Kerouac depicted as a perpetual bachelor's party. They all felt very fraternal towards him. Poems were a sharing activity. Welch's "I Sometimes Talk to Kerouac When I Drive" is perhaps his best poem. When Snyder shared a cottage with Kerouac in 1956, the former used to leave poems on a nail for anyone to read. Jack's descriptions of these frat houses evoke just that "booze and birds" atmosphere that is imbued with such nostalgia in later life. Looking back to the rosy time when the hangovers hurt less and there was always enough energy, love, and loyalty. You are getting old when you start to bury friends who shared all that. Welch went out into the wilderness alone to die and was a good enough woodsman to make sure he was never found. Snyder came back from the search for him a spiritually aged man.

Starting from tomorrow

The Iron Door is just down the road from the restaurant where they all sat in 1956 and Orlovsky made a Tower of Babel out of crockery and Jack said it was high enough. Across the road, behind its parking lot, is a supermarket where today I stood in line waiting for a checkout girl clad as a scarlet devil, red in horns, tights and tail, to tot up my purchases while she received bags of change from swaggering young rentacops with 44:40 Magnums strapped down on their hips.

The Iron Door (which has one) has all the conviviality of the average American suburban bar. Not a lot. It is a good place for a long think. No one is likely to interrupt your train of thought with an attempt at conversation.

I am thinking about the book and the film of *Heart Beat* and of the full autobiography which spans twenty-two years, starting spring 1947, Neal and Carolyn's first meeting in Denver. It supplies the background reality to Jack's novels and Allen's poetry. How the daily business of living was carried on amidst the freneticism. How flawed and driven men relied on female forgiveness and support to realize their potential. It is a firm and modest tale of female resilience and strength. It sits, four and a half inches high in typescript, newly assimilated, a couple of miles back up the palm-strewn rainy Saratoga highway. It concludes with the two men she loved so long and so well tapering out of her physical life, not with a bang, but a whimper. Neal, finally so deranged and unpredictable that she hardened herself to become deaf, for the sake of her children, to his pleas to return, rang her from Los Angeles. He was on the run and wanting home. Gently, she headed him south of the border, safe from arrest. A few weeks later his last mistress phoned on a Sunday morning, four days before his forty-fourth birthday. Dead in his T-shirt by the railroad track.

Jack phoned when he was maudlin and could outwit Stella's watchfulness. He ran up terrible bills. One night he called, late, just as Carolyn's aching head hit the pillow. He wanted one of his long, rambling, stop and start chats. It was nearly day in Florida. No, Jack, she said, not now. After she hung up, she had to tell him again. The third time the phone jangled, she put her head under the pillows. He never called again and twenty months later he was dead.

The Beat Generation never did very well out of the film industry. It was lumped together with juvenile delinquency as arbitrarily as cell mates are upon the coincidence of conviction. Car journeys and Miss Green were too close to hot rods and dope not to mean automatically switchblades, zip guns, and rat-packing a lone cop. The natural picaresque of *On the Road* has not been filmed. The tender, breathy, warm-night rush of *The Subterraneans*, the only Kerouac to go to Hollywood, is absent from a film which squarely ducks the racial issue. Leslie Caron's French accent was as far down the road to miscegenation as MGM would go in 1961. It took the "underground" film-maker Robert Frank to put the philosophy onto the screen in *Pull My Daisy*.

Norman Mailer reported immense sadness at the moment he realized that *The Naked and the Dead* was going to be bought by a producer who couldn't tell the difference between soldiers and marines. Perhaps we should not expect the movies to tell the truth. *Heart Beat*'s author hates the film's license, though. Ginsberg refused to let his name be used: he appears as Ira Streiker.

"Waiter! There's a turd in my soup!"

"Not quite Allen's *style*," said Burroughs, drily.

Nolte's Neal, despite the blond good looks, doesn't quite get over whatever it was that made people love him and excuse him, forgive him over and over again. Sissy Spacek weeps over her ironing board, looking about as haggard and work-weary as Jackie Kennedy. (Carolyn wrote, "As a woman, I desired and chose the primary role of traditional wife and mother, knowing individual expression of artistic talents could be harmonized not to conflict." As likely a heroine for the eighties as a black one was for 1961.) For whatever reasons – the loss of love as a child, the hardships and the jails – Neal was never able to match Carolyn's selflessness and dedication, but a woman who emerged less down-trodden is hard to imagine.

When Kerouac's "mother" appears in the film the audience immediately thinks he's living with a floozie. Memere was a dumpy Canuck matriarch who wore religious medals pinned to her slip, not a redhead in a negligée. The awesome power of the unsevered umbilical does not automatically mean incest. McClure said the picture of Jack and his mother reminded him of the stance certain primates took when their unit was bossed by an old she-ape. Beast imagery again: none the less telling. Jack's mother-fixation was part of the reason the ready-made Cassady ménage was attractive to him, but Carolyn didn't have a rota or flip a coin; there was nothing shifty or underhand about her brand of polyandry, just two men she cared for working shifts on the railroad. Two men placating angry driving personal gods (chessmen, Deerslayer, chessmen) and the redemptive powers of love.

I get down from my stool and signal the bartender and settle my tab and I go outside and start on foot up the steeply climbing Saratoga highway into the headlights coming out of the dark. After a mile I turn left and left again. The house is asleep but there is a sandwich in the kitchen and a light burning like a hint in the study.

I sit down at the desk on the breezeblocks and I bite into my sandwich and take a pull on my tall can of Bud and the rain hisses outside on the plastic cover over the little swimming pool where Jack used to amaze the kids by doing jack-knife dives into the blue water and I have got it. All alone in a sleeping house under a pool of Hopper light and I've got it. After all this time. I came to America with America in my head, found already and just awaiting proof-marks and, because I had never set myself such an ambition, I found the spring of the Beat Generation too. All those biographies and histories and all those lists and appendices and critical examinations and charts and facts and it was there all the time.

171

It is just putting in something of the self. The biker in his colors knows who his brothers are. Agreement, pleasure, odd illumination. I explain a stance; I am not a historian.

If there is any tradition, apart from nationality or unity in place, shared by Thoreau, Melville, Twain, Cooper, Whitman, Williams, Pound, London, Hemingway, Wolfe et al., then the Beats are throat-deep in it. Pen to paper in a land so vast it takes up a lifetime. For all their bilingual understanding of Celine, Proust, Shelley, Blake, Nietzsche, Dostoevsky, the Beats were Americans. Posterity and hindsight will see to it. *My* Beat Generation might not exist for another living soul, but the Beat Generation was not a chorus of fags, a Roman Catholic group, or an East Coast, Californian, or Internationalist movement. And anyone who wishes it to be any of those may, and will, see it as such. I tell you again it don't apply. Caw, caw, caw. No glot, clom Fliday. There is no truth and I am telling it. I think of the old father we never found. I am not innarested in your horrible condition. Nothing important ever dies and what they were about is continually discovered by succeeding generations. Neal Cassady is alive and well in a tortoise egg.

The rain runs on out of sight and the light comes down like a funnel over the typewriter in the quiet house and I've managed to put my finger on it at last. All that remains is to write it down. In the next room I hear Heather stir, breathing and quiet and smooth in her sleep and I am tired with the wind-tossing and the revelation and all that remains to do is to put it down, one word after another. So I will. Starting from tomorrow.

IV On Paper

The abuse was disgusting

During the tourist months Heather runs cultural vacation junkets around the European capitals. They are chiefly battalions of highschool students. The boys are all junior jocks filling the bidets with beer bottles, the girls are all self-conscious about the scrap iron clamped across their smiles. A teacher gets a free ride for enrolling a certain number of names. One professor I met pronounced himself very interested that I was studying American letters. His initial perplexity when I reeled off the names gave way to a certain Mid-American distaste when he realized who they were. He didn't think I'd find many people who thought that sort of writing had any value. He later sent me a book of Erskine Caldwell short stories. Hatfield-McCoy good ole boys copping a quick feel up a corn sack dress in between the tobacco field and the melon patch. The sort of thing you used to pass down the back row of the fourth form with the best bits marked. He knew colorful characters just like that, he said. I bet you do, Mr. Tourist Dollar.

The prophet is without honor in his own land. American English, perhaps more than the original variety, is Europe's second language. European bands don't record in Swedish or Dutch to reach a few million when they can sell to half a continent by singing in English. It was the French who first saw a major writer in Burroughs. The old Penguin trio, Ginsberg, Corso, and Ferlinghetti, are greeted with rapture in Berlin or Amsterdam. Paris bookshops carry *Sur la route* or *Les clochards célestes*, Oslo ones *I sotteranei*. Occasionally, of course, translations get a little out of kilter (when Dean jumps in his car and goes "gunning for girls," Italy, he is not plotting rapes at pistol point, hear?) "England digs me," said Kerouac. "Not U.S.A."

When the Beats arrived on the scene American poetry was dominated by a cosy little literary mafia who regularly reviewed, analyzed, and assessed each other's lines to the point of incestuous dizziness. The *"Kenyon/Partisan Review* Axis" Bruce Cook called them, after two of their favorite journals. To the Beats they were the "old poetmen confessing their crafty souls in craft." Stale, insular, introspective: the Establishment. As relevant to the Beat alleys and bars as the tuxedoed crooners were to the arrival of punk. To them the Beats were upstarts, a challenge to the status quo to be viciously put down as brainless nihilists: the threat. That game of Cowboys and Indians lasted for years. Outbreaks of firing may still be heard.

The initial wave of hostility towards the new wave produced a predictable result. Instead of swamping it, it made it more resilient. "The more you stamp," said Burroughs, "the more it spreads." Comment since has been more often malice and misinterpretation than constructive analysis. The informed enthusiasm that marked Gilbert Millstain's greetings for *On the Road*, in 1957, remained the exception. Ginsberg's clear and appreciative review of *The Dharma Bums*, like anything by a fellow Beat, was dismissed as merely partisan.

Dharma Bums is a late and recent book, he's weary of the world and prose. Extraordinary mystic testament, however, and record of various inner signposts on the road to understanding of the Illusion of Being.

The sentences are shorter (shorter than the great flowing inventive sentences of *Dr. Sax*), almost as if he were writing a book of a thousand haikus – Buddhist Visionary at times. He's had an actual religious experience over a prolonged period. This book puts it, for convenience, in the form of a novel about another interesting friend. (*The Village Voice Reader*)

To poor Kerouac it was all too much. He was just a simple drinking Canuck who liked to make books and here were people pitchforking him into wars of attrition. Reviling and rejecting *him*, for there was little technical camouflage in the Beats' work, the stuff contained the essence of the men. Publishing his books was, to Kerouac, like sending his children out into the world, unprotectable now, to make their own way. Jacky Duluoz views Irwin Garden's plans for an assault on Fortress America, Entrenched Old Poetmen Division, with some trepidation.

"All that literary stuff is just a drag. . . Irwin if you'd really seen a vision of eternity you wouldn't care about influencing American Civilization."

"But that's just the point, it's where I at least have some authority to speak instead of just state ideas and sociological hangups out of handbooks – I have a Blakean message for the Iron Hound of America." (*Desolation Angels*)

Desolation Angels is a novel, not factual reporting, but it contains probably the best portrait of Ginsberg when his youthful enthusiasm and new-found confidence were at their height. His ambitions for the movement were shared more by Corso or Orlovsky than by Kerouac. The reactions they evoked proved Kerouac's fears wellgrounded. Respect for learning and intelligence was "foreign to Beatdom" (Kerouac and Ginsberg at Columbia; Snyder, Holmes, Burroughs all with degrees; Ferlinghetti a Ph.D.), and the "Beat writers. . .lacking the catholicity of experience necessary to major literary achievement. . .are destined to a quick eclipse of fame." James F. Scott published those comments in the *American Quarterly* in 1962. James F. who?

Far from being "eclipsed" Kerouac's persona has become virtually synonymous with the American experience of the highway. In Tom Robbins' *Even Cowgirls Get the Blues*, the exploits of Sissie Hankshaw, she of the enormous thumbs which so fit her for her chosen career of hitchhiking, so impress, or threaten "Jack Kerouac" that he stays drunk for a week.

The hostility towards the Beats as a group reinforced their support for each other's stance. After the wave of interest began in 1957, even some of their old champions appeared to recant. Notably Kenneth Rexroth, whose series of articles from '57 to

'59 went from enthusiasm to testiness to downright sneering. "San Francisco's Mature Bohemians" was published in February, 1957, seven months before *On the Road*, and Rexroth was celebrating the mood of San Francisco and the emergence of a new force.

> But something different is going on in San Francisco. What Lipton has called our underground culture isn't underground here. It is dominant – in fact almost all there is. . . It is self-evident that this will produce a literature considerably different from what is done on a job passing the seven types of ambiguity to seminars of born idlers. (*The Nation*, vol. 184)

Kerouac was compared to Henry Miller, Celine, Durrell, Beckett, and even Nelson Algren.

By 1959, reviewing *Mexico City Blues*, Rexroth had turned his coat very decisively.

> Someone once said of Mr. Kerouac that he was a Columbia freshman who went to a party in the Village twenty years ago and got lost. How true. The naive effrontery of this book is more pitiful than ridiculous. . . One of the best poems in the book. . . 'I keep falling in love/with my mother.' It's all there, the terrifyingly skillful use of verse, the broad knowledge of life, the profound judgements, the almost unbearable sense of reality. (*New York Times*, 29 November 1959)

Time and erosion have suggested other reasons for Rexroth's disenchantment: a drunken Kerouac thrown out of his house in disgrace, Creeley, who was around during the events in *Dharma Bums* but who does not feature in the book, running off with Marthe Rexroth and tarring the Beats with Black Mountain's brush. It is all a long time ago and scarcely matters anymore. The Grand Old Man of San Francisco, with his fine white hair and his great W. C. Fields nose, always as old as the century, got to eighty-two and called it a day and his hurt pride is history now.

Ginsberg, for one, seems to have been genuinely taken aback by the sort of treatment they received. "Have I really been attacked for this sort of joy?" he asked, bewildered. After a nasty little set of jibes was published by the wife of his old professor in *Partisan Review* it's no wonder he was perplexed. Diana Trilling's "The Other Night at Columbia" must have given pleasure to one person, acute embarrassment to her husband Lionel, and little, if anything, to anyone else. She approaches the reading with the disturbed, adolescent Ginsberg, for whom she had so little sympathy when he was her husband's student, firmly in mind.

> . . .some twelve or fourteen years ago when Allen Ginsberg. . . had to be rescued and revived and restored; eventually he had even to be kept out of jail. Of course there was always the question, should this young man be rescued, should he be restored? There was even the question, shouldn't he go to jail? (*Partisan Review*, XXVI, Spring 1959)

This is the attitude of everyone in society whose money or status protects them from the loss of liberty over an indiscretion or a lapse. Jail, for the Mrs. Trillings of this world, exists to house people they regard as nasty. Keep these people firmly at arm's length. The very idea of seeing what they are actually *like* is anathema. Sufficient authority is delegated to uniformed minions to deal with the "beats" of this world.

Partisan Review also published Norman Podhoretz's infamous attack. Vituperation shading into paranoia. Heard once again are the shrill cries of that perennially endangered species, the Privilege Bird.

> . . .the Beat Generation's worship of primitivism and spontaneity is more than a cover for hostility to intelligence; it arises from a pathetic poverty of feeling as well. . . This is the revolt of the spiritually underprivileged and the crippled of soul – young men who can't think straight and so hate anyone who can. (*Partisan Review*, XXV, Spring 1958)

There was exactly that same "Ma the rough kids stole my rattle" tone in the first press reports on the Rolling Stones or the Sex

Pistols. An art form that is essentially confessional in tone and content is easily ridiculed. Seymour Krim, fast talker from the side of his mouth, shake it for the world, smartass commentator, although pulling his punches, got Podhoretz pegged as early as 1960.

> Podhoretz is a highly shrewd young guy who got an entrenched literary position at an early – perhaps too early – age; position means responsibility means gray hairs means no rockandrolling in print. Norman is a little teacherish for his years. (*The Beats*)

Disowned by Frisco's Elder Statesman, criminal or deranged as far as the academies were concerned, the Beats fared little better in the prestigious journals. "Howl", as far as Frederick Eckman, in volume 90 of *Poetry* was concerned, celebrated "several types of modern social and psychological ills" and therefore "the question of its literary merit seems to me almost irrelevant." So there. Mental states disturbed or altered are not a subject for literature, OK? Fall out, Lowell, Plath, Berryman, Huxley, Castaneda. . .

The criticism that the poetry editor of the *Saturday Review*, John Ciardi, poured on the movement ("little more than unwashed eccentricity") became a standing joke. Concerning the one aspect of the Beats' work he did endorse – their movement to liberate language and literature from Grundyism – he managed to get his texts all wrong. His article in defense of Burroughs, quoted on the jacket of the first edition of *The Naked Lunch*, published by Girodias (no. 76 in the Traveller's Companion Series), was provoked by the suit against the Beat magazine *Big Table*, brought by the U.S. Post Office. *Big Table* (named by Kerouac) came into being after the University of Chicago squealed in outrage when it saw what its university magazine was about to print and the student editorial board resigned *en masse* and founded the new journal. Ciardi's article called the first forty-nine sections of Kerouac's sound poem, "Old Angel Midnight" a "blurt" and "gibberish" and accused it of "dullness," but said Burroughs' work was ". . .writing of an order that may be cleanly defended not only as a masterpiece of its own genre, but as a monumentally moral descent into the hell of narcotic addiction." (*Saturday Review*, vol. 40, 27 June 1957)

As in the case of *Junkie* it was not lack of merit which prevented the publication of *The Naked Lunch* in Great Britain or the U.S.A., but frankness of material. Ciardi was so keen to defend the book on a didactic level he misinterpreted the text. For him, a book which treats heroin addiction realistically must of necessity be an exposé.

> Bit by bit the undertone of self-consuming horror leaps free of even surface realism and beings to develop through more fanciful perceptions: She seized a safety pin caked with blood and rust, gouged a great hole in her leg which seemed to hang open like an obscene and festering mouth waiting for un-speakable congress with the dropper, which she now plunged out of sight into the gaping wound. (*Saturday Review*, vol. 40, 27 June 1957)

Quoted out of context, Burroughs' satirical intent in this passage is lost.

> You know how this pin and dropper routine is put down: "She seized a safety pin caked with blood and rust, gouged a great hole in her leg which seemed to hang open like an obscene, festering mouth waiting for unspeakable congress with the dropper, which she now plunged out of sight in the gaping wound. . ."
>
> The real scene you pinch up some leg flesh and make a quick stab hole with a pin. Then fit the dropper over, not in the hole and feed the solution slow and careful so it doesn't squirt out the sides. . . (*Naked Lunch*)

Thus what Burroughs intends as satire is made to seem his own authorial attitude.

Ginsberg has been as much a target for technical ignorance as Kerouac. A. Alvarez dismissed *Kaddish* as nothing more than "good psychotherapy." Some things never change. Boston Public Library's committee turned down a newly published work once as ". . .rough, coarse and inelegant, dealing with a series of experiences not elevating. . .being more suited to the slums than to intelligent respectable people." The book was called *The Adventures of Huckleberry Finn*. This sort of critical ineptitude is often matched with a naive pomposity. Leslie A. Fiedler, when attacking Ferlinghetti, delivers an anecdote about the "poet professor" who was not astute enough to spot his love of quotation

. . .failed to recognize the obvious and deliberate echoing of Prospero's farewell speech in the following lines:

> and he is an old man perpetually
>   writing a poem
> about an old man
> whose every third thought is Death
> and who is writing a poem
> about an old man
> whose every third thought is Death. . .

The poem is called "He" and is clearly about William Carlos Williams thinking of Prospero (the whole farrago, I cannot help believing with some embarrassment, suggested by a critical essay of mine printed years ago in an eminently scholarly volume). (*Waiting for the End*)

The dedication "To Allen Ginsberg before 'The Change'" appears in Ferlinghetti's book *Starting from San Francisco* which contains "He." The reference is to Ginsberg's poem "The Change: Kyoto–Tokyo Express." Ferlinghetti's poem is not "clearly about William Carlos Williams" at all – Williams is a character in it, as are Shakespeare and Prospero. The lines "And he speaks of himself and he speaks/of the dead/of his dead mother and his Aunt Rose" should be more than enough to alert anyone who claims a knowledge of the work of Allen Ginsberg that the poem is about him seen in a tradition of poets, even if the references in the opening lines are missed.

He is one of the prophets come back
He is one of the wiggy prophets come back
He had a beard in the Old Testament
    but shaved it off in Paterson
He has a microphone around his neck
    at a poetry reading
    and he is more than one poet
    and he is an old man perpetually
      writing a poem
    about an old man
    whose every third thought is Death
    and who is writing a poem
    about an old man
    whose every third thought is Death
    and who is writing a poem
    Like the picture on a Quaker Oats box
    that shows a figure holding up a box
    upon which is a picture of a figure
    holding up a box.

Starting from San Francisco

The fabulous wordslinger

Gregory Corso was giving a reading in Cambridge (the Fens, not Mass.). As I climbed the stairs an American lady passed me, shaking her head and tutting.

Smashed before he even started, Corso finished one quarter of Teacher's and sent out for another during the reading. He was every inch the Beat poet that night, shuffling through his papers for minutes at a time and explaining, in a rather slurred voice, that he really should have done all that before the reading. I had found the new stuff disappointing: the man who invented penguin dust and who elegized Kerouac "you stood upon America like a rootless, flat-bottomed tree;" seemed to have lost

183

his sparkle. Heather, on the other hand, received an authentic tremor and staunchly defended the little living legend ever after. Men may want to punch him out but he seems to have a quality that makes women forgive him anything. Later, with Gregory seeing a hypocrite on every chair and falling off his own, it turned into one of those nights with too great an imbalance between various levels of intoxication, and a long drive to arrive somewhere in a pointless dawn. About Ginsberg, he had been violently vituperative, "that fucker, I'll kill 'im if he tries to get m'fucken kid away from me!" Allen's loyalty seems to endure under these curious provocations. He remains as tenderly exasperated as a paterfamilias with a teenager at the horrible stage, continues to argue Gregory's case and book him in for the odd stint at Naropa. The long-awaited *Herald of the Autochthonic Spirit* was dedicated to his children and their mothers: three kids, four mums. Ginsberg's copy is inscribed: "for my funny friend to the yummy end, love Gregory, San Francisco, 1981." The first few pages bear corrections in both hands. "Academy of Arts & Sciences" is corrected by Allen, who is very proud of his fellowship, to "Institute of Arts & Letters" and "porogative" to "prerogative." Gregory has deleted the lines from "though my output" down to "long before the poem" and changed "Gregorio" to "Gregore."

Now, a year later, on a harmless Wednesday, hunched over in his snuff brown jacket, stubbled of chin and the upper lip, nicotine stained, sucked in over the toothless top jaw, sloping through North Beach on his way to meet the school bus, is Gregory. Open, funnily enough, to the offer of a drink.

He balks at the door of the first bar I try to duck through. "I cain't go in 'ere. Got mad with the guy, shouted at 'im." Gregory is, these days, 86ed from quite a few of the North Beach watering holes.

In a bar with a longboat in the pool room and a motorcycle on a shelf we are tended by a lady with one of those beautiful earth-mother mantillas of hair down her back. She seems to have forgiven Gregory whatever trespasses he might have committed.

He requests a Scotch and sits demurely, one eye on the street, in case something that requires his attention might suddenly appear. He keeps an eye on the time: little Max must be met from school.

He talks lucidly and with an absence of braggadocio. I feel quite disconcerted until I realize that he's sober. Drunk he is everyone's idea of the wild bragging Beat, rather like the mask Kerouac wore to hide his shyness. This afternoon there is a clear glimpse of the quick-witted and charming *enfant terrible* he must have been thirty years ago. He seems to know nothing of the report of his trashing of his room in Naropa.

"Where'd you *hear* that?"

"Tom Clark's *Great Naropa Poetry Wars*."

He is full of praise for Mike Horovitz's Poetry Olympiad during which he read at Westminster Abbey. About his affairs, he's vague: despite sparse publication, he manages. *Spirit* sells so well in City Lights he can't understand why they aren't stocking the paperback. I forbear to ask him about the story that he burgled that particular bookshop and that Ferlinghetti knew but wouldn't prosecute. Yeah, he's around North Beach most of the time, now, except when he flies to Amsterdam or Boulder or Hamburg.

The ice cubes twirl in his empty glass. He looks, abashed, just like the "old crone" Charles Jarvis described in *Visions of Kerouac*. Then he lifts his head an inch or two and there is that sly, juvie, zoot suit glimmer in the corner of the wrinkled old hustler's eyes.

"Say," he drawls, coyly. "Could you stand me another drink?"

The Old Gregory is back again: what a relief.

". . .*all la vida es dolorosa*"

> I am the substance of my poetry. You honor poetry you honor me; you damn me you damn poetry. I am the poetry I write. (Gregory Corso, Voice of America Lecture)

185

Corso was the last of the founder members of the Beat Generation. He missed the early traumas. His coming of age was even harsher. *Gasoline* is dedicated to the "angels of Clinton Prison who, in my 17th year, handed me from all the cells surrounding me, books of illumination."

The great crime, which earned Corso three years in the slammer, was a Mickey Mouse affair. The tyro crook bought zoot suits and tipped big and laid low afterwards. The judge, alarmed by the use of the walkie talkie, cracked down on this application of technology to skulduggery. The excitement of the forties New York years he could only experience vicariously.

> Lucien was a very handsome young man, and this big red-haired fag was chasing Lucien all over. And Lucien finally just got tired of it, stabbed the man. The man yells out, "So this is how it happened." Not "This is how it happens," but "This is how it happened." Lucien goes with the bloody knife, up to Kerouac, who was his friend. And Jack says, "Oh-h-h, Go-o-o-d, Lucien, Lucien. Poor Jack, man. All right, you know what he did? He helped his friend out. Dropped the knife down the sewer drain somewhere. (*The Beat Diary*)

Later in his career the customary references to his fellows in the Beat Generation begin. "Power," which Corso published in 1960, is dedicated to Ginsberg just as *Reality Sandwiches* was "to the Pure Imaginary POET Gregory Corso."

Corso's Harvard friends brought out his first book, *The Vestal Lady on Brattle*, after he spent a year in Cambridge, Massachusetts. The juvenilia is all with time and the river. His character in *Desolation Angels* then is less phlegmatic about that loss:

> Raphael is screaming. "In the Greyhound Bus Terminal in Miami Florida! These new poems are all the poems I've got! And I lost my other poems in New York! You were there Jack! What'd that editor do with my poems? And I lost all my earlier poems in Florida! Imagine that! Balls on that!" It's the

way he talks. "For years after that I went from Greyhound office to Greyhound office talking to all kinds of presidents begging them to find my poems! I even cried! You hear that Cody? I cried! But they weren't moved! In fact they began to call me a nuisance all because I used to go to this office on 50th Street most every day begging them for my poems! It's the truth!"

Corso is not prolific. Six books of poems and a Paris novel. Eleven years between the last two: long consideration before *Elegiac Feelings American*. Rumors and contradictions about "lost" poems bought by academic archives.

Contact with Ginsberg introduced Corso to a Bohemianism to which he took like the proverbial duck. He became court jester, showman, surreal wit to the Beat Generation. The interaction of ideas began. Angels, roses, and sunflowers in everybody's poems. Corso got back from Europe in 1954 just in time for the Beat explosion. He provided some of the best copy for the reporters. Luce Publications quickly invented a "Beat Generation" which they could invite readers to ridicule.

Demanded Corso: "Man, why are you knocking the way I talk? I don't knock the way you talk. You don't know about the hollyhocks." Replied Haskins: "If you're going to be irrelevant, you might as well be irrelevant about hollyhocks." Countered Corso: "Man, this is a drag. You're nothing but a creep – a creep! But I don't care. I can still laugh and I can still cry. That's the way to be." "The hell it is," snorted Haskins. (*Time*, vol. 73, 9 February 1959)

It was then that the derogatory epithet "Beatnik" came into common usage. Corso's surrealistic epigrams, scornfully quoted, read as rather more lasting than most *Time/Life* pieces do a few decades later.

Would they like to make any comment? "Yes," said Corso. "Fried shoes. Like it means nothing. It's all a big laughing bowl and we're caught in it. A big scary laughing bowl."

187

Added Gregory Corso, with the enigmatic quality of a true Beatnik, "Don't shoot the warhog." (*Time*, vol. 73, 9 February 1959)

Corso's imagined reaction to a situation in which there is no common ground, merely scarcely informed preconceptions, is the basis for the poem which sprung some of the best of his "leather milk" images upon the world.

When she introduces me to her parents
back straightened, hair finally combed, strangled
   by a tie,
Should I sit knees together on their 3rd degree sofa
and not ask Where's the bathroom?
How else to feel other than I am,
Often thinking Flash Gordon soap –
O how terrible it must be for a young man
seated before a family and the family thinking
We never saw him before! He wants our Mary Lou!
After tea and homemade cookies they ask
What do you do for a living?
Should I tell them? Would they like me then?
Say alright get married we're not losing a daughter
we're gaining a son –
And should I then ask Where's the bathroom?
O God, and the wedding! All her family and her
   friends
and only a handful of mine all scroungy and bearded
just waiting to get at the drinks and the food –
And the priest! he looking at me as if I masturbated
Asking me Do you take this woman
for your lawful wedded wife!
And I trembling what to say Pie Glue!
                                   The Happy Birthday of Death

Rebellions against strictures of conventional form began long before the Beats' period of notoriety but continue to be associated

with them. If the Beat poetry has a common denominator it is
that the poem dictates its own length. It stops by itself. This
applies to the spare, intense verse of Gary Snyder, brevity
influenced by Chinese and Japanese models, and to the longer
and more rambling pieces by Kerouac and Ginsberg. "Marriage"
is in this tradition. It also supports Corso's claim that he has an
in-built sense of form. One hundred and twenty-nine lines long,
it is fully realized and never padded. It would profit from neither
expansion nor editing. The imagery is sharp and economical
throughout. The ideal American matron is evoked in seven
words: "aproned young and lovely wanting my baby." The secret
fears of the man without family ties come to life in one line: "all
alone in a furnished room with pee stains on my underwear."
The frank language, as in the image of the priest calling up
childhood confessions of self-abuse, are a successful casting off
of restraint, not an adolescent desire to shock or gesticulate at the
Establishment. The "I" is not a persona. Individual experience
serves as a microcosm of the human condition. "Marriage" has a
self-deprecating wryness that heads off pomposity. The poet sees
himself sitting stiffly on the parlor sofa, his famous mop finally
combed, his bladder bursting, in two minds whether to admit
being a poet. His "scroungy and bearded" friends show him up
at the wedding reception and the staff snigger and nudge when
he registers at his honeymoon hotel. The first person is not used
through lack of imagination. Corso can project.

> Waiting by the window
> my feet enwrapped with the dead bootleggers
>   of Chicago
> I am the last gangster, safe, at last,
> waiting by a bullet-proof window.
>
> I look down the street and know
> the two torpedoes from St. Louis.
> I've watched them grow old
> . . .guns resting in their arthritic hands.
>
> *Gasoline*

189

No proper poet is without the broad streak of compassion. Corso's is his main strength. Kerouac showed it in the awkward, opinionated urchin "Raphael Urso" who feels sorry for the future chow mein.

> . . .suddenly he sees chickens in crates in the inside dark Chinese store, "look, look, they're all gonna die!" He stops in the street. How can God make a world like that? (*Desolation Angels*)

Visiting a Mexican zoo Corso sees not animals in cages but caged animals.

> Long smooth slow swift soft cat
> What score, whose choreography did you dance to
>   when they pulled the final curtain down?
> Can such ponderous grace remain
>   here, all alone, on the 9X10 stage?
> Will they give you another chance
>   perhaps to dance the Sierras?
> How sad you seem; looking at you
>   I think of Ulanova
>   locked in some small furnished room
>   in New York, on East 17th Street
>   in the Puerto Rican section

Gasoline

Corso the Wordslinger was way ahead of his time. The surreal is a part of twentieth-century life now (see almost any advertizing hoarding). When Corso was making telling fun of images so wholesome they were Middle America's sacred cows, it was not.

> and so happy about me she burns the roast beef
> and comes crying to me and I get up from my
>   big papa chair
> saying Christmas teeth! Radiant brains! Apple
>   deaf!

190

God what a husband I'd make! Yes, I should get
  married!
So much to do! like sneaking into Mr Jones'
  house late at night
and cover his golf clubs with Norwegian books
Like hanging a picture of Rimbaud on the lawn-
  mower
Like pasting Tannu Tuva postage stamps
all over the picket fence
Like when Mrs. Kindhead comes to collect
for the Community Chest
grab her and tell her these are unfavorable
  omens in the sky!

The Happy Birthday of Death

Corso's humorist's logic had an impact on his contemporaries
that is only now becoming apparent: read his "Marriage" next to
the Kerouac *Paris Review* interview. The interviewer asks Jack
his taste in poetry: does he like Orlovsky's stuff? Then, apparently
unnoticed, Corso's far-flung gift for language sneaks on to the
stage after *years*.

Should I get married? Should I be good?
Astound the girl next door
with my velvet suit and faustus hood?
Don't take her to movies but to cemeteries
tell all about werewolf bathtubs and forked
  clarinets

KEROUAC: . . .There are some fellows in San Francisco that
told me that Peter was an idiot. But I like idiots, and I enjoy
his poetry. Think about that, Berrigan. But for my taste, it's
Gregory.

  Give me one of those.
INTERVIEWER: One of these pills?
KEROUAC: Yeah. What are they? Forked clarinets?
INTERVIEWER: They're called Obetrol (*Paris Review*, 43)

191

Luce Publications, having built the public image of the Beat Generation from scratch in the public mind, naturally lost no time in giving it the treatment for which they had set it up. Corso's surrealism was an easy target. Aware of the effects of his cavorting before the press, Corso well knew that his scatterbrained image meant that he would be depicted as talking so much gibberish. When Luce first started booting Corso, Ginsberg, and Orlovsky around they were supporting the magazine *Big Table*. Paul Carroll, introducing Corso's contribution to issue Number 5, saw both sides.

> Since he has become famous for being a fabulous word-slinger – "Fried Shoes," "Penguin Dust" – the poems he printed in this issue will probably shock and disappoint his admirers as well as his detractors. In their severity and quiet intuitions these poems are classic. The fact is that Corso is more intelligent than many give him credit for being: and he got off one of the best epigrams of the '50s. After having given Henry Luce the credit for the success of the Beat Generation, Corso was asked by a journalist: "Have you ever met Mr Luce?" "You don't have to meet him" snapped Gregory. "He's everywhere."

His discipline, he feels, is greater on the surface than that of Kerouac, Ginsberg, or Ferlinghetti and he feels this comes naturally to him.

J.L.: Do you have a built-in sense of form?
G.C.: Yeah, I know I do. Oh sure. The "bing bang bong boom" hit it, right, with the "Bomb" poem. I mean that was real music coming out on its own, and I don't have to knock myself out too fast with it, you know.
R.K.: But you don't worry around syllables or stress or. . .?
G.C.: I like to rhyme when I want to rhyme. When I don't want to rhyme I don't rhyme. It's all music.
J.L.:How did you get that sense of form? You never did cultivate it, never did study the sonnet?

G.C.: That's the whole shot; if I did I wouldn't have had it. I know the sonnet. . .I can do the sonnet, the sestina.

J.L.: It was there.

G.C.: Yeah, because it's obvious to be there, it's one of the simplest things. Just do what you want to do, right. And poetry, top shot, poesy. (*The Beat Diary*)

In his Voice of America lecture, when defending "writing from the top of your head," Corso used a phrase Ginsberg used about *Howl*. "If the poet's mind is shapely then his poem will come out shapely." Even collaboration with his revered Burroughs did not prevent Corso from making a disclaimer when he interfered with that "shapeliness" by dabbling in cutups in *Minutes to Go*.

After his early hardships, Corso never romanticizes the seamier side of life, but his awareness of it results in a vein of melancholy running through his work. He is ever aware of mutability whether in the persona of a beast of burden or as Gregory Corso.

> I am watching them churn the last milk
>   they'll ever get from me.
> They are waiting for me to die;
> They want to make buttons out of my bones.
>
> *Gasoline*

> Moaning: Oh what responsibility
> I put on thee Gregory
> Death and God
> Hard hard it's hard
>
> I learned life were no dream
> I learned truth deceived
> Man is not God
> Life is a century
> Death an instant
>
> *Long Live Man*

With the passage of time the elegy increasingly featured in the work of the surviving Beats. Corso had always written them: "Spontaneous Requiem for the American Indian," "Errol Flynn On His Death," and "Lines Written Nov. 22, 23 – 1963 – In Discord." The death of Jack Kerouac moved him both to write a threnody and to bring out *Elegiac Feelings American*. He found that to sing of Kerouac was also to "requiem America," so the poem concerns the two great Beat themes: redemptive love and the search for the mythical America.

> How inseparable you and the America you
> saw yet was never there to see; you
> and America, like the tree and the ground,
> are one and the same; yet how like a
> palm tree in the state of Oregon. . .
> dead ere it blossomed, like a snow polar
> loping the Miami –
> How so that which you were or hoped to be,
> and the America not, the America you saw
> yet could not see
> So like yet unlike the ground from which you
> stemmed; you stood upon America like a
> rootless flat-bottomed tree;. . .
> *Elegiac Feelings American*

And the asphalt seas are calling Heffalump to come back

D.O.: What do you think of American women?
W.B.: I think they're possibly one of the worst expressions of the female sex because they've been allowed to go further. This whole worship of women that flourished in the Old South, and in Frontier days, when there weren't many, is still basic in American life; and the whole Southern worship of women and white supremacy is still the police of America. They lost the Civil War, but their policies still dominate America. It's a matriarchal, white supremacist country. There seems to be a very definite link between matriarchy and white supremacy. (*The Job*)

With customary good sense the female sex mostly left the American frontier, with the attendant likelihood of being shot, frozen, starved, washed away, or scalped, to men. As a direct result, American literature has a tradition of novels dealing with male comradeship. The theme uneasily spans both the democratic ideal ("give me your poor") and the expansionism which tolerated the ownership of slaves and encouraged the extirpation of the Indians. This tension produced a genre: in it, two men share their existence out of comradeship, but if one of them has a dark skin any sexual overtones can be safely ignored – nobody was even going to *contemplate* miscegenation on a homosexual basis. The dominant role was usually the white man: the Lone Ranger and Tonto are hero and sidekick rather than friends.

Whitman lost his Washington clerkship because Anthony Comstock, founder of the Society for the Suppression of Vice, found *Leaves of Grass* immoral. It was 1882 before the book found a commercial publisher. Much of Whitman's "intense loving comradeship" was too overtly sexual for the taste of his times. On the other hand, the novel set in an all-male society which was an *enforced* condition – Indian fighting for Natty Bumppo and Chingachgook; whale-hunting for Ishmael and Queequeg; dual flight for Huck and Jim – was readily acceptable.

The "sidekick" tradition did not necessarily involve racial arrogance. Huck, unwittingly initiated into manhood when he apologizes to the man whose feelings he has hurt, despite the fact that he's black, feels better, not worse. Queequeg, that model of courage, grace, and dignity, is significantly a much larger man physically than Ishmael. *The Last of the Mohicans* (who, incidentally, wore their hair like hippies, not Hurons) is prefaced with the quote: "Mislike me not for my complexion." It is possible for an author to be aware of society's prejudices, even to write of them, without endorsing them.

Redemptive love between men in Beat literature finds various expressions, from Jack's platonic fascination with Neal to Allen's passionate sexual urge towards both of them. Commentators have their own Procrustean beds. Paul Metcalf, in an exchange with Ginsberg, wants Melville to be queer; Allen thought he was more Greek.

> Ishmael in bed with Queequeg: "Upon waking next morning about daylight, I found Queequeg's arm thrown over me in the most loving and affectionate manner. You had almost thought I had been his wife."
>
> And Melville, late in life: "For, Nature, in no shallow surge/Against thee either sex may urge. . ."
>
> All these unquestionably argue a homosexual drive. . .but one wonders: the urge was there, but was it ever given expression, and in what way is that important, i.e., the relation between urge and action? I suggested to Olson once, perhaps on a long whaling voyage, but he said, naw, those sailors were too dirty. . .It's simple humanity, not modern concept homosexuality. (*The Beat Book*)

Metcalf conveniently ignores Ishmael's reaction to Queequeg's somnolent cuddle: "the unbecomingness of his hugging a fellow male in that sort of style." Selective quotation can prove anything. The Beats brought a new frankness to this theme. Ginsberg's elegies for Neal are achingly sexual in their loss: "Tender Spirit, thank you for touching me/with tender hands/When you were young, in a beautiful body", but, like the majority of the members of the Beat Generation, Neal's real sexual orientation was towards the female. He didn't really, he said, "like cocks and men" and his rejection of Allen was what brought on the original case of the Denver Doldrums.

In his recent work, notably *Cities of the Red Night* and *Port of Saints*, Burroughs fantasizes a society in which the awakening desires of the adolescent male are directed exclusively towards his fellows, scorning girls. (The one heterosexual scene in *Red Night* is an orgy conducted for purposes of procreation.) Both books are a kaleidoscope of homoerotica and Boys Own Paper battles. Fucking and fighting down South America way. Bums and guns: Burroughs in heaven. The opposition is always as inept as that from a spaghetti Western (gunsels so bad at their chosen trade it's a mystery how they managed not to shoot themselves before Eastwood rode into town). Opponents, never presented as sentient human beings, merely as targets, shades of My Lai, are as easy to blow away as Mexican bandits. Coincidentally, the Wild Boys' favorite weapon was the Bowie knife.

Opposites attract but are a lot more difficult. To give love, support, or sexual pleasure to someone whose emotional and sexual equipment is very different from your own requires more than making love to a mirror image. To live permanently on the Island of Lost Gay Boys is to refuse to grow up. Cassady and Kerouac, with varying degress of success, did take the risks involved in becoming married men. Nevertheless, while admiting that they did not feel for each other what he felt for each of them, Allen did try to enroll them as honorary citizens of Whitmanville.

"I heard you, I sure do know it now," to Neal's speech, "I love you man, you've got to dig that; boy you've got to know." Whitman's adhesiveness! Sociability without genital sexuality between them, but adoration and love, light as America promised in Love. . . (*Visions of the Great Rememberer*)

"Those guys were all queer. They hated women," said one of Jack's old Lowell friends, who thought the Beat Generation had ruined his old highschool chum. Because its two major survivors are so well known for their sexual proclivities, some observers wish to see the group as a "chorus of fags." Ginsberg lists "Gay" as one of the subjects of special concern at the Disembodied School and Burroughs is one of the lecturers under that heading. The (unpublished) predecessor to *Junkie* was called simply *Queer*. Now while there were few queer junkies who could write, or who cared to, there were plenty of people who wanted to read about being one. Vicarious kicks in liberal circles. Very discreet sir of course under the counters of the Charing Cross Road truss shops. We are fascinated by your horrible condition. *Naked Lunch* is read by the colored handkerchief brigade as straight pornography. The sexual norm in Burroughs' books is casually promiscuous. In the days when they were still anonymous, one *TLS* reviewer got very sniffy about sex between men being presented in such a fast, nasty, and impersonal way. Burroughs can never be accused of being sentimental. Sing if you're glad to be gay, Bill? Fuck off. Whether Cassady is regarded as Dionysus incarnate or a streetwise Lothario whose reform school diplomas had made him less fussy about where his orgasm came from does not alter the fact that he was a compulsive womanizer who was immensely attractive to both sexes. Burroughs, with his advocacy of a gay state, and Ginsberg with all the propagandizing in *Gay Sunshine*, have entered gay politics, never an area of interest to Neal. Allen, after heavy aversion experiences re women "smell of Naomi all over me," struggled to come to terms with his sexual nature. Having done so, he made a virtue out of a necessity. He evangelizes, perhaps, a shade too enthusiastically. Orlovsky's entrée into the Beat group was as Allen's boy. Sexual activity for the Beats was, though, chiefly heterosexual. The undue emphasis that has been placed on the homoerotic has tended to obscure the greater importance of the redemptive nature of love. Sal and Dean are saved by the fact that they genuinely care for one another, and by the love of women. Their story is more representative of the Beats' philosophy than Burroughs' spurting brown boys.

Most close friendships in the Beats' novels are between heterosexual men. They often share the affections of the same women. When Jack and Julien plan to run away to sea in *Vanity of Duluoz*, it is to avoid the homosexual Franz Mueller. In *The Subterraneans*, Yuri Gligoric alienates the affections of Mardou Fox, but Leo Percepied forgives, acknowledging that making love to the same woman may be an expression of platonic love between them.

> Raphael Urso I liked quite well, too, in spite or perhaps because of a previous New York hassle over a subterranean girl, as I say. He respected me though he was always talking behind my back, in a way, tho he did that to everybody. (*Desolation Angels*)

Similar instances may be found in John Clellon Holmes' novels. In *Go*, Gene Pasternak has a brief fling with the wife of Paul Hobbes, causing the latter to exclaim to her, when he discovers that he has been cuckolded,

> Look, do you think I'm angry about you and Gene? Is that what it is? You know me better than that. . .I mean it, it doesn't matter to me! It's normal for you to be attracted to other men. It made me happy last night because you were acting freely, naturally. . . And you know how much I like Gene.

The later novel, *Get Home Free* (it takes its title from a children's street game), opens with Verger having taken over both the home and the mistress of his dead friend Agatson.

> . . .they were living together in Agatson's old loft in the West 70s, where May had remained after Agatson was accidentally killed under a subway train. She had gotten ownership because she was Agatson's last girl.

Kerouac exhaustively explored the theme of comradeship through the Cassady persona, especially in *On the Road* and his own personal favorite from the Duluoz Legend, *Visions of Cody*. The *ménage à trois* of 1952 he was rather reticent about: Carolyn was, after all, another man's wife. For him the logical extension of friendship between two men would be friendship between whole families, like the idealized memories of such he retained from his New England childhood. Sadly for him, the surrogate nuclear family of the Cassady household was the closest he ever came to his dream of the two of them, each a paterfamilias, in porch rocking chairs on some tree-lined street as American as Andy Hardy. Even *Time* , the magazine that had so derided the Beats in the early days, came to recognize that dream, though it took an obituary to do it.

> . . .Kerouac's final vision: he and his friend Cassady growing old together, living with their families on the same street in some quiet backwater. Very touching, and very American.

James Fenimore Cooper fantasies the last Mohicans. Kerouac dreams up Neal Cassady, as the last cowboy.

Accept loss forever

> He said that for him there was only one way to account for things – to tell the whole truth about them, holding back nothing; tell the reader the way it truly happened, the ecstasy and sorrow, remorse and how the weather was, and, with any luck, the reader will find his way to the heart of the thing itself.
>
> ". . .were any of the other characters in the book based on people you knew. . .?"
>
> "Sure. The whole mob. Based on. Not exact. . ." (*Papa Hemingway*)

> "This must be it, all right," Harrington said. "There's Kerouac." (*Nothing More to Declare*)

Kerouac always claimed the term "Beat" originated with him. Certainly it is his public image that is most associated with the Beat Generation.

> That wild eager picture of me on the cover of *On the Road* goes back much further than 1948 when John Clellon Holmes (author of *Go* and *The Horn*) and I were sitting around trying to think up the meaning of the Lost Generation and the subsequent Existentialism and I said "You know, this is really a beat generation" and he leapt up and said "That's it, that's right!" (*Playboy* vol. 6, no. 6, June 1959)

He said that in a speech at Hunter College which is probably the only one ever printed verbatim by both *Playboy* and *Encounter*. A decade later he felt the term had been debased.

> Oh the beat generation was just a phrase I used in the 1951 written manuscript of *On the Road* to describe guys like

Moriarty who run around the country in cars looking for odd jobs, girlfriends, kicks. It was thereafter picked up by West Coast leftist groups and turned into a meaning like "beat mutiny" and "beat insurrection" and all that nonsense. . . (*Paris Review*, 43)

Whatever the term was understood to mean, it was always synonymous with Kerouac. He was variously called the Beat Generation's apostle, poet, hero, laureate, prince, King Arthur. In 1959 Seymour Krim called him "King of the Beats" and that was the one that stuck the fastest. By the time of his death the appellations had grown more stately in tone. The *Time* obituary called him "shaman of the Beat Generation" and the *Washington Post* printed his last article, the day after he died, as "Kerouac: The Last Word From the Father of the Beats."

The close identification of man and myth reflects the extent to which his books were the chronicles of the group, but the Duluoz Legend, the heart of Kerouac's work, is not the story of the Beat Generation to the exclusion of all else. Drawing freely from his life and experience his instinctive process of exclusion, elaboration, and invention created the work of fiction.

Some of the changes are minor matters. Old Bull Lee's first marriage is mentioned in *On the Road*. ". . . he married a White Russian countess in Yugoslavia to get her away from the Nazis in the thirties. . ." Interviewed in 1974, Burroughs was asked about his first marriage.

> J.T.: What about the story that your first wife was a Hungarian countess?
> W.B.: She wasn't. Her name was Ilse Herzfeld Klapper, they were solid wealthy bourgeois Jewish People in Hamburg. She had to get out because of Hitler and went to Yugoslavia, and I married her in Athens to get her into the States. (*The Beat Diary*)

Old Bull is invested with the romantic past of an international dilettante. A marriage of convenience to acquire a passport is less glamorous than one which outwits Nazism. Wilhelm Reich, another spirit killed by the McCarthyites in their goddam Brooks Brothers suits, was one of his brief enthusiasms. He gives Old Bull an orgone accumulator.

> "Say, why don't you fellows try my orgone accumulator? Put some juice in your bones. I always rush up and take off ninety miles an hour for the nearest whorehouse, hor-hor-hor!". . . According to Reich, orgones are vibratory atmospheric atoms of the life-principle. People get cancer because they run out of orgones. (*On the Road*)

In a magazine article in 1977 Burroughs emphasized the fact that this was invention:

> I built my first orgone accumulator on a farm near Pharr, Texas, in the spring of 1949.
>   Kerouac described my orgone box in On the Road – a pretty good trick, as he never set foot on the south Texas farm. . . Like so much of Jack's writing, this makes a good story but is actually pure fiction. (*Oui*, vol. 6, no. 10, October 1977)

Kerouac molded members of his family into fictional characters just as he did the members of the Beat Generation. At the very end of his life he was reiterating the theme of *On the Road*.

> true adventure on the road featuring an ex-cow hand and ex-footballer driving across the continent north, northwest, mid-west and southland looking for lost fathers, odd jobs, good times, and girls and winding up on the railroad. (*Washington Post*, 22 October 1969)

This list is in his last article. The objects of the quest are significant. The wanderings are not pointless because they are a search for a grail. Odd jobs, girls, and the occasional good time are not exclusive to one geographical location but a lost father can only be in one place. There was a possibility that was open to Dean Moriarty which was not to the prototype of Sal Paradise:

the chance of finding the father. Leo Kerouac's death had left Jack with unresolved questions. One way to try to answer them was to cross and recross the vastness of a country often imbued with the mystique of a spiritual parent. The search for the self, the final conquest of the father necessary for full manhood, is externalized in a search for an actual man, a search conducted across the surface of a huge, challenging, and elusive America. The characters he based on his father are among his most fictionalized. They reflect the way he needed to think of the man at various times in his life. The rounded and believable head of the Martin clan in *The Town and the City* starts out roaring with joy, a huge and rumbustious figure in the eyes of his children. Gradually his fortunes decline until, afflicted by what his wife recognizes (though he cannot) as the male menopause, he watches in almost paralyzed fascination as his business is lost and his stature dwindles. When he visits his son in a military hospital he is scarcely recognizable.

Francis was astounded. As he hurried in the hall he passed a wet, shabby old man, who, with a meek and humble air, was looking back down the hall in a gape of hesitation, clutching a dripping straw hat with both hands. It was a moment of awful presentiment before Francis, turning back to this woeful old man, realized it was his father George Martin. (*The Town and the City*)

The Martins were "the Kerouacs of my soul" he said in *Book of Dreams*. Something of his own experience is invested in each of the five sons. At the family reunion for the father's funeral, written approximately two years after the burial of Leo Kerouac, Peter Martin turns his back on the past and sets out into the world, face to the elements. The book closes on Peter, like Lieutenant Henry, putting it all behind him.

When the railroad trains moaned, and riverwinds blew, bringing echoes through the vale, it was as if a hum of wild voices, the dear voices of everybody he had known, were crying: "Peter, Peter! Where are you going, Peter?" And a big soft gust of rain came down.

He put up the collar of his jacket, and bowed his head, and hurried along. (*The Town and the City*)

Papa Leo died before the rite of passage designed to defeat him could do so. Jack recommended that his mother did not read *The Subterraneans* because of the love scenes (especially, perhaps, because they were with a black girl). Yet it was in that book that he took his father's name.

The Town and the City echoes, in the symmetry of the title, those of Wolfe, a literary hero at the time. New York shaped the book. Kerouac was out of the archetypal small town (the population figure is less important than the tone of the collective mind). First he, as a college boy, then the whole family, what was left of it, went to the big city. Tore the roots up out of the wrinkly tar corners and wooden porches and the steaming coffee urn diners and the smoky mills of football practice lots and headed for the big city.

Yet Dr. Sax knew Massachusetts like the Brontës knew Yorkshire. They went, not to some Okie paradise by the ocean, but to the cold bleak towering and glamorous cityCityCITY of New York. And there Jack broke his leg and grabbed the excuse to get out of being bawled out by men of lesser intellect, men like "Lou Libble," a flubbering fat-lipped slobber of a pseudonym, and Leo died and they sent him back to lie among his Nashua cousins.

It was Kerouac's healthy streak of indolence that makes his early athletic endeavors important to an understanding of the beer-belly years. Once he had another way of garnering approval he could give up physical exertion. This is what makes eleven books in five years a heroic achievement. It was the act of a driven man who would rather have been out carousing but who needed to prove something to himself and to dead Leo. Later he would want to win over the critics and that would be why their grubby streetings would hurt him so, why the shrapnel of their easy scorn sliced into him in a way it could not the equally vilified Burroughs and Ginsberg. He did not have the defeat of the father to fall back upon.

"They rejected me," he mused, drunk and sad, after his last visit to Lowell High. Even then. Especially there.

Had he been truly down and out and on the road his early books would have had the purple patches you find in Woody Guthrie, but he was living out and writing a fantasy of emergent manhood, even when he was thirty. He took the substance of one man's life and made literature out of it. And all of us out there, in our dull and necessary jobs and day to day concerns picked up on it and said: this is about a man just like me, and yet it is, truly, poetry, and therefore it enriches my life like nothing else, for it gives me a renewed belief in the validity of my existence.

Kerouac always hankered for a family man status he never attained. He initially denied that the child his second wife bore after their separation was his. One look at Jan Kerouac's coloring, her eyes and her jaw, are enough to refute that. "His absence was all there was," she said. When she went to see him, late in his life, and he told her to write a book (she did, in fact: *Baby Driver*), he said to use his name. Too little too late. His letters to Carolyn urge that she should never leave Neal. If Neal should lose her, then of course Jack would lose her too. To some extent he was able to share Neal's family without making a commitment, to enjoy a domesticity without responsibility. He could never shoulder Neal's breadwinner burdens.

. . .Cassady's attic in San Francisco. I had a bed there. That was the best place I ever wrote in. It rained every day and I had wine, marijuana, and once in a while his wife would sneak in. (*Kerouac Biblio.*)

Yet the Kerouac who groaned at Corso's new son, "Oh Gregory you brought something up to die" was the old and disillusioned Kerouac. He liked children alright, telling stories and drawing cartoons for the little Cassadys, but responsibility frightened him because he'd never cut the umbilical, never spiritually prepared himself for fatherhood. By the Cassady fireside he could enjoy it all by proxy, Carolyn in the kitchen and the kids on the hearthrug. Perhaps he never even admitted this to himself or perhaps he did and that was why he preferred to hint that he was sterile (and therefore less of a man) than admit it. So, when he was trying to head down the road in the rain he dreaded that the Cassadys might split up, for then he would have no one to go home to: except Memere. And to return to Memere would be to return to being so small again that you have to do what women tell you. Back to Memere who forbade Ginsberg the house that Jack built from his royalties, who tore the phone out of the wall if he used it too much, who didn't like his friends and who never read his books and who nagged him about his drinking and about whom he dreamt sexually. She was part of that Catholic tradition which venerated the pious, long-suffering wife and mother as the highest aspiration for women. The world would never be happy, she said, until men got down on their knees and asked their women to forgive them. "Women live here," wrote Jack, "and the world is taken care of." Such ruthless old women often turn into the sort of Lawrentian tyrants who are vengefully drowned in flash floods. To Burroughs Memere was the epitome of matriarchy. Leo Kerouac died, clutching his belly and groaning, "Look after your mother" and the stage was set for Memere to skive in shoe factories while her "wastrel" son bummed around and then to grasp the tiller firmly when his ship came in. When she finally took to her bed he married a good Catholic girl who, by nursing Memere, accepted her mantle of suffering and so became worthy of little Jacky. Small wonder Kerouac shied away from taking on a family of his own.

Kerouac's works are frequently rites of passage, falling into, and through, love; leaving the womb of America for Europe, Mexico, or Africa; confrontations physical or spiritual (a new religious frame, or frightened self on a mountainside); leaving home for football and college or the Merchant Marine. *On the*

Road is a novel of initiation. This is why it is continually rediscovered: it is about the tools one may use to break into the world of the adult. Huck used a raft and a river; Sal and Dean use the travel technology of their time – gas guzzler and highway – to come to their greater maturity through confronting each other in depth, matching, in their talents and their failings, like two halves of a broken plate. The doer and the thinker: the driver and the observer in the seat beside him. Sal's moment of realization comes when he groans with fever in Mexico City and comes to just in time to see Dean abandoning him. "I realized what a rat he was," says Sal. A useful thing to know about one's alter ego. This knowledge gives Sal, in his turn, the strength to desert Dean, at the book's end, for Laura, his girl. Harry with Falstaff: I know you not, old man – rejecting the adolescent dream of gang acceptance for the adult responsibility.

Jack in life, of course, retraced his steps too often, ducking back, never quite charring his bridges thoroughly enough. So *On the Road*, an earlier work, is more mature and complete than *Vanity of Duluoz* or even *Big Sur*, the last one he ever brought off completely. *On the Road* is not memoirs. Like Peter Martin, the protagonist is last seen setting off down the road, chin lifted and feet firmly planted, with scarcely a backward glance. In reality, once Jack got where he was going he promptly set off back again. In *Desolation Angels* Duluoz can hardly wait to get off the mountain and back to the world and the beers and burlesques (goodbye solitude, meditation, and wilderness) and jumps for joy when the American familiarity of ocean garbage bobs alongside the ship heading for New York (so long American in Paris, soldier of fortune, romantic expatriate). In *Big Sur* he notes in surprise in his journal "already bored?" (farewell communing with Thoreau nature, drying out, and scribing the Joycean sea). Leo Percepied compares Mardou's sheets to Memere's and backs off (*adieu* momma's boy become bohemian lover across miscegenation lines). Ray Smith mutters his Zen koans knowing he'll ask for the last rites on his deathbed (exit Buddhist scholar who turned his back on ancestry and the old dominatrix Mother Church). Jack couldn't keep silent, couldn't bear exile, and was too open-hearted for cunning; he had to settle for serving after all. As Burroughs said, he didn't change all that much. He just became a fatter man sitting drinking beer with his mother.

If only, like Burroughs, Holmes, Ginsberg, and Ferlinghetti he had possessed the tools that the academic draws when he is issued with cap and gown and degree. The essay, the review, the manifesto, the carefully edited interview (the copyright of which you keep), instead of the chat shows and the tabloid interviews for which he had to present such a big drunk target in order to face at all.

What did he have when the vitriol started to drip? When even old buddies crafted careful, skilful, spiteful articles on a style which made a virtue out of blending content and form, which showed its means of propulsion there on the page, which, above all, denied the revision which is the hallmark of the academic?

He'd never stayed at Columbia long enough to get a badge for analyzing and dissecting and, by definition, criticizing a work. The Podhoretzes would have had to grin and bear it over the canapés if he had ever been in a position to do it *back*. He was a sitting duck for a hatchet job. There is no telling answer in all his work, just hurt and bewilderment and, later, bellicosity. It was as if a strong man was up against smaller opponents with belts in strange martial arts. It was the same when smart Quebecois or Parisians scorned his Canuck patois. He had no way to counterattack his tormentors. When they gave Jean Rhys the W.H. Smith Award in 1966 she was so neglected most people genuinely thought she was dead. The acclaim was not overdue, she said: "It has come too late." For Kerouac, after eleven books in five wilderness years, acclaim would have soothed the bitterness. Instead, he got the treatment any upstart gets from the established and he got in the way of the copy hungry. They called his detail irrelevant or repetitious and they tutted over his material and values while the mirror he held up to life sold them a lot of newspapers. In 1950 he had been a smiling eager young author in a suit. He even called himself "John." By the end of *Desolation Angels* he was a "famous writer more or less" and thoroughly sick of the whole subject. In the year that saw the publications of *On the Road* Kerouac settled down to live with his mother in Northport, settling finally for the guaranteed, suffocating support. Whenever he referred to the situation in his later books it is with that slightly shrill defiance of the man who is defending a position he knows to be untenable. *Book of Dreams*, begun in 1952 and published ten years later, shows his fellow Beats and his family constantly in his subconscious.

> Last night my father was back in Lowell – O Lord, O haunted life. . . He keeps coming back in this dream, to Lowell, has no job, no shop even – . . .but he's feeble and he ain't supposed to live long anyway so it doesn't matter. . . – it's mostly my mother talking to me about him – "Ah well, ah *bien, le vivra pas longtemps ça foi icit!*" "he won't live long *this* time!". . . I'm my father myself and this is me. . . – but it *is* Pa, the big fat man, but frail and pale, but so mysterious and un-Kerouac – but is that me?

> In Kerouac's *Book of Dreams*, begun in 1952, his mother entered his world of fantasy both as Angel and his Truth, and as a hateful old lady whose grave he dug up to plant marijuana. But he also dreamed of being a child again, lying with Memere arm in arm, Jack crying afraid to die, his mother blissful, with one leg "in pink sexually out between me." (*Kerouac*, Charters)

The dream diary provides a supplement to the novels and a key to their interpretation. Kerouac's original conception of the Beat Generation came from his childhood perception of his parents' social life.

> . . .the Beat Generation goes back to the wild parties my father used to have at home in the 1920s and 1930s in New England that were so fantastically loud nobody could sleep for

blocks around and when the cops came they always had a drink. (*Playboy*, June 1959)

The most important characters in his books are based on either fellow Beats or fellow Kerouacs. The glimpses we are given of his subconscious show that sometimes he scarcely distinguished between the two.

now I'm almost California SP and Cody and my father mingled into the One Father image of Accusation is mad at me because I missed my local, my freight, I fucked up with the Mother Image down the line, I did something childish (the little boy writing in the room) and held up iron railroads of men – . . .grimy Pop-Cody is already at work, he may fuck up in his own tragic night but by Jesus Christ when it's time to go to work it's fucking time to go to work – (*Book of Dreams*)

By the time he wrote *Vanity of Duluoz* Papa Leo had acquired the status of John Wayne. Recalling his own time under observation in a naval hospital visiting the "wet, shabby old man. . .with a meek and humble air" has given way to

. . .my Pa, father Emil A. Duluoz, fat, puffing on cigar, pushing admirals aside, comes up to my bedside and yells "Good boy, tell that goddamn Roosevelt and his ugly wife where to get off! . . .You tell these empty headed admirals around here who are really stooges of the government around here that your father said you're doing the right thing," and with this, and while being overheard by said admirals, stomped out fuming on his cigar and took the train back to Lowell. (*Vanity of Duluoz*)

"Admirals," in the plural, standing around the bedside of one disturbed volunteer seaman gives the piece no extra authenticity. The father who had been such a major influence thus comes full circle. Seen clearly in sadness and honesty, he was buried in a novel, as he was in life, before his son had proved himself. Years later, when that son had failed to succeed him, he was restored to the sentimental stature he enjoyed when Jack was a child.

Kerouac wrote about his contemporaries more than any of the others. His influence on their writing was considerable. Burroughs' and Ginsberg's most famous titles were supposedly Kerouac's ideas.

> Jack liked *Naked Lunch*, he'd suggested the title and helped type the manuscript in Tangier with Ginsberg; (*Kerouac*, Charters)

> Jack Kerouac, new Buddha of American prose,. . . Several phrases and the title of *Howl* are taken from him. (*Howl*)

The recognizable pseudonym is the open secret of the Duluoz Legend. Identifying Allen Ginsberg as Leon Levinsky in *The Town and the City*; Carlo Marx in *On the Road*; Alvah Goldbook in *The Dharma Bums*; Adam Moorad in *The Subterraneans*; and Irwin Garden in *Desolation Angels*, *Big Sur*, *Book of Dreams*, and *Vanity of Duluoz*, has always provided an extra esoteric dimension to the reading of Kerouac. Clues are usually provided: Allen Ginsberg's other given name is Irwin; Marx and Levinsky are Jewish names. Kerouac did this throughout his writing life and he included the lesser members, who are often absent from the work of the others. The nature of the Beats as a disparate group is vital to an understanding of his work.

For the last twelve years of his life, once *On the Road* had established an income from writing, Kerouac lived mostly with Memere, there was no longer the need, or the excuse, to get away in order to get a job. His wanderings were severely curtailed and his mother's hostility towards his former associates meant that he saw much less of them.

After the Cassady "two sticks" bust Memere barred drugs from the house. She wrote to Ginsberg in Paris threatening him with the FBI if he contacted Jack or mentioned his name in his "dirty" poetry books. Such ridiculous strictures on his private life did not, however, stop Kerouac quarrying the Beat Generation to build the Duluoz Legend.

Burroughs was Will Dennison in *The Town and the City*; Old Bull Lee in *On the Road*; Frank Carmody in *The Subterraneans*;

Bull Hubbard in *Desolation Angels* and *Book of Dreams*, and Will Hubbard in *Vanity of Duluoz*. Never an habitué of North Beach, he is notably absent from *The Dharma Bums* and the San Francisco sections of *Desolation Angels*.

Cassady only ever appeared under two pseudonyms (he is mentioned in *The Subterraneans*, though he does not appear, as Leroy). After *On the Road*, in which he is the basis for Kerouac's most famous character, he is always called Cody Pomeray. Any slightly sinister Conan Doyle implications are absent from *The Dharma Bums*, *Big Sur*, *Desolation Angels*, *Book of Dreams* and of course, *Visions of Cody*.

Gregory Corso enters the saga quite late, as Yuri Gligoric in *The Subterraneans* and Raphael Urso in *Desolation Angels* and *Book of Dreams*.

Lawrence Ferlinghetti is given his mother's family name, Monsanto, in *Big Sur*, which is largely set in the seaside cabin he loaned Kerouac in 1960. He is Danny Richman in *Book of Dreams* and the character of Larry O'Hara in *The Subterraneans* is a composite of him and Jerry Newman, with the latter in more prominence, as Kerouac spent the three weeks in the summer of 1953 in New York, although the book is set in San Francisco.

> – old Larry O'Hara always nice to me, a crazy Irish young businessman of San Francisco with Balzacian backroom in his bookstore where they'd smoke tea and talk of the old days of the great Basie band or the days of the great Chu Berry –
>
> So we all did go to Larry's. . .when the party was at its pitch I was in Larry's bedroom again admiring the red light and remembering the night we'd had Micky in there the three of us, Adam and Larry and myself, and had benny and a big sexball amazing to describe in itself – when Larry ran in and said, "Man you gonna make it with her tonight?" (*The Subterraneans*)

This change of location accounts for the appearance of Frank Carmody and of Yuri Gligoric even though Corso first visited San Francisco in 1956, Burroughs, circa 1960.

John Clellon Holmes (Tom Saybrook in *On the Road* and James Watson in *Book of Dreams*) resident in the fifties either in New York or Old Saybrook, Connecticut, puts in an appearance in the fictitious "San Francisco" milieu of *The Subterraneans*.

Michael McClure only appears in the San Francisco books. In his brief appearance in *The Dharma Bums* he was Ike O'Shay, in *Desolation Angels* and *Big Sur* he was Pat McLear. When they first met, at the time of the emergence of the Beat Generation in the media, Kerouac could write of professional jealousies.

> We come back to the coffee place where Irwin is back waiting, and here simultaneously in the door walk Simon Darlovsky, alone, done with his day's work as an ambulance driver, then Geoffrey Donald and Patrick McLear the two old (old established) poets of San Fran who hate us all – . . . McLear, 20s, young, crew cut, looks blankly at Irwin. . . (*Desolation Angels*)

By 1960, however, such things would appear to have been forgotten. Duncan is Robert Duncan respectively.

Peter Orlovsky's first appearance is in the Duluoz Legend in *The Dharma Bums*, when Kerouac did not take the trouble to invest him with the dignity of a full pseudonym. ". . .Sometimes Alvah and his new buddy George played bongo drums on inverted cans." In *Desolation Angels*, however, Kerouac fleshes out the character of Simon Darlovsky (this name is also used in *Book of Dreams*) fully.

Later stars in the Beat firmament are also represented. Lew Welch was characterized in *Desolation Angels* and *Big Sur* as Dave Wain "that lean rangy redhead Welchman."

Kerouac's attitude to homosexuality is much discussed by people anxious to "prove" that he was the way they want him to be. He was attracted to the "black lace and warm mystery" kind of female sexuality, but his athleticism and good looks made him as attractive to homosexual men as he was towards women. The subject was viewed with greater openness and tolerance in

Beat circles than it was in Catholic Lowell. When it crops up in his books Kerouac's tone is not enthusiastic.

> Irwin Garden was an artist like me, the author of the great original poem "Howling," but he never needed solitude like me. . . Irwin was never without his own immediate entourage . . .beginning with his companion and lover Simon Darlovsky . . .the blond Russian blood boy of 19 who originally was not queer but had fallen in love with Irwin and Irwin's "soul" and poetry, so accommodated his master – (*Desolation Angels*)

Gary Snyder appears in *Vanity of Duluoz* under his real name, as Jarry Wagner in *Desolation Angels* and as the protagonist of *The Dharma Bums*, Japhy Ryder.

Kerouac has a scene in *The Dharma Bums* which indicates the cross-fertilization of ideas between the poets at the time.

> ALVAH: Haven't you seen Ray's new book of poems he just wrote in Mexico – "the wheel of the quivering meat conception turns in the void expelling tics, porcupines, elephants, people, stardust, fools, nonsense. . ."
> RAY: That's not it! (*The Dharma Bums*)

That this poem actually exists, as part of *Mexico City Blues*, is the sort of fact which promotes confusion over whether the books are "novels."

> 211th Chorus
> The wheel of the quivering meat conception
> Turns in the void expelling human beings,
> Pigs, turtles, frogs, insects, nits, Mice,
> lice, lizards, rats, roan
> Racing horses, poxy bucolic pigtics,

Other San Francisco poets who appear in Kerouac's work include Philip Lamantia (Francis Da Pavia in *The Dharma Bums*, David D'Angeli in *Desolation Angels*), Kenneth Rexroth,

who hated the portrait of himself as "Rheinhold Cacoethes" in
The Dharma Bums and Philip Whalen (Warren Coughlin in
The Dharma Bums and Ben Fagan in *Desolation Angels* and *Big
Sur*).

Lucien Carr's appearances in Kerouac's books reinforce the
importance of the early New York years. Kerouac described
Carr's youthful exuberance in the last volume of the Duluoz
Legend.

> . . .like one night in Bangor Maine Claude get aboard the
> Whitlaw yatch [sic] with Henry Whitlaw (acquaintance of
> Johnnie's) and they, fifteen, simply pull the plug out and sink
> the yatch and swim ashore. Pranks and stuff like that. A wild
> kid. A guy in New Orleans lends him his car, and Claude,
> fifteen, no license, nothing, wrecks it utterly on Basin Street.
> (*Vanity of Duluoz*)

The persistent attentions paid the blond and heterosexual Carr
by Dave Kammerer (sometimes spelled Kammarer) who had
known Burroughs in St. Louis, drove Carr to arrange to go to sea
with Kerouac. They were photographed together by the future
Edie Kerouac, feet up on a fountain plinth in what was intended
to be their farewell pose. According to Kerouac's version in
Vanity of Duluoz, Kammerer found out about the plan and
wanted to join them. In any event, they never sailed and in the
summer of 1944 Carr stabbed Kammerer to death on the banks
of the Hudson River. He rolled the body into the river and then
went to ask the advice of Burroughs, which was get a good
lawyer and give yourself up. He was not psyched up to do that
yet so he called on Kerouac. They dropped the knife down a
drain and went out for a drink before Carr surrendered. Kerouac
was consequently booked and imprisoned as a material witness.
This event was the direct cause of his first marriage. He could
not get bailed out any other way. He paints the picture of
himself as a rugged seaman, married from jail with a gun-toting
detective as witness.

215

. . .I was let out of jail for 10 hours to marry my first wife in a hot New York afternoon around Chambers Street, complete with best man detective with holstered gun – . . .the rugged evil-looking seaman in tow of a policeman being married in a judge's chamber (because the D.A. thought the fiancée to be pregnant). . . (*Desolation Angels*)

Kerouac wrote of these events in *The Town and the City*. Kammerer appears as Waldo Meister, whose spiritual impoverishment is symbolized by his having only one arm, and by his cruel treatment of defenseless pet cats. Kerouac played down the drama; Waldo Meister falls or jumps to his death from a high window. Kenneth Wood, the character based on Lucien Carr, makes his entrance soaking wet, coming through a window fleeing someone who has just punched him in the nose. Kerouac never tired of telling this tale, and in later life, he embellished it with gunfire.

Claude came in through the fire escape. . .there were gunshots down in the alley – Pow! Pow! and it was raining, and my wife says, here comes Claude. And here comes this blond guy through the fire escape, all wet. (*Paris Review*, 43)

Carr was called Kenny Wood in *The Town and the City*, Sam Vedder in *The Subterraneans*, Damion in *On the Road* and Julien Love in *Book of Dreams* and *Visions of Cody*. As he gets drunk in *Big Sur*, Duluoz's new girlfriend seems like an androgynous version of his old friend.

all I can keep saying as I swig from my bottle is "Julien, you're talking too much! Julien, Julien, my God who'd ever dream I'd run into a woman who looks like Julien. . .you look like Julien but you're not Julien and on top of that you're a woman, how goddam strange"

In *Vanity of Duluoz* Carr is called Claude de Maubris. He is also referred to as Claude in the *Paris Review* interview when everyone else spoken of is given their real name. John Clellon

Holmes has said that all the others were very protective towards Carr after his release from prison (he was sent to Elmira State Reformatory for two years). The original dedication to *Howl* (mimeographed by Marthe Rexroth in 1955) included the line "Lucien Carr, recently promoted Night Bureau Manager of New York United Press." This line was included in the first printing of the City Lights edition. Its subsequent deletion seems to imply, as does the pseudonym in the Kerouac interview, that Carr, with a promising career and a family to support, felt discretion was desirable rather than risking public association with the Beat Generation. Only in recent years, with the survivors of the group growing increasingly respectable and events in the forties taking on a historical perspective, has Lucien Carr given interviews. His rehabilitation seems to have been swift and thorough. In *Desolation Angels* he is depicted as the head of a nuclear family, which Duluoz enjoys at second hand, just as he had Cassady's.

– I'd spend the day talking to Wife Nessa and the kids, who told us to shush when Mickey Mouse came on TV, then in'd walk Julien in his suit, open collar, tie, saying "Shit – imagine comin home from a hard day's work and finding this McCarthy-ite Duluoz here."

Kerouac regarded himself as the chronicler of his generation, the Duluoz Legend as encapsulating the flavor of his times as well as the sum of his experience. In *Vanity of Duluoz* (really his last book, most of *Pic* having been written twenty years before it was published) he wrote, half seriously, that most of the work in erecting the Beat Generation monument had been his: ". . .(a point of pride with me in that I've worked harder at this legend business than they have) – Okay, joke. . ." His portrayals of his friends depend on their relationships with him; versions of themselves shone through the prism of how they stood in relation to Jack Kerouac. Many owe most of their fame to the Kerouac reality. Neal Cassady would have a limited legend if he had not been incarnated as Dean Moriarty.

Kerouac cherished the idea that he would one day publish a uniform edition of the Duluoz Legend. He was never to accomplish this, but a conscientious reader may create, with the available guidelines, what Kerouac wished it to be: the official history of the Beat Generation.

My work comprises one vast book like Proust's except that my remembrances are written on the run instead of afterwards in a sick bed. Because of the objections of my early publishers I was not allowed to use the same personae names in each work. *On the Road, The Subterraneans, The Dharma Bums, Doctor Sax, Maggie Cassidy, Tristessa, Desolation Angels, Visions of Cody* and the others including this book *Big Sur* are just chapters in the whole work which I call The Duluoz Legend. In my old age I intend to collect all my work and re-insert my pantheon of uniform names, leave the long shelf full of books there, and die happy. The whole thing forms one enormous comedy, seen through the eyes of poor Ti Jean (me), otherwise known as Jack Duluoz, the world of raging action and folly and also of gentle sweetness seen through the keyhole of his eye. (*Big Sur*)

The obsession's in the chasing and not the apprehending

The station at San Jose has that air of settled calm that falls on suburban stations in the daytime hours between the two peaks of traffic. The booking hall is high-ceilinged and cool and sells good color postcards of lions. The trains have water coolers and no toilets and seats in two tiers and when you doze over the *San Francisco Chronicle* or the *San Francisco Examiner* or get mesmerized gazing out of the sealed window at the backs of the buildings, the debris along the sandy sidings, the diesel-stained blown weeds in the lots beside the track, where the hoboes used to hide as the freights gathered speed, there comes a sharp metal rap and out of the reverie you look down into the face of a smart and sassy uniformed young conductor, the blue uniform with vest and cap scarcely altered since Neal wore it on the old Southern Pacific and rode only as far as Watsonville.

That is all the past now.

That is one with the skyscrapers and the Pennsylvania truck stop at five in the morning when the waitress hissed at the short order cook to come out of the kitchen and take a look at her, with her long blond hair and her lofty model's walk and I saw a sideburned man, fresh at that hour, eating a block of white bread doused in gravy and there were blue seashell rings on sale on the wrong side of America.

It is one with the fall colors and with Akron and Indianapolis and Burroughs' St. Louis and Kansas City, Kansas, and Kansas City, Missouri. It is now with the Archway and the Plains, with the Colorado State Monument where there are canyons within canyons and the hairpin bends are dizzying to drive. It is with the brewery in Golden and the snow and the kiss on the top of the Rockies and the Mormon temples so white in the salt desert sun that you spend ten dollars in the pharmacy on River Rat shades.

It is one with Vegas, with Barstow and Bakersfield and San Bernadino. It is one with the bleached bones of Death Valley and the meadow by the Little Big Horn and the graves sown along the side of the Donner Pass and the disappeared buffalo. As the man on the jukebox, with the holes in his ears and the graying braids down to his waist said, you can die from the cold in the arms of a nightmare. At least Kerouac told me that when I was fifteen so finding it out over and over again wasn't all the trouble it usually is. At least when your own personal El Jadida comes along it does not come completely unexpected. And if you learn these lessons properly you develop a judgement you can trust and you learn to trust it. So when, in that West Village bookstore a few thousand miles away I knew that I couldn't go to Edson Cemetery in Lowell, Massachusetts, even though the stone that is flat to the ground says "he honored life," couldn't go to a public slab of land where they left flowers and feathers and coins and half-full beer cans, I had enough to go with it, El Jadida notwithstanding.

Now it is nearly all over and that is alright because nothing can last but there is something else that instinct tells me I must ask; another small investment of myself in risk. It is something to do with Mailer's unregarded authority. It is something to do with Holmes' beat man wagering the sum of his resources. A great deal of English reserve and a lot of personal courtesy awarded me make no small issue of it. I was right not to go to Edson and make a fool of myself in public: I am right now to ask something in private.

There is a pile of luggage by the slick, newly acquired little BMW in the rutted driveway where John Montgomery, the rapping mountaineer, once dumped a load of hardcore. Soon there will be the spectacular ride down the coast, the beaten blue silver of the ocean under the moonlit cliffs, a drink in the Nepenthe ("beautiful cliff-top restaurant with vast outdoor patio"), and Hearst's *Xanadu* and a Chinese motel and then the canyon, Laurel guns-and-coke Canyon under the Hollywood sign, where they pop off at the armor-plated asses of the police choppers swooping low over the winding road, but when the coyote comes picking among the mesquite they leave him alone. Carolyn and Heather and I are together in the back room of the ranch-style bungalow in Los Gatos. Heather is ready for the road, in a flared skirt fitted over the hips and the famous wool shawl and the long blond hair framing her face. She is watching me very closely without appearing to, a trick women pair-bonded to unregenerate writers apparently pick up very quickly. It was she who photographed me at Père Lachaise, by the grave of the Lizard King. I think she knows what this is about. Carolyn puts her head on one side as I speak, then smiles and goes to a tall gray-green metal cabinet and unlocks it. It is a nice, neat little wooden casket, and on the side it says:

REMITA AGENCIA GAYOSSO, S.A. ROSAS MORENO 151 MEXICO 4, D.F. CONTIENE CENIZAS DEL SR. NEAL CASSADY, JR. REMITIR A INHUMACIONES LOPEZ AT'N SR. FILIPE LOPEZ MESONES NO. 45 SAN MIGUEL ALIENDE GUANAYATO

She opens the box and takes out the small silk sack and puts it in my hand.

It feels just the same weight that a bag of bullseyes did when I was a child, I think. A lump of mutability. In smoke or to the worms, all of us, books or no. It is a very dense weight in my hand. Caw caw caw. No, on second thoughts, it feels nothing at all like something ordinary, safe, and familiar when you were small. Lord Lord Lord.

"The right place to scatter them has never presented itself," says his widow. "He always wanted to come home, so perhaps, they'll stay here. . ."

"Adios, King," said Jack. "All ashes, all ashes again," said Allen.

Outside there is a sleek little silver car with a bag of cameras and a big hat on the back seat and there are singing roads that go on forever. With your map on your lap to help me decide. The best way to see America.

The sparkler dims on the prairie.

Hic calix.

Appendix 1

Chronology of the Works of Jack Kerouac

ORDER OF COMPOSITION

The Town and the City   1946–9
Pic*   Originally begun 1951
On the Road   1948–56 (chiefly written 1951)
Visions of Cody   1946–52
Doctor Sax   July 1952
Book of Dreams*   begun 1952
Maggie Cassidy   early 1953
The Subterraneans   October 1953
San Francisco Blues   April 1954
Some of the Dharma (unpublished)   1954–5
Wake Up (unpublished)   1955
Mexico City Blues   August 1955
Tristessa   1955–6 (two parts, not a revision)
Visions of Gerard   January 1956
The Scripture of the Golden Eternity   May 1956
Old Angel Midnight   28 May 1956
Desolation Angels*   begun 1956
The Dharma Bums   November 1957
Pull My Daisy   March 1959
Book of Dreams   completed 1960
Lonesome Traveler   compiled 1960
Desolation Angels   completed 1961
Big Sur   October 1961

* Title listed twice.

223

Satori in Paris   1965
Vanity of Duluoz   1968
Pomes All Sizes (unpublished)   compiled 1960
Pic   completed 1969
Scattered Poems   1945–68 posthumously compiled in 1971
Two Early Stories   1939–40 posthumously published
Heaven and Other Poems   circa 1955–62 posthumously compiled,
                    1977
San Francisco Blues   April 1954, posthumously published 1983

ORDER OF PUBLICATION IN THE U.S.A.

The Town and the City   1950
On the Road   1957
The Subterraneans   1958
The Dharma Bums   1958
Doctor Sax   1959
Maggie Cassidy   1959
Mexico City Blues   1959
Visions of Cody (limited edition of 750 copies)   1960
The Scripture of the Golden Eternity   1960
Tristessa   1960
Lonesome Traveler   1960
Book of Dreams   1960
Pull My Daisy   1961
Big Sur   1962
Visions of Gerard   1963
Desolation Angels   1965
Satori in Paris   1966
Vanity of Duluoz   1968
Scattered Poems   1971
Pic   1971
Old Angel Midnight   1973 (UK only)
Visions of Cody   1972
Two Early Stories   1973
Heaven and Other Poems   1977
San Francisco Blues   1983 (UK only)

APPENDIX 1

THE DULUOZ LEGEND

The fourteen books of the Duluoz Legend are based on the events of Kerouac's life. Their titles are given below, followed by the date of the period with which they are concerned.

Visions of Gerard   1922–6
Doctor Sax   1930–6
Maggie Cassidy   1938–9
The Town and the City   1935–46
Vanity of Duluoz   1939–46
On the Road   1946–50
Visions of Cody   1946–52
The Subterraneans   Summer 1953
Tristessa   1955 and 1956
The Dharma Bums   1955–6
Desolation Angels   1956–7
Lonesome Traveler   1950s
Big Sur   Summer 1960
Satori in Paris   June 1965

Appendix 2

Selected Pseudonyms
in Books Discussed in the Text

The following abbreviations of book titles are used below: *Big Sur* – *Sur*; *Book of Dreams* – BOD; *Maggie Cassidy* – MC; *Desolation Angels* – *Angels*; *The Dharma Bums* – *Bums*; *Doctor Sax* – *Sax*; *The First Third* – FT; *Gates of Wrath* – *Wrath*; *Get Home Free* – GHF; *The Naked Lunch* – *Lunch*; *On the Road* – OTR; *The Secret Swinger* – SS; *The Subterraneans* – *Subs*; *The Town and the City* – T & C; *Tristessa* – *Tris*; *Vanity of Duluoz* – VOD; *Visions of Cody* – VOC; *Visions of Gerard* – *Gerard*; *The Yage Letters* – *Yage*.

WILLIAM SEWARD BURROUGHS Dennison (*Go*); W. Lee, Willy Lee (*Yage*); William Hubbard (FT); Will Dennison (T & C); Old Bull Lee (OTR); Frank Carmody (*Subs*); Bull Hubbard (*Angels*, BOD); Will Hubbard (VOD); Bull (VOC)

NEAL CASSADY Hart Kennedy (*Go*); Dean Moriarty (OTR); Leroy (*Subs*); Cody Pomeray (*Bums*, *Angels*, BOD, *Sur*, VOC)

GREGORY CORSO Yuri Gligoric (*Subs*); Raphael Urso (*Angels*, BOD)

LAWRENCE FERLINGHETTI Larry O'Hara (composite, *Subs*); Danny Richman (BOD, VOC); Lorenzo Monsanto (*Sur*)

ALLEN GINSBERG David Stofsky (*Go*, GHF); George Muchnik (SS); Leon Levinsky (T & C, *Wrath*); Carlo Marx (OTR); Adam Moorad (*Subs*); Alvah Goldbook (*Bums*); Irwin Garden (*Angels*, BOD, *Sur*, VOD, VOC)

JOHN CLELLON HOLMES Paul Hobbes (*Go*, GHF); Mack Hamlin (SS); Tom Saybrook (OTR); Balliol MacJones (*Subs*); James Watson (BOD)

JACK KEROUAC Gene Pasternak (*Go, GHF*); Jan Grehore (*SS*); Peter Martin *et al.* (*T & C*); Sal Paradise (*OTR*); Leo Percepeid (*Subs*); Ray Smith (*Bums*); Jack Duluoz (*Angels, Sur,* VOD, VOC); Jack (*BOD*); 'Ti Jean'/Jack Duluoz (*Gerard, MC, Sax*)

BILL CANNESTRA Bill Agatson (*Go, GHF*); Bill Genovese (*SS*); 'William Cannestra' (*Wrath*)

LUCIEN CARR Kenneth Wood (*T & C*); Damion (*OTR*); Sam Vedder (*Subs*); Julien Love (*BOD, Sur*); Claude de Maubris (*VOD*)

ROBERT DUNCAN Geoffrey Donald (*Angels*)

ALAN HARRINGTON Ketcham (*Go*)

HERBERT HUNCKE Albert Ancke (*Go*); Herbert Huck (*FT*); Junky (*T & C*); Elmo Hassel (*OTR*); Huck (*BOD,* VOC)

RANDALL JARRELL Varnum Randam (*Angels*)

DAVE KAMMERER Waldo Meister (*T & C*); Emil Duluoz (*Gerard, MC, Sax,* VOD)

PHILIP LAMANTIA Francis DaPavia (*Bums*); David D'Angeli (*Angels*)

MICHAEL McCLURE Ike O'Shay (*Bums*); Patrick McLear (*Angels, Sur*)

JOHN MONTGOMERY Henry Morley (*Bums*); Alex Fairbrother (*Angels*)

LAFCADIO ORLOVSKY Lazarus Darlovsky (*Angels*)

PETER ORLOVSKY George (*Bums*); Simon Darlovsky (*Angels, BOD*)

KENNETH REXROTH Rheinhold Cacoethes (*Bums*)

ALBERT SAIJO George Baso (*Sur*)

GARY SNYDER Japhy Ryder (*Bums*); Jarry Wagner (*Sur*)

LEW WELCH Dave Wain (*Angels, Sur*)

PHILIP WHALEN Warren Coughlin (*Bums*); Ben Fagan (*Angels, Sur*)

Index

INDEX

INDEX

INDEX

232

INDEX

INDEX

INDEX

INDEX